ELIZABETH LOWELL

CHAIN LIGHTNING

MIRA

ISBN 1-55166-538-7

CHAIN LIGHTNING

Copyright © 1988 by Two of a Kind, Inc.

MIRA and the Star Colophon are trademarks used under license and registered
in Australia, New Zealand, Philippines, United States Patent and Trademark
Office and in other countries.

Visit us at www.mirabooks.com

Printed in U.S.A.

For the people of Australia fair dinkum!

Chapter 1

❧❧❧❧❧❧

"**W**hat you need is a lover."

Mandy's head snapped up from the papers scattered across her desk. The movement was so sudden that it sent her silky, chin-length black hair flying, but a single glance told her that it was too late to deflect Anthea. The tiny dynamo who stood next to Mandy was already in overdrive; Anthea had that special gleam in her eyes, the one that came only when she had found a new "project." Mandy stifled both a sigh and a smile, pulled her scattering thoughts together and put away the masculine image that had sprung into her mind at the mention of a lover.

A thatch of unruly, sun-cured blond hair, strong, lean hands, jade-green eyes that never smiled.

"That's a wonderful idea," Mandy said cheerfully. "I'll stick up a bank and take my pick of the bachelors at the OCC auction tomorrow night." In neat, slanting printing she wrote on her calendar for the following day: Rob bank. Buy lover. Soonest. "Anything else? Have you found a replacement for Susie yet? Should I rob another bank and double the next receptionist's salary?"

"I have two excellent candidates."

Mandy was careful not to inquire whether Anthea's candidates were for the position of OCC receptionist or that of lover for one Samantha Blythe. Mandy prayed that it was the former. She didn't want to be the focus of her boss's unpredictable charitable impulses, especially on the subject of men. The last thing Mandy wanted was another waltz around a marriage ring with the kind of easy-smiling, honey-voiced liar her husband had been.

"Both of them are presentable and skilled," Anthea continued, numbering attributes on small, immaculately kept hands. "One of them was recently widowed and the other isn't married."

A neutral sound from Mandy was more than enough encouragement for Anthea to continue her summary of the candidates. Nothing in her voice or demeanor gave a clue as to which position the candidates were slated to fill— office worker or bedroom athlete.

"Both of them had very clean, neatly kept hands, which is essential," the older woman said crisply. "They both look strong and healthy, but it's hard to tell without trying them out. On the whole, I don't think either one will require on-the-job training. They seemed to be self-starters."

Mandy made a strangled sound.

Anthea continued without a pause, not noticing the look on her executive secretary's face. "Education and a sense of humor would be nice but aren't necessary. After all, no one expects anyone in that position to do more than take directions and follow through with a one hundred percent effort and no shilly-shallying. In the final analysis, all the job really requires is cleanliness, a generous portion of stamina and a willingness to take direction without sulking."

"Stamina?" Mandy asked faintly, banishing the images in her mind and wondering if Anthea was taking her usual bluntness to new highs. Or lows.

"But of course. Stamina is vital if the job is to be adequately filled."

"It is?"

Anthea gave Mandy an exasperated look. "Dear girl, do

you have any idea how many receptionists I've lost because they had delicate constitutions? Too many. Now I look for someone sturdy. When you applied for the job I almost didn't hire you. You looked frail. Too thin. Too nervous,'' Anthea said with typical bluntness. ''If it hadn't been for that determined chin and those haunting gold eyes of yours, I would have turned you down without a tryout.''

Mandy started to speak, then realized it was futile. Anthea was in full sail.

''I was wrong,'' Anthea continued without a pause. ''You've been with Our Children's Children for eighteen months and never taken a sick day, even after I doubled your work load by making you into my girl Friday.'' The older woman blinked and focused suddenly on Mandy. ''You've never taken a vacation, either, come to think of it. No wonder you've looked so wan lately.''

''You haven't taken a vacation, either,'' Mandy pointed out, sidestepping the implicit question as to why she had looked so washed-out for the past week or so. If her middle-of-September memories showed on the outside, she'd have to wear more makeup. Nobody in her new life knew what had happened almost two years ago. Mandy preferred it that way. Pity was her least-favorite emotional flavor. ''If you're feeling guilty about being a slave driver, may I point out that it has been four years since Sutter has had more than five days off in a row—and those days were spent traveling to some other desperate spot on the globe.''

For a moment Anthea looked startled. ''No. It can't have been that long!''

''Four years, two months, ten days and—'' she glanced at the clock ''—fifteen hours and thirty-two minutes, to be precise. The latter is by his reckoning, but I certainly wouldn't care to argue the matter with him.''

Anthea's faded green eyes narrowed suddenly. ''Did he call while I was out?''

''Twice. Once from the airport and once from his condo. He said, and I quote, 'If Aunt Ant has signed me up for any more expert testimony on Capitol Hill, I'll box up the entire Senate and send it C.O.D. to hell.'"

Anthea sighed. "Poor boy. He does hate cities and committees. But he's so very impressive...."

Mandy barely caught herself before she muttered, "Amen." D. M. Sutter was very impressive indeed, whether it was as a land reclamation specialist, as a futurist or simply as a man. In the eighteen months she had worked for Our Children's Children, Mandy had seen Sutter only occasionally, always unexpectedly, and each time she had been unnerved by his sheer presence.

It was more than simply a matter of size. Mandy had known many men taller than Sutter's six feet one inch, or more heavily built than Sutter, with his lean muscularity, but none of the bigger men could have commanded attention in a crowded room just by standing quietly. Sutter could, and did. He had a rapier intelligence and unflinching pragmatism that showed in his jade-green eyes and in his face, tanned by foreign suns and drawn into harsh lines by having seen more human greed, suffering, fear and stupidity than any man should have to see.

"I got the feeling that Sutter wanted to go someplace... clean," Mandy said softly.

Shrewd, pale eyes measured Mandy. Few people except Anthea ever saw beyond Mandy's quick smile and sassy one-liners to the very private, intelligent and vulnerable woman beneath.

"You sound as though you would like to go there, too," Anthea said speculatively. "Somewhere clean."

For an instant the luminous amber of Mandy's eyes was darkened by shadows. There was no place on earth like that for her because wherever she went, her memories also went. But that wasn't Anthea's problem. So Mandy smiled and shook her head, denying the shadows in her eyes and making her shiny black hair fly.

"Not me. I've got three reports to run through my magic machine," Mandy said lightly, gesturing toward her word processor. As she did, she saw a familiar figure from the corner of her eye. "And a stack of letters as big as Steve's ego to—"

"Hey, I heard that!" Steve interrupted, calling from the doorway.

"—and a new picture to add to your finished projects' gallery," Mandy finished blithely, as though she had neither seen Steve nor heard his outraged yelp.

"A finished project?" Anthea asked. "Was Susie accepted by an agency?"

"Susie?" Steve asked simultaneously, forgetting about his wounded ego. "Did she call?"

Mandy's smile became compassionate rather than teasing as she turned toward Steve. The young lawyer was a walking cliché—tall, dark, handsome—but the cliché failed to cover his unguarded ego. He had fallen for Anthea's former receptionist and most recent "project." Unfortunately for Steve, Susie had seen only the dreams in her own eyes, not those in his. Though only eighteen, Susie had the face, body and discipline to become an international cover girl. What she had lacked was contacts and the thousands of dollars required to pay for a portfolio of highly professional photos to leave with agencies. Anthea had supplied the contacts, the cash and the plane ticket to Manhattan.

"Susie just signed on with an international modeling agency," Mandy said. "They're sending her to Paris on Tuesday."

Steve's mouth tightened, then curved into a sad smile. "That's what she wanted. I'm happy for her, I guess."

"Be happy for yourself," Anthea said crisply. "Susie was too young to settle down. Better that she find out what she's made of in New York than make herself and some decent young man such as you utterly miserable by getting married in California."

"Is that the collection of international precedents on the use of rivers that flow through more than one country?"

Mandy asked quickly, changing the subject and gesturing toward the thick, dark folders gathered under Steve's arm.

He grabbed the new topic like the lifeline it was. Anthea had many fine points, but finesse wasn't one of them. Sutter was the same, impatient with people who lacked the common sense to avoid life's more obvious mine fields. Mandy, who had stumbled into one of those fields when she was Steve's age, had a great deal of sympathy for the young man's unhappiness. He was lucky to have escaped a bad marriage, but he was too young and too inexperienced to appreciate that fact. Mandy wasn't.

"Here's every precedent I could find," Steve said, flopping the bulging folders on Mandy's desk. Papers went flying in all directions. "Oops. Sorry about that."

"You'll be even sorrier when I tell you that the very papers you're carpeting the ceiling with are your entire presentation to the Senate Committee on Foreign—"

"Then don't tell me," Steve interrupted quickly. "What I don't know won't hurt me, right?"

Wrong, thought Mandy. *Ignorance can not only hurt, it can kill.* But she hadn't known that at his age, so she could hardly blame him now.

"When you're finished picking up the mess," Anthea said to Steve, "come into my office. The delegate from Belize has raised some ridiculous tribal legal precedent to prevent us from building that fish farm."

Steve swore. "Have you hinted that ten percent of all profits will go to him?"

"He wants half."

"Sutter would raise hell," Steve said.

"Sutter would like to feed the old bandit to the fish," Anthea said calmly. "However, if we waited for perfect leaders and perfect solutions, nothing would ever get done."

The phone rang. Mandy reached for it immediately.

"If that's Mr. Axton," Anthea said quickly, "I'm out."

"For how long?"

"Until he arises from his dead posterior and writes OCC a check that will make me smile."

Mandy mentally added another zero to the figure she had been prepared to give Mr. Axton. Though most of the Sutter wealth was tied up in OCC's charitable trusts, enough remained to make Anthea a wealthy woman. Her childhood friends were even more wealthy. Mr. Axton was one of them. He had been trying without success to persuade Anthea to have dinner with him.

"You should auction yourself off at the fund-raiser tomorrow night," Mandy said. "I have a pair of silk harem pants that would raise more than Mr. Axton's posterior."

Anthea looked thoughtful for a few moments, then smiled widely. "The auction. Of course. Why didn't I think of that?"

"You did, remember? No one else would have had the sheer brass to ask men like that to auction themselves off for charity and eager divorcées." Mandy grabbed the phone on the fourth ring. "OCC, may I help you?" Pause. "I'm terribly sorry, Mr. Axton. Miss Sutter just stepped out." Pause. "Four zeros should do nicely, not including the two to the right of the decimal point." Pause. "Of course it's exorbitant, but I'm afraid Miss Sutter has a weakness for grand gestures—she makes so many of them, as you know."

Steve snickered. Anthea merely arched her silver eyebrows.

"That's very generous of you, sir. I'm sure she'll appreciate it."

Anthea waited impatiently until Mandy hung up the phone. "Well?"

"Thirty thousand," Mandy said succinctly.

"Lovely," purred Anthea. "The man is a scholar and a gentleman. I look forward to dinner with him. Make that two dinners."

"Two?"

"Oh, yes. He has wonderful hands." Pale green eyes

focused sharply on Mandy. "You can always tell a man by his hands, dear. If you don't believe me, look at Sutter's someday. My brother might not have had the sense and grit that God gave a goose, but no one can say the same of his son. Pity the boy hasn't found a woman. I hate to see good genes go to waste."

"I thought you didn't approve of marriage," Steve said as he stacked a handful of the flyaway papers on Mandy's desk.

"Marriage?" Anthea smiled. "My dear boy, it will come as a great surprise to the men and women of this benighted world that marriage is a necessary precursor to conception." She turned to Mandy. "Do you have Susie's picture or did you put it on my desk?"

Mandy retrieved a folder from the out basket. "Right here."

"Good. Help me hang it while Steve chases paper. That makes two completed projects this week, you know." Anthea's lean, lined face settled into satisfied lines. "Lovely, just lovely. It couldn't have happened at a better time...."

Mandy followed her boss, torn between the desire to upbraid Anthea for her abrupt treatment of the lovelorn Steve and an impulse to hug the tiny dynamo for caring enough about the various people who crossed her path to take a hand in their personal destinies. An unintentionally imperious hand, to be sure, but very helpful all the same.

The south wall of Anthea's office was given over to photos of all sizes and settings. Their only similarity was that each featured a person who had been helped by a timely application of Anthea's money. There was a young man who had worked his way through journalism school and applied for the position of reporter at various papers in California, only to discover that having a car was a requirement for the job; without a job, he couldn't afford a car. Anthea had supplied the latter, the *Los Angeles Times* had supplied the former, and the young man had begun his career.

There was a picture of a young divorcée who had worked her way through school waiting tables while caring for her young child. All that had stood between her and a Ph.D. in psychology had been enough time off to write her dissertation. Anthea had supported the young woman until the dissertation was finished and accepted.

Susie's picture went next to the most recent of Anthea's successfully concluded "projects," a man and wife who had saved money all their lives in order to open a small restaurant, only to see their savings vanish when their accountant stepped on a plane to Rio with his mistress on one arm and a satchel full of money on the other. Anthea had replaced their stolen savings to the penny.

"Do you think their restaurant will be a success?" Mandy asked.

Anthea made a dismissive gesture with one hand. "Whether it is or isn't, the important thing is that they had the gumption to go after what they wanted. Most people don't. They're either too lazy or too frightened to reach for their dreams."

Carefully looking only at the picture, Mandy bit her lip and prayed that the heat rising in her face wouldn't show. She knew that Anthea's words hadn't been meant for her, but Mandy also knew that she was among the people who were too frightened to reach for their dreams.

Water still terrified her. She was better about water than she had been since the accident. Two months ago, for instance, she had managed to take a bath rather than a shower for the first time in nearly two years. Granted, the water had been only inches deep and it had taken her so long to screw up her courage and get into the tub that the water had been cold, but it had been progress all the same. Now she could step into a tub that had four inches of water in it without having to wrestle with fear while the bathwater went cold. She had tried six and then eight and then ten inches of water in the tub, only to panic at the feel of water climbing above her waist. It had taken her until last week to work back up to five inches of bathwater.

Some progress, she told herself derisively. *At this rate you'll be seventy before you ever get your face in water again.*

The thought of having her face covered by a cold, clutching, killing liquid made white replace Mandy's bright flush. She was more afraid of water than she was ashamed of being afraid. The source of her fear was as real as death. If she spent the rest of her life taking shallow baths or showers, so be it. She was alive, she had found a way to make a living that didn't involve water in any way, and she was able to sleep through the night without seeing the ocean surge up to claim the small plane—water rising slowly, slowly over the fuselage windows while she struggled to free herself and her husband, and then the endless black slide down into ocean's depths that had once fascinated and now repelled her.

Mandy blinked and realized that Anthea was looking at her as though expecting an answer to a question that had been asked.

"Are you all right?" Anthea repeated. "You look as though you've seen a ghost."

"Really?" asked Mandy, rallying. "Quick, give me a mirror. I've always wanted to see what kind of ditsy broad went around looking for ghosts."

Anthea's eyes narrowed. She started to say something, paused and finally turned back toward her gallery without a word. Seeing the faces of the individuals she had helped always made her feel as though life were more than an unremitting battle against poverty, greed and indifference. Somewhere out there, scattered across the face of the earth, were people who smiled more often because Anthea had smoothed one of the razor edges off their lives. She smiled more often, as well, taking pleasure from the pleasure she had brought.

Feeling anticipation of her next projects fizz softly in

her blood, Anthea looked affectionately from picture to picture. With luck and a little arm-twisting in the right places, Mandy soon would be up there with the others, smiling. Unfortunately, Sutter wouldn't be among the glad of heart. But then, Sutter rarely was glad about anything.

Even knowing her nephew as well as Anthea did, however, she was a bit taken aback at just how much he *dis*-liked the plan when she bearded her tawny tiger in his own quarters a few hours later.

"You did what?" Sutter demanded.

With an equanimity that few people could have mustered, Anthea faced the man looming over her. D. M. Sutter was always impressive, but with a brassy beard stubble, stone-green eyes, and eyebrows sun-bleached to a metallic gold—and teeth bared in what only an optimist would call a smile—Sutter looked frankly dangerous. The fact that he was wearing jungle-stained khaki shorts and no shirt at all did nothing to make him appear less malevolent. The lean, hard-muscled length of the man wasn't precisely soothing, either. It tended to remind people that the deceptively graceful tiger routinely dined upon the much bulkier, more obviously muscled water buffalo.

"I entered you in the OCC charity auction tomorrow night," Anthea said with outward calm. "Actually, you'll be the centerpiece. A surprise offering, as it were. A piece de resistance."

It sounded more like a coup de grace to Sutter. He muttered in fragments of languages Anthea was quite happy not to understand. He glared down at her. She was standing in front of him with her customary regal poise, serene in the rightness of what she was doing.

"Aunt Ant, you are my favorite person, living or dead, and—"

"Butter won't get it done, my boy," she interrupted with relish, stealing one of his favorite phrases. "You have been nominated and elected by acclamation and that, as they say, is that!"

"Anthea," Sutter said softly, knowing that yelling at the little tyrant wouldn't budge her, "what in God's name gives you the idea that I will stand around with my thumb in my, er, *ear*, while a pack of overwealthy, overwrought divorcées bid on what they hope will be my...services?"

"Three weeks of vacation."

He blinked. "Say what?"

"Three weeks at the location of your choice, during which time you do absolutely nothing you don't want to do. By definition, a vacation."

"Are you serious?"

"Very."

Sutter's cool green eyes assessed the woman in front of him. Although his aunt wore four-inch heels, she was still nineteen inches shorter than he was and weighed less than half what he did. He knew that the disparity in their sizes no more worried her than a wolverine worried about taking on a grizzly over a choice morsel of meat. Anthea knew, and Sutter had learned, that in most situations temperament counts for more than muscle. Sutter might be a nasty piece of business for the rest of the world to confront, but for the woman who had taken in a surly, near-violent teenager and had taught him the meaning of constructive discipline, intelligent dreams and clear-eyed affection, for this woman Sutter had only love.

And frequent bouts of exasperation.

This particular bout was right up against the precipice of true anger, however. Anthea had never interfered in Sutter's private life before. It had been an unwritten law between them; she didn't choose his women and he didn't choose her men. He could hardly believe that she had casually chosen to rearrange their mutual relationship at this late date.

"Anthea."

The word was hard-edged, the tone whiplike. He was tired, hungry, jet-lagged and as close to losing his temper as he had been since a wealthy Brazilian had offered to rent him a pair of eight-year-old twin girls for a night of casual recreation. Sutter had purchased the girls in thin-lipped silence, taken them to a Catholic convent, and then he had returned for a very brief, no-holds-barred chat with the man.

Closing his eyes, Sutter took in and released a long breath. What Anthea had done was aggravating, exasperating, irritating, maddening and presumptuous; but it wasn't evil. She didn't deserve the razor edge of a tongue honed in some of the world's most brutal places. Slowly he counted to ten in a language that had no numeral system. As an abstract intellectual exercise in controlling unruly emotions, it had few peers.

"Someday you'll push me too far," Sutter said finally, softly. "I don't know who will be sorrier when that happens—you or me."

Anthea let out a hidden breath and smiled very gently at the man who had become the son she had never borne. "I hope I'll never truly anger you, Damon. You're the center of my heart, you know."

Sutter's long, callused fingers touched her cheek lightly. "Without you, I wouldn't have had a heart." He grimaced. "All right, Ant. I'll be your damned sacrificial goat for the Our Children's Children bachelor auction. Once. Please don't ask me to do it again."

"I won't. That's a promise, Damon."

He smiled crookedly at the nickname she rarely used, just as he rarely called her Ant anymore. He bent and brushed his lips over both of her soft, faintly powdered cheeks.

"I'll make the travel arrangements tonight," Sutter said, straightening and stretching at the same time. "I hope whoever buys me doesn't expect a romantic tour of jet-set ports of call. What I have in mind for my holiday is less cloying."

"Let me make all the arrangements, dear. You look as though you would welcome a few hours of sleep."

Sutter's lips shifted into a hard curve. "I'll sleep better if *I* make the arrangements. If you know where I'm going, you'll have a full schedule of work set out for me when I arrive. That's not my idea of time off."

Anthea managed to look hurt and amused at the same time. "Not this time. It will be a true vacation for you."

"I know. But you don't. That's why it will be a true vacation."

Anthea's pale green eyes shifted focus for a moment as she considered ways of overcoming her nephew's stubbornness. None came immediately to mind, so she gave in gracefully. After all, there were many routes to any goal.

"Whatever you say, dear. Do get some sleep. You look grim rather than dashing. Any rational woman would think twice about bidding for you."

Sutter's eyes narrowed while he watched Anthea exit his condominium as unexpectedly as she had arrived. He didn't know what had lit a fire under her thin, aristocratic rear, but he sensed that she wasn't finished with him quite yet.

Chapter 2

❧❦❧

Mandy looked quickly around the crowd, seeking Anthea. The movement made the thousands of tiny black bugle beads on her dress shimmer. Bias-cut, long-sleeved, high-necked, utterly backless and slit to the thigh, the dress nonetheless managed to look sensuously elegant rather than sexually provocative. But then, at the price the designer was asking for it, the dress had to do something more than just glitter. Mandy frowned as she remembered the cost. For the tenth time that evening she wondered how she had allowed Anthea to talk her into modeling Sharai's exclusive, costly creation.

Simple, Mandy told herself dryly. *You took one look at the dress and fell in love. The fact that Sharai is one of Anthea's former projects simply made the offer more impossible to refuse.*

A subtle flash of blue caught Mandy's eye. That would be Alice, one of the two receptionist candidates. Sharai had decreed that Alice wear a slinky cerulean dress that made her look like a blue candle flame burning in the crowd. The other candidate—Jessica—was breathtaking in red silk pants and a beaded strapless top. Apparently Anthea hadn't been able to decide which of the two women to employ, so she had hired both. Jessi was working as receptionist while Alice was learning the basics of Mandy's job. When Mandy had pointed out that soon she would have nothing to do, Anthea had laughed and said that the more quickly Alice could take over routine office duties, the more quickly Mandy would be freed to work with Anthea on her various personal and OCC projects.

Suddenly Mandy stopped scanning the crowd. Her abrupt stillness wasn't the result of a conscious choice to stop looking for Anthea; it was simply that Sutter was impossible to catalog and pass over in a single glance, even though he was seated in the shadows of the orchestra pit a few rows away. He wore a black suit coat, a dress shirt of a linen so fine that its surface was smoother than summer silk, and a rich black tie. The midnight color of his suit served to intensify the blondness of his thick, sun-cured hair, which in turn made his tanned skin seem very dark by contrast. Instead of making him appear civilized, the expensive clothes served only to heighten the aura of primal, barely leashed masculinity Mandy had sensed in Sutter the first time she had seen his picture on Anthea's desk.

OCC left Sutter out in that Brazilian jungle too long. I wonder if those cold green eyes can see in the dark.

Mandy forced herself to continue scanning the crowd, then sat down as swiftly as she could, feeling as though Sutter had been staring at her and at the same time telling herself that she was being foolish. Sutter was hardly likely to stare at her. She had spoken perhaps twenty words to him since he had returned, those words consisting of "yes, sir," "yes, sir," and "yes, sir," repeat as necessary.

A flurry of anticipation rippled through the crowd as the lights dimmed and the auctioneer stepped onto the stage to introduce the first of the bachelors who had volunteered to be auctioned off in the name of Our Children's Children. As though pulled by invisible strings, the crowd leaned forward for a better view of the stage. Jewels flashed and glittered in the low light, plush foldout chairs creaked, and conversations died throughout the large auditorium. The auctioneer was wearing another of Sharai's creations. Every movement of the auctioneer's body sent exotic tongues of luminescence licking through rich green fabric, defining the curves beneath without actually revealing their precise proportions. As a bit of seductive witchery, it was stunning.

"Good evening, ladies and gentlemen," the auctioneer said. "I have a mirror at home, so I know those gasps of admiration aren't for me. The gown I'm wearing is by Sharai. As some of you may know, Sharai gives ten percent of her profits each year to OCC. In return, OCC does its best to send clients her way. Several of the OCC staff are also wearing Sharai's creations tonight, compliments of the designer."

That was the cue for Mandy and five other women throughout the crowd to stand up and pirouette slowly in the prearranged spotlights. The dresses displayed the range of Sharai's elegant evening creations while the auctioneer gave a few facts as to price and availability of each costume. Silently Mandy kept telling herself that she needn't be shy—the audience certainly would be looking at the flashier dresses worn by the other women rather than at the relatively demure black dress she herself had chosen to wear.

Mandy repeated the comforting thought to herself for half of the required pirouette, then shivered involuntarily to a stop when she saw Sutter watching her from the shadows of the orchestra pit. Suddenly she felt naked, stripped of defenses, clothed only in a transparent shaft of light. The feeling was so unnerving that she swayed like a dark orchid in a sultry breeze. The movements sent networks of black lightning over the dress with each shivering breath she took. There was a flurry of appreciative applause from people who thought that the seductive swaying had been planned rather than involuntary. Mandy forced a stiff smile to her lips and prayed for the spotlight to black out before she did.

The spotlights snapped off, leaving only the auctioneer visible. There was a round of applause for the dresses. Mandy was so relieved to be invisible again that it was all she could do not to fall. She sat down in a rush, her face flaming and her heart beating far too fast.

"Gowns by Sharai!" the auctioneer said enthusiastically, leading a final round of applause. When silence came again, the auctioneer began speaking in a clear, trained contralto that carried easily to every corner of the music hall. "I'm sure you'll be as generous in your bidding as you were in your applause, so let's lead the first lamb to the altar."

There was scattered laughter.

"As you know," the auctioneer continued, "OCC, Our Children's Children, is a nonprofit foundation dedicated to promoting rational national policies of resource use, policies that will result in decent lives for our children and for our children's children. OCC was founded and funded by Jason Charles Sutter and Alicia Jean Sutter, the parents of Anthea Jean Sutter, who is the present administrator of OCC's diverse global projects. Foremost among those projects is what the press calls a 'think tank' located amid the redwoods in northern California. At present, the OCC retreat houses thirty-one academic, political, artistic and business leaders whose sole task is to…think. If that sounds easy, you're welcome to apply for the next opening. At last count there were more than one hundred applicants for each vacancy."

Mandy felt her heartbeat slow and the trembling in her body subside as the auctioneer's voice and the blessed darkness concealed her from Sutter's view. The man unnerved her. There was no explanation for it and no way to get around it. Even looking at his picture made her uneasy. He was precisely the kind of man that her husband Andrew had been—powerful, impatient, both scholar and man of action—only Andrew had worked for a university rather than for a charity. He had been an oceanographer renowned for his incisive intelligence and lofty academic principles.

What a pity Andrew's principles didn't preclude adultery. Maybe then I wouldn't have spent a night of horror adrift on a cold sea. Maybe then I would have had a child to laugh with rather than the company of nightmares.

Maybe.

And maybe it all would have happened anyway. Maybe it wasn't a lack of principles that sent Andrew on the prowl. Maybe it was the simple fact that his student-bride didn't know how to please a man. Maybe if I'd been better in bed none of this would have happened.

Maybe. Oh, God, maybe....

Mandy shuddered violently but didn't try to suppress or deny the churning of her thoughts. She had learned the hard way that whatever she suppressed during the day returned to haunt her in the darkness of her dreams. Once she had understood that, she had begun to grapple more successfully with her emotions. All that remained now was for her to accept the fact that there was more than enough blame to go around in life and much too little joy. Andrew had failed her and she had probably failed Andrew and she had certainly failed their unborn child. Having acknowledged that, she had nothing left to do but live the rest of her life as best she could.

A wave of laughter called Mandy from her bleak thoughts. Her head snapped up as the auctioneer waved her index finger from side to side at the audience, imitating a parent chastising a child.

"Naughty, naughty," the woman murmured. "What I meant to say is that a good man is hard to find, rather than vice versa. The first of our hard—that is, *good*—men is Dr. Anthony Streano. He is Tony to his friends and has been known to respond to other names on rather more intimate occasions. I leave it to the lucky last bidder to discover what names and which occasions!''

The crowd laughed again while a man of middle age and height walked onto the stage. He smiled briefly before he took a seat at center stage in a pool of white light. Silence descended again while the auctioneer recited his "vital statistics" in a sultry contralto that found double meanings in the most innocent phrases. As the last of the appreciative laughter died down, she described the "date" Dr. Streano had donated—a star-studded gala film opening in Hollywood.

"Remember," concluded the auctioneer, "the money you bid goes directly to OCC. Each bachelor pays all costs for his proposed outing, just as he would on a more traditional date. There is no limit to the number of dates you may acquire, so bid often, and bid high! Your children's children will thank you."

The auditorium's lights came up again so that the bidders could be spotted. The auction opened at one hundred dollars and rose quickly to one thousand. Finally a blushing, beaming woman not quite old enough to be the good doctor's mother walked up onstage to claim him. The doctor smiled, introduced himself and murmured something that made the woman glow. Grinning, laughing and attempting to ignore the occasional risqué comment from the audience, the pair exited the stage.

For the next half hour the bidding went briskly, as everything from a VIP tour of Disneyland to a Malibu barbecue to a ski weekend at Vail was auctioned. The men took the auctioneer's spicy teasing in good humor, plainly both gratified and chagrined to be in the position of seller rather than buyer in the dating game. The women, for their part, enthusiastically exploited the opportunity to see men on the sexual auction block for a change.

Mandy watched man after man walk onstage, sit down and smile while his attributes were numbered and his "favors" were auctioned off like a glorified box lunch. Some of the men were four-year veterans of the auction, but most had never before participated. Fully one-third of the purchased dates resulted in long-lasting relationships, a fact that tended to seriously deplete the pool of available bachelors OCC could call upon.

"Our final bachelor before we break for a champagne intermission is Jeremy Stanhope, owner of Stanhope Electronics and patent holder of a nifty little process that allows our computers to work ten times as fast as they used to. Jeremy is a newcomer to our auction, so let's make him very welcome."

A tall, thin, obviously shy man walked slowly onstage while the audience applauded. He looked uncomfortable in his black tie and shifted restlessly from side to side while the auctioneer read his vital statistics. He was offering a week-long cruise on one of the "Loveboats" that plied the waters between Washington and Alaska. As the "date" was described, an appreciative murmur went through the crowd, followed by an enthusiastic hand. Because the costs of the excursion would be borne by the bachelor rather than by OCC, and the bids tended to reflect the cost of the date itself, the electronics tycoon's cruise amounted to a generous, if indirect, donation to OCC's coffers.

The bidding began at six hundred dollars and went rapidly higher. As had been the case with the previous auctions, the women who were too shy to bid outright had conned friends and family into bidding for them. Mothers bid for their daughters' birthday gifts and vice versa. The OCC auction was only in its fourth year, but already it was the most popular and lucrative of the many events on OCC's fund-raising calendar. The fact that the event had been preceded by a free champagne and caviar reception increased both the attendance and the generosity of the ultimate bids.

After the intermission, during which more champagne and canapés were consumed, the bidding intensified. In the second half of the auction, the "dates" offered were uniformly expensive vacations that often were unusual and always hotly contested among the bidders. As the bidding became more spirited, so did the innuendos. The comments from the audience went from flirtatious to nearly salacious. Good taste was skirted but never breached, and the men took the sexy teasing with comic-opera leers that brought laughter from the audience.

When the auctioneer introduced the last bachelor listed on the program, a former tight end for the Rams, by saying that this was one man who matched his job description, the audience shouted with laughter. Variations on the sporting theme—holding penalties, game-winning touchdowns, incomplete passes, hands-on scrimmages and punting for distance—were all explored by the auctioneer and the audience. The man himself was both huge and beautifully proportioned. He was offering a ten-day surfing safari to Hawaii. The bidding was a machine-gun blur of numbers that finally resolved into a three-cornered war among a trim matron, a blond society girl and Sharai.

Ten minutes later the bidding was over. Five thousand dollars poorer, Sharai walked onstage in a dress that looked like water flowing over her, giving the impression that with the next step, or the next, some of the feminine secrets lying beneath the cloth would be revealed. They never were, but the dress kept every man hoping. The former jock took one look at Sharai's near six feet of height and generously proportioned body, joined the wild applause and then casually scooped up the designer and carried her offstage in his arms. The look of surprise and then pleasure on Sharai's face made it clear that she believed her money well spent.

As soon as the thunder of applause diminished, the auctioneer spoke again. Her voice had lost its bantering, teasing tone.

"This brings us to the end of our scheduled program, but not to the end of our bachelor auction. We are truly privileged to have with us tonight a man who has dedicated his life to working for Our Children's Children. Whenever politics or war or natural disasters threaten OCC's overseas projects, this is the man who is sent to clean up the mess and put things back into working order again. Unfortunately, not all governments have been appreciative of his efforts on behalf of the earth's children—he has been harassed, shot, beaten and jailed. He has also received more awards, citations and jeweled medals than one man can wear. He told me earlier tonight that of the two—being harassed or being applauded—he would take the former. Nonetheless, he has volunteered himself and a truly spectacular Australian mystery vacation to some lucky and generous woman. Ladies and gentlemen, I give you Damon McCarey Sutter, internationally renowned futurist and director of Our Children's Children's overseas projects.''

As one, the audience came to its feet in a storm of applause. Mandy was among the first to stand. Sutter might unnerve her but she, better than anyone in the audience, understood what he had done for the success of OCC's projects in countries that most people didn't even know existed. The three months he had just finished in Brazil had been brutal. There were few places on earth where the gap between the rich and the poor was so wide, deep and final.

Sutter walked across the stage with the same lithe stride that had served him so well in jungles, deserts and mountains. He had made too many speeches in front of too many wealthy and powerful people to be bothered by stage fright. Yet, despite his best efforts to be charitable, he knew that there was a razor edge to his smile. He knew because the auctioneer was giving him the sideways, wary glances that people usually reserve for large, fanged animals that have been carelessly left unchained.

It's all for a good cause, he reminded himself for the twentieth time as he sat down, hoping to end the unwanted applause. He worked for OCC because he believed in it, not because he wanted to be known as a benefactor of worthy causes.

Suddenly Sutter spotted a svelte redhead sauntering down the aisle and taking a front-row, center seat. The body was by the best personal fitness instructors. The jewels were by Tiffany. The dress was by Sharai, purchased outright rather than merely modeled for the evening. The woman was stunningly turned out, unbelievably self-centered and had been pursuing Sutter with equal parts of energy and shamelessness for more than three years.

The redhead was not noted for her charitable nature. Sutter had little doubt that she had come tonight for the sole purpose of acquiring him for a few uninterrupted weeks of intense pursuit. As his name hadn't been on the program, there was only one way she could have discovered that he was auctioning himself off to the most generous bidder.

Damn Anthea, anyway! If that redheaded barracuda has the last bid, my so-called vacation will be undiluted hell!

Furious, Sutter reached up with outward casualness and tugged on his left ear. It was a signal of long standing between himself and his aunt. Whoever used it was calling for help in being extricated from an impossible social situation.

"Go see what the dear boy wants."

Anthea's unexpected purr of satisfaction at Mandy's elbow slid easily through the crowd's noise, making her jump. She hadn't even seen Anthea come down from the side aisle to stand beside her.

"But—" Mandy began.

"Quickly!" interrupted Anthea crisply. "The auction is about to begin and then it will be too late."

Bewildered, Mandy stepped out into the aisle, only to stop as a small, surprisingly strong hand gripped her forearm.

"Tell him if he wants me to make the last bid, he must

also let me make the travel arrangements for his mysterious Australian holiday.''

Mandy gave her boss a blank look, then responded to a less-than-delicate push by hurrying down the aisle toward the stage while the audience continued its enthusiastic standing ovation for D. M. Sutter. Just as people were beginning to sit down again, Mandy walked up the stage steps in a subtle glitter of black beads and discreetly touched the auctioneer's arm.

"Message for Sutter," Mandy said quietly. "Urgent."

"It can't wait?"

"You know how it is with hard men," Mandy retorted. "You take 'em where you find them."

The microphone picked up her words and relayed them all over the auditorium, much to the audience's amusement. Mandy wanted to go through the floor but the boards were much too tightly fitted for that. Given no other choice, she brazened it out when Sutter hooked his index finger in an imperious, sexy gesture for her to come to him.

"It's not that he's rude," Mandy said clearly, knowing the microphone would do the rest. "It's just that none of the five languages he speaks is English."

Laughter echoed and reechoed through the auditorium. Sutter slanted Mandy a smile that was frankly dangerous as he crooked his finger again. Mandy knew better than to tease the tiger twice. She walked across the stage toward him, drawing on every bit of her insouciance to hide her underlying nervousness. Though the bodice of her dress was demure enough for a matron twice her age, the front slit showed glimpses of long, well-formed legs and inviting hints of thighs clad in the sheerest of black silk stockings. The rear view of Mandy was frankly breathtaking. Her back was shapely, smooth and defined by a faint shadow along her erect spine. The shadow deepened enticingly just before the fabric began again, clinging to her hips in a dark glitter of beads.

Mandy was grateful not to be presenting Sutter with the costume's back view. Even seated and wearing evening clothes, Sutter radiated the kind of raw physical presence that sent up warning flares telling her to beware of getting close. Yet there was no help for it. She had to get quite close to Sutter or run the risk of broadcasting every word of their conversation over the auditorium's sensitive sound system.

"You beckoned?" she murmured, bending down until her mouth all but brushed Sutter's ear. With each breath she took, the clean, male scent of him spread through her body, making her knees oddly weak. She swayed.

Sutter's hands snaked out with shocking speed, holding Mandy by the waist. His grip was powerful and his fingers were so long that they met in the small of her back. Male fingertips found smooth, naked skin, drawing a gasp from Mandy. The low cut of Mandy's dress seemed to bother Sutter not one bit. There was strength in his grip but no sensuality. He moved his head sharply, seeking Mandy's ear beneath the silken curtain of her chin-length hair. His breath was as warm as his words were cold.

"Tell my sainted aunt that if Sissy buys me she finally will have succeeded in making me lose my temper."

Mandy had no trouble deciding that the "she" referred to was Anthea, not the mysterious Sissy. The icy tone of Sutter's voice and the steel quality of his grip on her convinced Mandy that the time for teasing the tiger was long past. There was only one way she was going to get beyond the reach of his powerful, unnerving presence, and that was to gather her scattering wits and tell the man what he wanted to hear.

"I think Anthea already knows," Mandy murmured. "She said, quote, 'Tell him if he wants me to make the last bid, he must also let me make the travel arrangements for his mysterious Australian holiday,' unquote."

What Sutter whispered next into Mandy's ear didn't bear translating, much less quoting to his maiden aunt.

"Is that yes or no?" Mandy asked with a coolness that was sheer bravado.

Sutter jerked his head back from her scented, swirling hair. For the benefit of the audience he smiled, but Mandy was close enough to see his eyes. She shivered and wondered how a man whose hands were so warm could have eyes like green ice.

"Yes," he hissed.

Mandy nodded her understanding because she knew she would stammer if she tried to speak. She turned and walked away, but with each step she felt Sutter's icy eyes boring into her naked back. Silently pitying whoever bought Sutter's vacation—and his unnerving, short-tempered company—Mandy hurried across the stage.

"Is the Australian vacation still on?" the auctioneer asked, covering the microphone before she spoke.

"You bet. The sooner the better. If I had the money, I'd buy the ticket myself and launch him with a bottle of champagne over his thick prow."

The auctioneer smiled as she looked from Sutter's hard, handsome face to Mandy's flushed cheeks. "Honey, didn't you know? The best ones always bite, and they bite in all the best places."

Mandy looked first shocked, then intrigued despite herself. The thought of Sutter's mouth closing on her flesh in sensual teasing made sudden heat expand deep inside her, flushing her from breast to thighs.

"*Bon appétit!*" Mandy muttered, and hurried from the stage, her cheeks burning.

Laughing, the woman turned back to the audience. "Relax, ladies, the Australian outing is still up for bid. Better move fast, though. The next phone call could change things and take this elusive hunk of steamy jungle beyond your reach forever. Before the bidding begins, Mr. Sutter requested that I warn you—the three weeks will be spent in one of the most little-known resorts in the world, a place where only a severely limited number of people are permitted to stay each year. The accommodations won't be luxurious. Leave your diamonds and designer clothes at home. You will be sleeping in a tent. You will be permitted to carry no more luggage than fits into a backpack, and that includes your purse. If these restrictions don't discourage you, then you are just the lady to accompany D. M. Sutter on his Australian mystery vacation.''

If the women in the audience were discouraged, it didn't show. The bidding was opened by the stunning redhead. Her bid was equally stunning.

''Five thousand dollars.''

The auctioneer picked up the bid without missing a beat and began skillfully working the audience. The next bid wasn't long in coming, nor in being topped.

''Six thousand,'' called the redhead.

''Is that Sissy by any chance?'' Mandy asked Anthea.

Anthea's low purr of satisfaction was the only answer.

''I gather Sutter doesn't want to spend three weeks with her,'' Mandy said.

Anthea laughed. ''The woman is a two-legged barracuda who loves nothing but her own reflection in the mirror. But even reflections have their uses.''

Mandy hesitated but knew she should warn her boss that this wasn't the best way to fill OCC's coffers. ''Anthea, Sutter is furious. Not hot furious. Icy furious. Why did he volunteer himself if he dislikes being auctioned off so much?''

The older woman winced. ''He didn't volunteer himself. I did.''

''My God,'' Mandy said faintly, looking at her boss in disbelief. ''Do you have a death wish?''

''So long as Sissy doesn't have the last bid, everything will be fine,'' Anthea said with more determination than real self-assurance.

''The cost of keeping everything fine is seven thousand dollars,'' Mandy muttered, ''and climbing fast. The women in this place must be blinded by the spotlights.

Anyone with two eyes could see that going on vacation with Sutter would be like inviting a hungry tiger to take the first bite of your hamburger.''

Then Mandy thought of what the auctioneer had said and winced.

Anthea laughed and patted Mandy on the arm. ''You needn't worry. I suspect Sutter has arranged a vacation that will keep him at arm's length from his 'date' while still showing her a piece of the world that few people ever get to see. In fact I suspect he—'' Anthea broke off abruptly. ''That's it. No one is going above Sissy's eight thousand.'' Anthea's fingers tightened on Mandy's arm. ''Bid ten.''

''What?''

''I can hardly bid on my own nephew, can I? Do it!''

''T-ten,'' Mandy said.

''Louder!''

''Ten thousand dollars!''

There was a long pause while the audience swiveled to see the new bidder. At Anthea's prod, Mandy held up a trembling hand.

''Eleven,'' Sissy said coolly.

Anthea's elbow dug into Mandy's ribs.

''Eleven five,'' Mandy said.

''Twelve.''

''Twelve five.''

''Thirteen.''

''Fifteen thousand dollars,'' shot back Mandy, not waiting for Anthea's response.

The audience murmured. There was scattered applause.

Mandy didn't even notice. She was looking across the footlights at Sutter's calm face and burning green eyes. The idea of the shallow, glittering Sissy buying Sutter as though he were a designer dress irritated Mandy unreasonably. The man might be impossible in a social setting, but he was undeniably brilliant and of proven physical courage. She doubted that Sissy was interested in those particular qualities, however. No doubt the only thing Sissy burned to know was whether Sutter's stamina extended to areas other than chopping through jungles for weeks on end.

And then Mandy heard the echo of her last bid rippling across the audience. She turned to Anthea with a stricken look. The older woman smiled and squeezed Mandy's hand in silent reassurance.

Sissy hesitated for a dramatic moment, looked over at Mandy and the tiny woman standing next to her, then turned back to the auctioneer.

"Fifteen thousand dollars," the auctioneer said. "Do I hear fifteen thousand five hundred? Fifteen five, anyone?"

Sissy sat down.

"Sold for fifteen thousand dollars to Samantha Blythe!"

There was a burst of applause.

"Well, go on," Anthea said, prodding Mandy. "Go up there and claim your prize."

Wide, cognac-colored eyes fixed on Anthea. "What?"

"Sutter," Anthea said. "You're supposed to walk off-stage with him."

"But I didn't—"

"Of course you did," interrupted Anthea. "Everyone here heard you. Now get up there before you embarrass him."

"Embarrass? *Sutter?*"

The thought was so ridiculous and at the same time so delicious that Mandy laughed aloud. She was still smiling widely when she walked onstage, followed every inch of the way by the spotlight, her long legs gleaming in their black silk sheaths. In a glittering, slithering cloud of black fabric, she came to a halt a few feet away from Sutter.

And crooked her finger at him.

Chapter 3

Even two weeks later, the memory of that moment was enough to make Mandy shiver. Sutter's sudden, dangerous smile was burned indelibly into her memory, as was the feel of his hand on the naked small of her back as he escorted her offstage; but it was his eyes that haunted her. Gem hard, dismissive, saying as plainly as the words he had whispered in her ear that he thought she was silly and inconsequential.

That's your free one, little girl. You pull a stunt like that again and you'll feel like grass after an elephant stampede.

She had looked down his tuxedoed length to his polished calfskin shoes and then back up, all the way up to those cold eyes. *You needn't be so sensitive about the size of your feet. If they weren't elephantine, they wouldn't fit so neatly in your mouth.*

The memory of her retort made Mandy groan silently. She put her hands over her face, shutting out the sight of her empty desk. She had always had a quick mind and even quicker tongue, but never had she regretted the result quite so much. Sutter unnerved her. Half the time she wanted to hide when she saw him.

And half the time she couldn't resist the urge to needle

him into noticing her. Thank God he had gotten a head start on his three-week vacation by leaving four days ago.

"Why did I crook my finger at him in front of all those people?" Mandy asked herself for the thousandth time. "What on earth made me think I could embarrass him? How do you embarrass a rock!"

Even the memory of Sutter's granite self-assurance irritated Mandy. Instead of becoming angry at her mocking gesture, he had simply stood, slid his hand up beneath her hair to the nape of her neck and smiled while he had found and casually stroked the sensitive, vulnerable knot of nerves, sending visible goose bumps marching over her arms. One golden eyebrow had lifted at her response, his glance had moved over her as though stripping away the dress, and then he had turned aside with an utter lack of interest. She could still hear his passionless, cutting words.

You didn't buy a lover, baby, though God knows you're hungry enough to have robbed a bank for it. Maybe you could buy a piece of Sharai's jock. Two on one looks about his style.

Heat flushed Mandy's face now as it had that night when she had realized that Sutter had read the flip note on her calendar: Rob bank. Buy lover. Soonest.

Mandy had to give Sutter full marks for good manners, though. He had hustled her offstage before he walked away from her, leaving her to field teasing, prying questions from the women who had surged up from the audience to congratulate her.

She had started to explain that she had purchased Sutter for his aunt, not for herself, but Anthea had arrived and shaken her head slightly. With a rather grim smile and hot cheeks, Mandy had endured the twittering congratulations in silence.

"Mandy? Yo, Mandy. Anyone home behind those two-hundred-proof eyes?"

"Alcohol isn't stable at anything much higher than a hundred and eighty proof," she said automatically to

Steve, her mind elsewhere. "It sucks water out of the air, diluting the mixture until—"

"Lady, you know some really weird things," Steve interrupted, flopping some folders down on her desk. "Here are the precedents Anthea has been jumping up and down to get."

Mandy blinked and focused on the present, shutting out the disturbing, unnerving memory of Sutter's wickedly male smile and utterly cold eyes. "She has?"

"Steve," Jessi called from Anthea's office, "where are those precedents? Anthea has the premier's personal secretary on the phone!"

Steve snatched up the folders before Mandy could touch them. "Coming right up!"

With a stifled sigh, Mandy watched Steve disappear. No wonder she had been brooding over Sutter lately. She had no work piled up on her desk, nothing to think about except the anniversary of the day two years before when her life had come apart.

Anything was better than dwelling on that. Even Sutter.

The phone rang. Welcoming the distraction, Mandy reached for it. As she held it to her ear she heard Alice's voice saying, "OCC, may I help you?"

Mandy replaced the receiver with a gentleness that was at odds with her mood. She could take anything but inactivity. Since Alice and Jessi had come to OCC, Mandy's own work had been divided up and handed out to them. Despite repeated assurances and hints of better things to come, Anthea had given Mandy nothing new to do. As a result, Mandy had had far too much time with her own thoughts.

Two years ago today, minus a few hours.

Stop it! It's over and done, dead and buried. It happened and nothing can be done to change it.

Yes. And it happened two years ago today.

The pen Mandy had been holding slipped from her fingers to roll across the desk and off the edge onto the floor.

With unfocused eyes she watched the pen bounce softly on the carpet. Memories turned uneasily, unquiet ghosts rippling through her mind. Her skin went pale and her heart beat too quickly. Automatically she forced herself to breathe more deeply, more easily, bringing color back into her face, telling herself that there was nothing to be upset about.

It's just a day like any other. Just a day. If there were a grave to visit you'd go and stand and think about it all over again. But there isn't a grave, so you'll sit at home and think about it over and over until you're numb and then you'll sleep and get up and it will be another day like any other day, one more day, another day farther from yesterday. And someday it will be far enough.

But not today. Today it's too close.

Abruptly Mandy stood up and began pacing around the large office, touching desks and chairs at random, wanting…

Out.

She stood utterly still, surprised by the fierceness of her desire to be outside, in the open, free. It had been a long time since she had felt so trapped.

Same day, different year. I shouldn't have tried a deep bath this morning. Too deep. The water triggered too many memories.

A shudder ripped through Mandy's body. Suddenly she looked around, knowing that she had to have something to do or she would go crazy. She strode into Anthea's office to demand work. Anthea, Jessi and Steve were bent over the folders, which had been spread across a large library table. Apparently the premier's secretary had had his question answered, for Anthea was no longer holding a phone.

Anthea glanced at her utilitarian watch. "You're a few minutes early, but I suppose it's best. Airport traffic can be so unpredictable."

"What?" Mandy asked.

"Airport traffic," Anthea said briskly.

"Why do you care about—"

"The flight leaves in two hours."

"The flight?"

"To Sydney."

"Where?"

"Australia."

"*What?*" Mandy demanded, knowing how Alice had felt during the free-fall down the rabbit hole.

"Isn't this where I got on?" Anthea smiled serenely. "Get your purse, Mandy. This is where you get off."

"Anthea, what are you talking about?"

"The flight," said Steve, barely suppressing a wide smile.

"The flight?" Jessi said instantly, laughing.

"To Sydney," Steve said.

"Where?" Jessi asked, deadpan.

"Australia," Steve said.

"*What?*" Jessi asked, right on cue.

Mandy smiled despite herself. "I sounded that bad, huh?"

"Nothing that my vacation won't cure," Anthea said, crossing the room.

Just as Mandy opened her mouth to ask, "*What?*" she caught herself, disappointing Steve and Jessi. Anthea pulled a brilliant pink-and-black-striped backpack from her executive closet and plopped the bag softly on the desk. Mandy eyed the backpack dubiously.

"I didn't know zebras came in pink," Mandy murmured.

"They don't," Anthea said calmly. "This is a tiger stripe."

"Oh. Well, that explains it."

Anthea smiled and patted Mandy's hand. "That's what I like about you, dear. You understand me."

"I do?"

"You certainly do."

"That's frightening. When did you say your flight left?"

"I didn't, so we'd better hurry."

Mandy snapped her mouth shut, knowing she was in a losing battle. When Anthea was in high spirits, even Mandy's quick tongue had to take a back seat.

"Okay. Purse. Airport. Plane. Sydney," Mandy said. "I'll carry the tiger."

"Hold my calls," Anthea said over her shoulder.

For three weeks?

But the thought went no further than Mandy's smiling lips as she followed Anthea. She didn't want to puncture Anthea's high-flying mood; the prospect of a three-week vacation in Australia would be enough to make anyone slightly giddy. If it weren't for Sutter's presence at the other end—and the plane flight itself—Mandy would have envied her boss. Even with the flight and Sutter's uncertain company waiting at the other end, the thought of Australia was still enough to make Mandy dream. It had been so long since her horizons had been bounded by anything but office and apartment walls, memories and fear.

"This way, dear. We'll take my car," Anthea said.

A few minutes later Mandy tossed the backpack in the trunk of Anthea's sleek two-seat Mercedes.

"Are you sure you don't need more luggage?" Mandy asked. "For you, surely Sutter would bend his rules."

"It's all right. I guarantee I won't be inconvenienced by Sutter's rules in the least."

Anthea's sweeping assurance left no room for questions. Mandy closed the trunk and slid into the driver's seat.

"How about your passport?" Mandy asked. "Did you ever get that problem with it straightened out?"

That was why Sutter had left early; he hadn't had the patience to wait while his aunt untangled red tape.

"I finally called Senator Martin Thurgood. He took care of everything."

"What was the problem exactly? You never said."

"No, I didn't, did I?"

Mandy waited.

Anthea rummaged in her purse for the car keys. "There you are. Better hurry, dear. Sometimes these international flights are overbooked."

Mandy took the keys automatically. "Mr. Axton guaranteed you a seat, didn't he?"

"The seat is guaranteed," Anthea agreed.

"Since he owns a huge chunk of the airline, I don't think you need to worry about getting bumped. The way Mr. Axton feels about you, he'd probably throw out the captain first," Mandy said dryly.

Anthea simply smiled.

The drive to the airport took only twenty minutes. Mandy let Anthea off at the curb, then zipped across five lanes of traffic to find a space in the one-hour parking lot. She grabbed the vivid backpack out of the trunk, slammed down the lid and raced on foot back across five lanes of traffic. The first-class window was closed, telling Mandy that Anthea had already been checked in. She followed the directions to the gate, expecting to catch up with Anthea. She wasn't at the security checkpoint, however.

"Did a tiny silver-haired lady come through here?"

"Yes, ma'am," said the guard, smothering a smile. "Captain took her through himself on a cart. She had the wrong flight time. They're holding the plane."

"But I've got her luggage!"

Mandy tossed the backpack and her purse on the conveyor belt to be X-rayed. She hurried through the arch, didn't set off any alarms, grabbed the backpack and purse and set off at a run despite her high heels. At first she thought there was no one at the designated gate. Then she spotted a glint of silver hair at the end of the tunnel leading to a huge Boeing 747.

"Anthea!"

"Hurry up, dear. They're waiting for you."

Mandy ran down the slanted tunnel and held the backpack out to Anthea. She ignored it, taking Mandy's purse instead. She stuffed a fat business envelope into the purse and gave it back to Mandy.

"Everything you need is inside. Now hurry along."

"What?"

"Don't worry about a thing," Anthea continued, rolling over Mandy's objections as she guided her employee toward the plane's entrance. "I'm having your mail and newspaper held, Jessi will water your plants, Steve is taking your car in to be serviced and Alice will pick up your dry cleaning. Was there anything else needing your attention in the next few weeks?"

Openmouthed, unable to say anything, Mandy simply shook her head.

"Ms. Blythe?" called the stewardess from the opening. "I have to close the door in one minute."

"Run along," Anthea said. "Four hundred people are waiting for you." Suddenly she stood on tiptoe and gave Mandy a hug. "Enjoy your vacation. You've more than earned it."

"But I—"

"Shoo," Anthea interrupted firmly. "Steve and Jessi are waiting to help me hang another picture on my wall. Your picture."

Purse in one hand, pink-and-black tiger-striped backpack in the other, Anthea's latest project moved toward the waiting plane in a daze.

"And, Mandy," called Anthea clearly over her shoulder, "don't forget what I said about finding a lover. Australian men are marvelous!"

"Is your name D. M. Sutter?"

"Would it do any good to deny it?"

The man laughed. "Sorry, mate. Afraid not. I saw your picture on the telly last night."

Cursing under his breath, Sutter descended the last step leading away from the airplane, careful not to touch the metal handrail. Late September was spring in Bundaberg, but in the northeast corner of the Australian continent, spring was a relative term. The tropical intensity of the sun brought everything it touched up to a burning heat—including handrails.

"You a reporter?" Sutter asked, eyeing the tall, muscular, heavily tanned young man in front of him with little favor. Australian reporters made their American counterparts look like well-mannered choirboys.

"No worries, mate. My name's Ray. I'm a dive instructor over on Lady. I picked up a message for you along with your diving gear."

At the words "dive instructor" the grim look vanished from Sutter's face. He smiled and held out a tanned, callused hand. "Thanks for picking up my tanks for me. We had to dodge some early monsoon storms on the way from Kununurra. Took twice as long as it should have. Is the plane ready?"

"Just one more passenger and we can leave. Let's weigh you in."

Sutter followed Ray into the small air-conditioned passenger terminal. At a gesture from Ray, Sutter stepped onto a scale with his backpack in his arms. Ray's eyebrows went up. He gave Sutter's deceptively lithe length a reassessing look.

"You're a diver, right enough," Ray said.

Sutter's eyebrow lifted in a silent question.

"All muscle," Ray explained. "You weigh fifteen kilos more than you look."

"Is that a problem?" Sutter asked, remembering the strict weight restrictions for the flight to the island.

Shaking his head, Ray added Sutter's weight onto the running total he was keeping for the plane. "No worries, mate. We've got seventy kilos left on this run. Unless your wife is built like you, we'll do fine despite the heat."

"I don't have a wife."

"Right. Your Sheila."

"I don't have a Sheila."

"Then you've got worries, mate," Ray said, putting away his clipboard. "She's the one we're waiting for."

"Bloody hell."

Trying not to smile, Ray handed a folded piece of paper to Sutter. He eyed the note suspiciously, wondering what his aunt was up to now. The "early start" on his vacation had turned out to be two days of flying, followed by three solid days and most nights of slogging through some of Australia's choicer slices of tropical hell while discussing rain patterns and animal migrations with the most enigmatic natives Sutter had ever met anywhere on earth. He had a week's growth of itchy beard and hadn't washed himself in the same time—unless he counted periodic drenchings from Australia's early monsoon rains—and now he was standing around on a blistering cement apron in one hundred degrees Fahrenheit and ninety-five percent humidity, waiting for...just what the hell was he waiting for?

Muttering, Sutter unfolded the paper and read silently: *I'm sending my latest project. She needs a vacation as much as you do.*

The handwriting was both elegant and subtly imperious. The latter element was underlined by the sweeping signature.

Anthea.

Sutter looked at the horizon and silently counted to one hundred and thirty in the language that had no numbers. Ray watched from beneath his battered bush hat with the same deeply wary look the auctioneer had used.

And two goats is twenty. I don't need this. A near moon and a rising sun is twenty-one. I need a bath, a night's sleep, a good meal and a drink. Plus two goats is twenty-three. I need peace and quiet. And a pregnant goat is twenty-five. I need to be left alone. I need a vacation, not one of Anthea's damned projects! And a full moon is twenty-eight....

It was several minutes before Sutter's eyes focused on

the sugarcane fields that surrounded the small airport. The cane was in all stages of production from bare red earth furrows to saw-toothed plants taller than the tallest man. Beneath a heat-shimmering sky of towering clouds, varying stages of the cane's growth glowed in different shades of green, beginning with a pale chartreuse and progressing through a green so dark it was just short of black. With each movement of the hot, humid wind, the deceptively slender cane leaves shivered and swayed.

The wind shifted, bringing with it the rich aroma of Bundaberg's only claim to fame—a rum distillery.

"You wouldn't happen to have any of the local product on hand, would you?" Sutter asked at last, focusing on Ray.

"Huh?"

"Rum," Sutter said succinctly.

The diver's wariness vanished in a compassionate male smile. "Right. Got it in my kit bag. Follow me, mate. It will be too late to dive by the time we reach the island anyway."

For the thirtieth time in as many hours, Mandy refused an airline attendant's polite offer of food and drink. In the eternity since Anthea had blithely launched her latest project, said project had watched two in-flight movies, listened to everything from elevator music to Bach on the earphones and told herself repeatedly that she was sitting in a theater, not in an absurd piece of metal suspended by unknowable forces forty thousand feet over water so deep that it was almost entirely unknown to man.

On the whole, Mandy had been quite pleased with her handling of the trans-Pacific flight. She had managed to convince herself for several hours at a time that she was safe, if not quite sane. The flight on the 747 had been so long it had finally put her in an odd kind of trance, too tired to be actively frightened while the huge plane had chased midnight across half the world, never catching it, falling slowly farther and farther behind until an iridescent orange dawn had caught the airliner over the South Pacific.

Other people had looked out the window and murmured grateful appreciation of the glorious light sliding over the ocean. Mandy had closed her window shade and had kept it that way until the plane landed in Sydney. Every instant of the trip she had reminded herself that once the ocean went by, she was going to enjoy herself. Australia was the perfect destination for someone afraid of water—it was the driest continent on earth. After the landing she had walked off the plane with a soaring sense of pride and accomplishment that had lasted all through Customs and Immigration.

Then she had been directed to her connecting flight. Sydney wasn't her ultimate destination. A place with the unlikely name of Bundaberg was. Her flight was to leave in twenty-eight minutes. The plane was not a 747. It wasn't even half of one. It held less than one hundred people. If she hadn't been nearly dead from jet lag and a lack of food and sleep, she never would have allowed the too-helpful crew to lead her aboard, tuck her into a front seat and hand her a magazine. She hadn't exactly read the magazine during takeoff—she had tried to crawl between its pages.

After the first half hour of tightly clenched fear, her mind had slowly regained control of her body. She hadn't exactly relaxed, but she had been able to force her fingers to turn magazine pages rather than to dig uselessly into the armrests. Food was still impossible to consider, much less to eat; fear-induced adrenaline had killed her appetite beyond hope of easy resurrection. Even water nauseated her, so she had simply endured the dryness in her mouth. The light-headedness that had finally set in after thirty hours of absolute fasting was rather welcome. It took her mind off the size of the plane.

Mandy blinked, trying to remember what she had been attempting to read. Slowly her eyes focused on the creased, twisted pages in her lap. The map detailing Australian airlines' domestic routes was indecipherable now, ruined beyond any hope of use. She closed her eyes and prayed that Bundaberg was somewhere in the center of the outback, where water came no deeper than occasional puddles left by even more occasional rains.

The plane landed with no fuss and only a slight barking of the tires. While everyone else milled and descended the staircase that had been wheeled into place, Mandy breathed shakily and sat in her seat, telling herself that her ordeal was finally over. This was it. It was all done, finished, and she hadn't disgraced herself. Tomorrow— whichever day that might be, for she had lost track of time somewhere in the endless midnight over the ocean—tomorrow she would feel proud of her accomplishment. Right now all she wanted to do was to crawl into bed and sleep for a week.

"Miss Blythe, are you well?"

Mandy lifted her head and smiled wearily at the anxious attendant. "Jet lag," she said. "My stomach is somewhere over Hawaii and my brain is still in California. The rest of me isn't worth a bent penny."

The woman smiled. "Let me get your rucksack. The pink striped one, right?"

"Yes. Thank you."

Slowly Mandy stood up, feeling as though she were using a body that was on temporary loan rather than the one she had lived in for nearly twenty-eight years. The sunlight pouring in the airplane's open door was so bright that she pulled sunglasses from her purse. The lenses were utterly black, contrasting starkly with the pallor of her skin, but the glasses reduced the sun's tropic glare to a bearable level.

Mandy closed her hand over the rail of the rolling metal staircase, only to yank her fingers back. The rail was uncomfortably hot, and the air was so steamy that it was an effort to breathe. Very slowly she went down the stairs, sensing the attendant hovering helpfully behind. Finally her feet touched the apron. The solid feel of the earth was like a benediction to Mandy. She had never liked flying even before the accident; afterward, airplanes had become something she endured only because she wanted to be able to look herself in the mirror and not see a complete coward staring back out—just a partial coward.

With a sigh Mandy started toward the terminal, not even seeing the man who stood impatiently to one side, watching her. Sutter's eyes had narrowed into unwelcoming slits of green when he recognized Mandy slowly descending from the airplane. The rum he had drunk had loosened the muscles in his neck but hadn't otherwise improved his disposition. The last thing he needed right now was three weeks of one-liners from Anthea's smart-mouthed assistant—even if she did have the most elegant, sexy back he had ever seen or touched.

Sutter didn't need Mandy, but he was stuck with her. There was no help for it. She was there and he was there and Anthea was wisely beyond reach. Swearing beneath his breath, Sutter covered the few yards separating him from Mandy.

"Get your tail in gear," Sutter said in a clipped voice, grabbing her arm just above the elbow. "We've got to weigh you in. Where's your luggage?"

Mandy stared at Sutter, too thick-witted to do more than hear his words. Barely. Understanding or answering him was beyond her.

"Here you go, mate," the stewardess said, handing over Mandy's backpack. "She must be an experienced flier. She didn't bring anything more than this."

Sutter took the backpack, grimaced at the color, grunted his thanks to the stewardess and resumed hustling Mandy toward the small terminal. Before her body could adjust to the cool impact of the air conditioning, Sutter had lifted her onto the scale's low platform, shoved her purse and backpack into her arms and let go of her.

"Sutter?"

He ignored Mandy, looking only at Ray.

"No worries, mate. I've got diving gear that weighs more than your Sheila."

"She's not mine," Sutter snarled.

Mandy flinched.

Ray looked over Mandy's trim, womanly length. Even Mandy's dense sunglasses couldn't dim the impact of Ray's smile as he helped her down from the scale. Despite her exhaustion Mandy smiled in return; Anthea had been right about Australian men. Compared to Sutter, they were marvelous.

But then, so was a rabid gorilla.

"There's a good 'un," Ray said soothingly, steadying her. "Tough flight?"

"Yes," Mandy said, her voice cracking from dryness and relief that her torment had ended.

"No worries, luv," Ray said, giving her arm a reassuring squeeze as he removed the backpack. "Earl will have us out to Lady before you can say vegemite. Just don't try eating the stuff. Bloody awful. I've got to stow your gear now, but if you need anything on Lady, ask for Ray."

Rather mournfully Mandy watched as the handsome, energetic young man vanished through a back door in the terminal. She hadn't understood much of what he had said, but his smile had been like the local air conditioning— nearly overwhelming yet basically wonderful. She turned her attention back to Sutter. His mouth made as thin a line as his glittering jade eyes.

"Look, you have no idea how sorry I am," she said wearily, pushing the sunglasses up on her forehead so that she could rub her aching eyes. "Believe me, this wasn't my idea." She tried to smile placatingly at Sutter, but her lips kept curving down rather than up.

Sutter's glance was more comprehensive and less approving than Ray's had been. All that kept Sutter from venting his anger and frustration over his ruined vacation was the certainty that Mandy was on the ragged edge of exhaustion. There wasn't a bit of sauciness left in her.

Obviously Anthea had been right; Mandy needed a vacation as much as he did. Equally obviously, she hadn't been prepared for this one. The conservative suit, nylons and heels she was wearing fairly screamed of Anthea's old-fashioned office.

"How much warning did you get?" Sutter asked reluctantly, feeling unwilling compassion stir for the wilted waif standing in front of him, silently pleading with him not to be angry.

"Warning?" Mandy made a choked sound and shook her head.

"She means well," Sutter said, taking Mandy's arm again and hustling her toward the door through which they had just entered the terminal. "C'mon, kid. They're waiting for us. You can flake out on the way over."

Mandy barely had time to pull her sunglasses into place before she stepped into Bundaberg's natural outdoor sauna. It took a moment for her to realize that Sutter was taking her toward the landing strip, not the parking lot. She slowed. His grip on her arm tightened.

"Is the car around at the side?" she asked.

"What car?"

"The one that…oh, no. *No.*"

Behind her sunglasses, Mandy's eyes widened in horror. Ahead of them was a plane that looked like an overgrown white dragonfly. The tiny twin engines were revving, making conversation impossible as Sutter dragged her closer to the open passenger door. She tried to speak but was too exhausted and too frightened to make her tongue work. Her legs weren't working very well, either, but Sutter didn't seem to notice. He simply swept her along, ignoring her futile attempts to stop. When it came time to scramble into the plane, she balked. She couldn't do it. She simply couldn't.

"N-no," she stammered. "I d-don't like small planes."

"If you think this is small, wait until you see the runway at the other end. Come on, get in," Sutter said impatiently, wanting to get out of the sun. "We've waited an hour for you already."

Mandy tried to think, to explain, but all she could do was stare in horror at the little plane that seated eight, including the pilot. Suddenly she felt herself being boosted aboard. She tried to fight, but it was like her worst nightmares; her muscles turned to sand, every movement was in slow motion except the world around her and it was hurtling forward so fast that nothing could stop it or the lethal crash that waited for her. With the last bit of her willpower Mandy turned to Sutter, forcing herself to speak.

"S-Sutter, p-please! I'm t-terrified of f-flying!"

"Cute, real cute," Sutter said curtly, stuffing Mandy through the fuselage door with more muscle than ceremony. "You're so terrified that you flew halfway around the world on one plane and then flew up the length of the Australian continent on another, right? So knock off the bad comedy and get your butt in the damn seat."

He boosted himself in right behind Mandy, sat her firmly in her seat just behind the pilot and flopped down in the seat next to her. The sound of the engines changed in pitch to a mechanical scream. Mandy only wished she could scream, as well, but her mouth was too dry, her throat too constricted.

"S-Sutter..."

He hadn't heard her aching whisper. She grabbed his wrist, trying to make him understand.

"Listen, honey," he snarled, jerking free. "I haven't slept in three days, I haven't bathed in a week and the last thing I ate was a lizard charred in a camp fire. I'm sure as hell in no mood for any more of your silly jokes. Give it a rest!"

Mandy tried to speak again but her mouth was too dry, the engines had become too loud, and the earth itself was hurtling away beneath her. Within minutes the plane

turned and headed out over the sea. She closed her eyes
and prayed that she would die in the crash rather than be
trapped alive in the fuselage, sinking, drowning, no one to
hear her screams but a dead man who had never loved her.

Chapter 4

❧❧❧❧❧

To Mandy the sound and smell and feel of the plane were part of a nightmare revisited. There were vibrations shaking her, too much noise for a scream to be heard and no voice left with which to scream, no strength, nothing but the empty sky above and the uncaring sea below.

Nightmare and memory became one and the same, hammering at her, shaking her, until all she could do was endure as the devastating past rose up and overwhelmed her....

Mandy wheeled her bike off the early-afternoon ferry to Catalina Island. She stepped onto the left pedal and swung her leg easily over the seat, feeling happy and healthy and very much alive. Early summer clouds swelled silently overhead, pushed up from the Mexican tropics by a southerly wind. The unusual humidity didn't bother Mandy. Nothing could bother her today. Humming softly, smiling at people she passed, Mandy began pedaling toward the campground that was halfway up the island, closer to the tiny airstrip than to the small resort town of Avalon.

She pedaled faster than usual, eager to give Andrew the good news. Her husband had been unusually moody lately. His research hadn't been going well. At least, that was what he had blamed his bleak silences and sudden outbursts on in the past. Once she had thought Andrew's dark mood had to do more with the fact that his forty-second birthday had come and gone—placing him securely within that dread territory called middle age—with no baby in sight despite nine months of trying. But when she had mentioned his age and lack of a child as a possible source of his temper, he had stormed out of the house, leaving her to wait up until 3:00 a.m., when he had come in smelling of alcohol and smoke from nameless bars.

That had been the first time he had come home in the early hours of the morning, but not the last. It had happened more and more frequently during the past nine months. Andrew's forty-third birthday—and their fourth wedding anniversary—was tonight. That was why Mandy had begged, wheedled and bullied the doctor to get an early answer from the lab so that she could surprise her husband by arriving early on the island that lay only twenty-six miles off the coast of California.

Mandy and Andrew had honeymooned on Catalina, diving along its steep, rocky sides, seeing ocean life that was far more varied and abundant than the marine life to be found off mainland Southern California's heavily populated and often heavily polluted shores. The honeymoon had been one of the happiest times of Mandy's life, despite the fact that the pleasures of marital sex hadn't lived up to their advance billing. The ocean had more than compensated for the awkwardness she felt during her husband's swift, turbulent lovemaking.

The novelty of her sexual inexperience had quickly worn off for both herself and her husband, leaving little to take its place but her efforts to understand what had gone wrong. The ocean's novelty had never worn off for Mandy. The siren call of the green-shadowed depths sank more deeply into her soul with each dive.

At least we have that in common, Mandy thought.

The insight startled her. She and Andrew had a lot more

in common than diving, didn't they? He had been her faculty adviser while she got her Ph.D. in oceanography. He had encouraged her, respected her work, tried to seduce her repeatedly and unsuccessfully and had ultimately married her on his fortieth birthday. His second marriage. Her first. The fact that there had been no children from the first marriage had reassured Mandy at first; Andrew's demanding schedule left little enough time for a wife, much less for children.

But Andrew wanted children. Desperately. Mandy hadn't been ready for immediate motherhood. She had wanted time to adjust to juggling marriage and her burgeoning career as an ocean resource specialist for the state of California. Yet before her marriage was more than a few months old, fights had begun over when to have children, fights that left Mandy angry and crying and confused. In all the time before their marriage, she and Andrew had talked of their joint careers, of exploring the oceans of the earth together, of teaching and dissertations and the color of the sea fifteen fathoms down on a sunny day.

Never once had Andrew mentioned wanting children at all, much less immediately after marriage. Just as Mandy had naively assumed that sex would be wonderful after marriage, she had assumed that Andrew shared her desire that she establish herself in her field before she took a leave of absence to have children. She had been wrong. Andrew had wanted her to throw away her pills the day they were married. The fact that she had just been given an important grant to study the dietary habits of the Pacific sea otter had meant nothing to Andrew. The fact that her work might ultimately be used to determine whether or not that endangered species survived had also left him unmoved. He had wanted her pregnant, period. Everything else came second.

Mandy had thrown her pills away the day her work on the otters was complete. She had assumed that her marriage would improve immediately. And it had, until her period came.

After her third period had come, she had gone in to see her doctor, received a thorough checkup and been told to come back in nine months if she hadn't conceived. Nine months later she had returned. After an exhaustive series of tests it had been determined that her fertility was all that it should be and then some. She was told to send her husband in for tests.

Andrew had flatly refused.

It doesn't matter now, Mandy told herself, pedaling fiercely. *I'm almost two months pregnant and everything is all right. I can tell Andrew and see him smile at me again. He'll be a good father—God knows he really wants children, which is more than you can say for a lot of men.*

The thought of their future baby made Mandy smile and then laugh. She couldn't wait to feel the baby move, to give birth and to hold the baby in her arms, to teach her child to swim and to read and to ride a bike, to share with her child the beauty and mystery of the shimmering sea. She couldn't wait to tell Andrew, either, to see his delighted smile, to know that she had finally given him something he desperately wanted.

Anticipation made Mandy impatient with the miles between herself and her husband. She wished that she had been able to call him, but that hadn't been possible. She wished that she had flown over with him in their little plane a few days ago, but if she had, she wouldn't have been able to get the lab report back until next week, and she had wanted the report in time for it to be a birthday and anniversary present in one. Besides, she really didn't enjoy flying, especially in a small plane, which was another thing she and Andrew argued about. He took her unease as a slap at his abilities as a pilot, and nothing she had been able to say had convinced him otherwise.

That's all in the past, Mandy told herself firmly. *Now that I'm pregnant, he won't be so touchy about his age, his abilities, his career. Everything. We'll be able to laugh together again.*

Mandy's thoughts veered back to the coming baby. Mentally she began making lists of things to do, things to put on hold for a year, people to tell, papers to be rushed before she was too big to do the research. She was still making lists when she wheeled into the campsite where Andrew had been for three days. No one was in sight. She bit her lip, then sighed. He was probably out diving with one of the locals.

Deflated, Mandy parked her bike beneath a big bush at the back of the campsite and headed for the tent. The first thing she noticed was the compressed-air tanks propped against a nearby boulder. The second thing she noticed was the components of two wet suits strewn across the ground between the tanks and the tent, as though whoever had worn the suits had been in a terrible rush to get out of their neoprene prisons. The third thing she noticed was an oddly shaped scrap of fuchsia cloth dangling from a guy rope near the tent's entrance. Puzzled, she pulled back the tent flap and stepped in.

It took a moment for Mandy's eyes to adjust from full sun to the tent's dim interior light. Her ears had no such problem. She heard the feminine voice with awful clarity.

"Oh...more...harder...harder...!"

Mandy barely recognized Andrew as his hips slammed rhythmically into the girl who was squirming frantically beneath him, both of them panting, her nails raking down his naked back as her body bucked and then went rigid. Mandy's horrified cry was lost beneath the noise of her husband's climax and that of his partner. The difference in the light level inside the tent registered on the girl, however. After a few more cries, she opened her eyes lazily.

"Oops," she said.

"Huh?" he said.

"When did you say your wife was coming over?"

"Tomorrow."

"I think she decided to come early."

"She never comes," Andrew said, laughing. "That's why I like getting off with you. You like it the same way I do, hot and fast."

"Hon, I'm not fooling. We've got company."

Andrew followed the girl's glance, shifting onto his elbows in response to his partner's pushes. He squinted into the light streaming through the open tent flap.

"Mandy?" he asked.

Her only answer was a choked sound of rage and hurt and disbelief.

With a muttered obscenity, Andrew rolled off the girl. "What the hell are you doing here today?"

Mandy could hardly believe what she was hearing. "I think a better question would be what *she* is doing here."

"What she's doing here is fornicating, and she's doing it a hell of a lot better than you ever do," he retorted, peeling off a condom and dumping it in an ashtray.

The words slid past Mandy's anger, slicing into her until she couldn't speak for the pain.

"Hey, hon," the girl said, stretching, "I think I'll give this whole scene a pass, know what I mean? Righteous wives just aren't my thing."

The girl grabbed a scrap of fuchsia cloth from the foot of the sleeping bag. The cloth turned out to be a bikini bottom, which she wriggled into before brushing past Mandy on the way out. The tent shivered as the girl snapped the other scrap of fuchsia cloth off the rope.

"Thanks for the use of the diving gear," the girl called from outside the tent. "Catch ya later."

Mandy looked down at her husband, who was pulling on a pair of wet swimming trunks. She wasn't able to say anything or even think of anything to say; all she could do was try to cope with the anger, humiliation and disbelief that were shaking her.

This can't be happening.

But it was.

"Mandy, Mandy, Mandy," Andrew sighed, running his hand through his thinning hair. "Well, you were bound to find out sooner or later. The miracle is that it wasn't sooner."

"Find out?"

The dry rasp of Mandy's words surprised her. That couldn't be her voice. That couldn't be her husband, the father of her child, still slick from another woman's body. She made a low sound of pain and wrapped her arms around herself.

"You're so damned naive," Andrew said, exasperated and almost sad at the same time. "It used to fascinate me how anyone as brilliant as you could be so dense about men and sex. I kept fantasizing how great it would be to initiate you, to know I was getting something no other man had ever had. And then I thought what bright kids we'd have together. So I married you and took you to bed and—" he shrugged "—well, it wasn't great and it didn't get any better. I didn't have the patience to teach you how to please me and you didn't have any interest in learning." He sighed. "So I found my sex elsewhere. That shocks you now, but you'll get used to it. And I'm careful, Mandy. I learned my lesson with my first wife. I don't bring anything home but memories, and they're not contagious."

Mandy didn't realize that she was shaking her head in automatic denial until Andrew cursed and came angrily to his feet.

"Grow up, Mandy! Stop looking at me like I've just drowned your favorite kitten. I don't know of one man who doesn't step out on his wife—and I know of damn few wives who don't return the favor! But they live together in relative harmony and raise kids anyway, because nothing human is perfect and they're grown-up enough to know it!"

For a long time Mandy looked at her husband, then asked raggedly, "What about love?"

"What about it?"

Mandy closed her eyes. "Then why did you marry me?"

"I was nearly forty and I panicked. Like every other fool since Adam, I thought an injection of young tail would make me young, too. But I couldn't get in your pants without a ring. Then I decided, what the hell, why not? I wanted kids. I wanted them a lot. I didn't want to grow old alone and die knowing that nothing of me lived on."

Silence stretched, then stretched more, until Andrew asked tiredly, "Any more questions?"

Mandy shook her head.

"You sure?"

She nodded, but she felt as though she had been torn in half and was watching herself from a distance—talking, breathing, all the normal gestures and signs of life. But nothing felt real. The tent wasn't real. She wasn't real. The moment wasn't real.

"Great," Andrew said, looking relieved. "Let's go diving. It's not too late to bag something for dinner."

As though at a distance Mandy heard herself say, "I'll eat on the ferry."

Her husband looked at his diving watch. "No, you won't. You can't pedal back in time to catch the last ferry. Come on, Mandy," he coaxed. "Suit up. The only thing we're good at together is diving. You'll feel better once you're down there." He smiled ruefully. "You know, if you'd taken to sex with a tenth of the instinct and skill you show for diving…" He sighed. "Well, you didn't, and I need a lot of sex and that's the way it is."

"No."

"No what?"

"If you think I'm going to crawl into my wet suit—the wet suit that your little sand bunny just peeled off—you are crazy."

Mandy's words were as quiet, flat and blank as her eyes. She still had the eerie feeling of being divided in two—

half of her screaming soundlessly in pain and anger, the other half watching with unnatural calm.

"Fine," Andrew said curtly. "So we'll have hamburger."

"Like hell."

He rubbed his forehead in sudden pain. "Mandy, I've got a real splitter. Could we put this on hold?"

"You can put it where the sun don't shine," she shot back. "I'm going home right now if I have to swim."

"If I break camp and take the gear, there will be too much weight in the plane."

"Who said anything about breaking camp?"

"Mandy—"

"If we hurry," she interrupted, her voice brittle, "in a few hours you can be back here grunting and sweating on top of little miss loose thighs."

"Why don't you stay and watch? Maybe you'd learn something about how to make a man feel like a man!"

Mandy spun around and left the tent, heading for the airplane.

It wasn't that easy, of course. Andrew couldn't believe that his young wife wouldn't change her mind once she had cooled off. Mandy endured the arguments and pleas and insults because there was no other choice, no place to go, nothing she could do but wait for Andrew to give in or for tomorrow's early ferry to leave the island, whichever came first.

It was Andrew who finally gave in, sometime in the lost hours before dawn. Grim-faced, unnaturally pale, he strapped himself into the little plane. The tiny strip was unmanned and not set up for night takeoffs, but Andrew had flown in and out of Catalina so many times that he didn't even hesitate. The small plane leaped into the air, climbed, executed a crisp turn and headed for the mainland.

For once Mandy wasn't nervous about being in the little plane. She was more afraid of what her husband's next cutting justifications for adultery might be than she was afraid of the plane itself. A swath of city lights glittered on the mainland horizon, a beacon of life and color beyond the blank darkness of the sea. Next to her Andrew piloted the plane in silence, his hands too tight on the controls. Several times she thought he was going to speak, but beyond kneading his neck and left shoulder from time to time, he concentrated exclusively on flying.

Gradually Mandy became aware that Andrew's breathing had changed. Simultaneously she realized that the altitude of the plane had changed, as well. Instead of flying level, they were descending. The plane had lost so much altitude that the mainland's glittering lights were barely a tiny thread across the darkness. It was as though Andrew were going for a landing, yet there were no lights below, no airport, nothing but the black sea.

"Andrew? What are you doing?" She turned and saw him. "Oh, God! Andrew!"

His face was bathed in sweat and his mouth was flattened in a grim line of pain. He was flying one-handed. Before her horrified eyes he groaned and went limp. Instants later the plane ripped off the top of one wave and bounced onto the peak of another and then another, skimming the surface of the sea like a flat rock thrown by skillful hand.

But unlike a rock, the plane could float. For a time. Long enough for a dazed, battered Mandy to realize what had happened. Long enough for her to claw off her harness and her husband's. Long enough for her to pull futilely at his slack body, wrenching with all her strength and calling incoherent prayers, trying and trying to pull him out the buckled passenger door, kicking at the door with her feet and screaming and yanking at Andrew's dead weight.

Suddenly cold water surged upward, engulfing the white wreckage, pulling the fuselage down and down, taking her and her immovable burden with it....

* * *

Sutter lifted his attention from the fascinating patterns of indigo and glittering silver reflections that gave the sea around the Great Barrier Reef so much visual variety. Each difference in color represented a change in the depth of the sea, a change caused by the presence of the tiny animals that were in the process of further enlarging the greatest mass of material ever assembled by any life-form anywhere on the face of the earth. From orbital distance, even the most dense metropolitan sprawls of humanity didn't register on the human eye; the Barrier Reef did. More than twelve hundred miles long and sixty stories from bottom to wave-combed top, the reef formed a 100,000-square-mile fringe to Australia's northeastern edge.

And just off the nose of the plane, only a few minutes away, lay tiny Lady Elliot Island, a scuba diver's paradise. Elation surged within Sutter, making him smile. He had wanted to go to Lady Elliot since the first time he had heard of the island twenty years before. Now it was finally within reach, the southernmost coral island of the immense Great Barrier Reef complex, an island that was no more than a tiny mote decorated with white breakers, lime green lagoons and an ocean so clear that he could count more shades of blue than he had words to describe.

The plane banked, shutting off Sutter's view of Lady Elliot Island. Eagerly he leaned to his left, over Mandy's lap, peering out her window. The plane straightened, shifting his weight unexpectedly. He bumped into Mandy.

"Excuse me," he said loudly over the engine noise, "I..."

Sutter's words trailed off as he realized that Mandy hadn't noticed him. She was rigid in her seat, her hands clenched together, her face gleaming with sweat. It occurred to him that he couldn't remember her moving at all during the flight. She hadn't even crossed and recrossed her ankles or shifted her purse or rummaged inside it for a comb or a piece of gum. It was as though she were a statue.

"Mandy?"

There was no answer. Sutter touched Mandy's hands. The chill of her skin shocked him; the plane was too small to be air-conditioned, which meant that the interior temperature was well into the eighties. There was no reason for her to be so cold.

If Mandy felt Sutter's touch she didn't show it. Nor did she appear to notice the plane's descent. She was unnaturally still, as white as the coral beaches and landing strip below, her skin icy to the touch.

Abruptly Sutter understood that Mandy hadn't been joking at the Bundaberg airport; she really was terrified. Even as he reached out automatically to comfort her, he overrode the impulse, forcing his hands back to his sides. So far she had somehow managed to control her terror. Anything he did might snap that fragile restraint and send her into a bout of hysterical screaming. The pilot didn't need that kind of distraction at the moment—there was a hard crosswind blowing and the coral landing strip was little more than a white line gnawed through the sturdy she-oaks that had colonized the island.

The pilot crabbed in, compensated for the relatively calm air between the she-oaks and dropped down onto the crushed coral runway, dumping speed as fast as he could. Sutter's eyes widened when he saw why the pilot was in such a hurry to stop—a colony of terns was nesting on the far half of the strip.

The pilot knew precisely what he was doing. He stopped short of the birds with room to spare. He shut down the engine, popped open the side window for ventilation and stretched. The passenger sitting next to him hopped out, followed by the pilot himself. In order for the four people seated behind Sutter to exit, he had to get out first, for until his seat was folded down, there would be no way for anyone in back to scramble out of the plane. He looked over at Mandy. She hadn't moved.

Sutter got out quickly, helped the remaining passengers out and then climbed back in. Mandy neither moved nor acknowledged her surroundings in any way.

"Mandy, it's all right. We've landed."

Sutter's voice was low, soothing. She didn't seem to hear him. Slowly he removed her black, oversized sunglasses. Her eyes were wide, unfocused, dilated, and what he had thought was sweat was actually a slow rain of tears. Gently he stroked her white, cold cheek.

"Mandy, you can come back now. It's all over. You're safe."

He repeated the words many times, touching her very carefully, telling her that she was safe. After a few moments she shuddered once, violently, like a swimmer struggling up from the black depths to the surface of the sea. Slowly her eyes focused on Sutter.

"That's it, golden eyes. Look around. You're safe," he murmured, smoothing the back of his fingers down her cold cheek once again. "Ready to get out now?"

Mandy fumbled at the fastening of her seat belt, but her hands were shaking too hard to accomplish anything. Sutter took care of the buckle with a swift motion, then eased her from the seat, taking most of her weight when her legs proved to be as uncertain as her hands had been.

"Lean against the frame while I get out, okay?"

Before Mandy managed to nod, Sutter had slipped out and was turning to lift her onto the blindingly white coral runway. Carefully he set her on her feet.

"Can you walk?" he asked.

He watched her lips form the word *yes*, but before she could speak she crumpled. He caught her, lifted her into his arms and began to walk toward a small building that was all but hidden by she-oak trees.

Ray, who had been unloading the plane's small baggage compartment, saw Mandy faint. He sprinted forward.

"What happened?" he demanded.

"Jet lag," Sutter said laconically. "Which tent is ours?"

"This way. Need a hand?"

The idea of turning Mandy's limp form over to anyone else was frankly distasteful. Sutter shook his head in curt refusal. Then, realizing how rude the gesture had been, Sutter added in his best Australian accent, "No worries, mate. She's not that big."

Ray hesitated, smiled slightly and led Sutter at a brisk pace along a crushed coral pathway. As he walked, Sutter shifted Mandy until her head was supported by his chest. He kept her tucked in close, dividing his attention between the path and her white face. The slow, even movement of her breast against his left hand told him that she was breathing well, despite her pallor. He hurried between tents and a few spartan cabins, barely noting the dive gear propped everywhere. There were curious glances from a few well-bronzed, husky young men lounging in front of one tent, cans of Fosters Lager firmly in hand. A wave-off from Ray told the men that things were under control.

"In you go," Ray said, pulling aside a ragged tent flap.

Two single mattresses rested on the tent floor, one to each side. The clean white sheets, neatly folded white blankets and oversize white towels looked rather incongruous against the worn canvas.

"Usually there are double bunks," Ray explained hastily, "but they're all taken. This tent wasn't rented because it was a spare that needed mending. Wind can blow bloody hard here. We got the worst rips repaired, but—"

"It's fine," Sutter interrupted, laying Mandy on one of the mattresses and propping her feet instead of her head on the pillow. "I'm still surprised you fit us in on such short notice. Anthea must have moved heaven and earth."

Ray grinned. "Don't know about heaven, but there was a hell of a to-do here until we found a place to put you."

He knelt beside Sutter and looked at Mandy's pale, delicate face. "You sure she's all right?"

Sutter held his fingers against the pulse in Mandy's throat. The flow of blood was steady, even and reassuring. There was nothing to suggest that anything more than exhaustion and fear was at work on her body. Color began coming back into her face even as he watched.

"She's coming around right now."

"Water is in the thermos by your bed. I'll go out and tell the blokes what's what—unless you need me?"

Sutter shook his head, never lifting his intent green gaze from Mandy as he stroked her smooth cheek. Long, dense black eyelashes fluttered. She murmured and turned toward the source of the slow, gentle caresses that were warming her cheek. Her lips brushed the back of his knuckles and her breath sighed warmly across the sensitive skin between his fingers.

Desire coiled suddenly, heavily, in Sutter. He told himself it was only that Mandy had aroused his protective instincts—and then the memory of her elegant, naked back and the satin gleam of her skin beneath the stage's spotlight came to him. A hot shaft of desire pulsed through him, pushing his shorts into a new shape. It was a response that had occurred more than once when he had looked at Mandy.

I need this like I need the bends. Damn Anthea! How did she know that Mandy turns me on? Did I somehow give it away during the few days I was in the office? I spoke less than twenty words to Mandy, and all of them were strictly business.

There was no answer to Sutter's silent question except the hard thrust of desire lying heavily between his legs, tightening his body until he ached.

Too bad Mandy isn't like whatsherfanny, the glamour girl Anthea shipped off to New York. But Mandy isn't the type for fast affairs and faster goodbyes, and that's all I want from a woman. So stand down, John Thomas. There's nothing doing with this woman.

Mandy nuzzled against Sutter's hand. He yanked it back as though she had bitten him. Even so, the sensory impact of her lips burned on his skin, making a mockery of his attempts to control his unruly sex. Sudden anger rushed through Sutter, anger at himself for not understanding that Mandy truly had been afraid, anger at Anthea for meddling by throwing matches and gasoline together on a remote coral island, anger at his pulsing body for demanding something it wasn't going to get and pure masculine rage at Mandy that she could arouse him simply by being alive.

Three weeks. In a tent. Listening to her breathe. God, I'll go crazy.

But first I'll throttle my damned meddling aunt!

Mandy made a low sound as she swam up from the depths of her nightmare. Her eyes opened, focused, and her breath came in sharply. Sutter's green eyes were very close to hers, watching her with something that looked like anger.

"What…?" Mandy asked, wondering what she had done wrong now.

"You fainted," Sutter said in a clipped voice. "How do you feel?"

Slowly Mandy looked around. She was in a tent and a wind was gusting, alternately belling out the canvas sides and collapsing them again. The screened flap of the tent's front opening was in shreds that fluttered with each movement of the air. Beneath the wind came the sound of distant surf. The unmistakable smell of the sea was rich in the humid air.

"We didn't crash," Mandy said.

"You seem surprised."

She looked at him blankly. "Crashes happen."

"Not very damned often or people wouldn't fly." Sutter came to his feet in a powerful, impatient movement, not wanting to stay any closer to Mandy than he absolutely had to. "Feel like sitting up?"

Slowly Mandy brought herself into a sitting position. Sutter clenched his hands into fists to keep from reaching for her. He wanted to help her, sure, but not half as much as he wanted to feel her in his arms again. The knowledge only fed his anger. He should have let the handsome, solicitous Ray haul Mandy to the tent and nurse her to consciousness.

Sutter's instant, savage rejection of that idea did nothing to take the sharp edge off his temper. The rational part of his mind calmly pointed out that jet lag, fatigue and lack of sleep were taking their toll of him as surely as they had of Mandy. The irrational part of his mind told the other part to get stuffed—his long-awaited vacation had been ruined and he was in no mood to be gracious about it.

"Dizzy?" he asked curtly.

Mandy shook her head. All she felt was utterly drained.

"Good. Why don't you get in your suit while I get Ray to walk you down to the lagoon. You can take a ride in the reef boat or go for a lazy swim in some of the most beautiful water in the world. You'll feel much better and—"

"No," Mandy said, shuddering. "The only thing that scares me more than small planes is the ocean."

"Then the reef boat—"

"No. I can't take anything smaller than the *Queen Mary*."

Sutter's last hope of a decent vacation evaporated, and with it went his temper.

"Let me get this straight," he said coolly. "I've spent a lifetime trying to get to the Great Barrier Reef, and my sainted aunt has fixed it so that I'll be locked up in a tent for three weeks with an amateur comedian who's afraid of her own shadow!"

"I'm not so hot on the idea myself," Mandy retorted, feeling strength return on a rush of anger. "I'd rather spend the time in a cage with a hungry tiger than trapped here with you!''

"I sense an area of agreement emerging," he said sardonically. "If you get your butt in gear, we can stuff some tranquilizers down your throat and get you back to the airfield before Earl takes off for the run back to the mainland. We'll give you some for the road, too. With luck, you'll be safe in your little burrow at home before the last of the pills wear off.''

"Never," Mandy said, her voice climbing. "I will never get on that little white plane again!"

"Fine. I'll charter a boat."

"No. It won't be big enough."

"Then I'll blindfold you so you won't know the difference," he shot back. "Or are you afraid of the dark, too?"

"Go to hell, Sutter."

"You're the one who would like it there—it's dry and there's not a pair of wings in sight!"

Chapter 5

"How's the little Sheila doing?" Ray asked, his blue eyes vivid with health and good humor.

Sutter grunted. The quarter-mile walk from the tent to the "dive shop"—little more than a small shed—had taken some of the edge off Sutter's temper, but not enough. He looked longingly through the dark green fringe of narrow she-oak leaves, trying to catch a glimpse of the fantastic coral reef he had come so far and waited so long to see. Though invisible from where he stood, the presence of the sea was palpable in the brine-laden air, the distant murmur of breakers, the crushed coral lying white and pure beneath his feet.

"Any chance of a dive today?" Sutter asked wistfully.

"Sorry, mate. It's blowing too hard to take out the dive boat. The only other way to get out is to walk out through the lagoon to the reef at low tide and dive off the far side. But it will be dark by the next low tide."

Even as Sutter swore, he knew it was just as well that he didn't go diving. He was too tired and too edgy to dive. "What about tomorrow?"

"S.S.D.D." Ray saw Sutter's lack of comprehension and smiled. "Same manure, different day."

Sutter's mouth kicked up at one corner.

"If it's windy," Ray continued, "most of the blokes are going to walk the reef tomorrow morning and dive off the wall. You're welcome to come along. The Sheila, too, if she's up to it. Walking the reef both ways in diving gear takes it out of you."

"I doubt that Mandy will feel like taking on the sea," Sutter said sardonically.

"She did look a bit like old beer," Ray said. "But we'd better go over her diving gear as well as yours just the same. That way when the fancy takes her, she'll be ready to go."

The next hour of checking equipment to see how it had survived the baggage handlers on two continents went a long way toward smoothing Sutter's ragged temper. Not for the first time in his life, Sutter wondered if diving weren't all that had kept him sane in a brutally crazy world. It was months since he had gone diving in anything but Brazil's opaque jungle rivers. As a form of release, that kind of river diving served its purpose, but only barely. He hungered to feel the cool, clean sea sweep around him in shades of blue, buoyant salt water taking the weight of the world from him and giving him the incomparable gift of flight.

By the end of the hour Sutter had relaxed completely, and Ray had accepted Sutter as a member of the informal fraternity of scuba divers. Sutter's ease and expertise with the gear, his critical attention to detail and his wry stories of the drawbacks of diving in unknown jungle rivers all had combined to make the young diver watch Sutter with growing interest and admiration.

"Looks like your Sheila bought herself all new gear to meet the Lady," Ray said, setting the last of the equipment aside and looking at it with mild envy. "Only the best, too."

Sutter grunted. He was certain Anthea had bought the expensive wet suit, tanks, mask, fins and all the rest. He also had no doubt that everything would fit Mandy perfectly. Anthea left no detail overlooked when she committed herself to a project.

Suddenly the sound of children's laughter burst into the dive shed's masculine silence. Sutter's head snapped up in surprise.

"That's the Townehome lot," Ray said. "Family comes here every year. The girl was nearly born here, but we got Linda to the mainland in time."

"They sound a little young for diving."

"Ted and Linda swap off the nanny duties. One dives, the other wades." Ray glanced at his dive watch. "Time for tucker. Do you know where you eat?"

"No, but with only a few buildings on the whole island, the cafeteria can't be hard to find."

"It's just back of the office, which is just below the bird sanctuary and facing the lagoon."

Sutter smiled. "Got it."

He stood, stretched and walked back down the coral pathway, past the handful of small, frankly plain cabins and wind-battered tents. There were two bathhouses, one per sex, although the men on the island probably outnumbered the women four to one. Lady Elliot was not for the casual tourist; the accommodations were spartan, the island utterly isolated, and if you didn't like diving, there was little else to do other than walk laps of the tiny island. Even walking slowly, he doubted that it would take Mandy more than an hour or two for a complete circuit. She was going to be one very bored tourist before the three weeks were up—maybe even bored enough that a boat or plane ride to the mainland would be welcome.

As Sutter approached the tent that had been hastily set up within a she-oak grove and at a distance from the other tents, his long stride slowed to a crawl. He wasn't looking forward to the next few minutes. Mandy had been as much a victim of Anthea's good intentions as he had. He owed Mandy an apology and he knew it. He just didn't know how to phrase it.

"Mandy?" Sutter said quietly, not wanting to startle her by walking in unannounced.

No answer came.

Concerned, Sutter pushed aside the ragged flap and looked in. Mandy lay on her side, deeply asleep, her hands tucked beneath her chin and her knees slightly bent. Her dark hair was fanned across the pillow like a silky forerunner of night. Her suit jacket had been discarded, her blouse was half-pulled out from her waistband, and her skirt had crept halfway up her wonderfully sleek thighs. One of her shoes was still on. The other teetered on the edge of slipping off her toes.

Silently Sutter knelt next to the mattress and eased off Mandy's shoes. Beneath the thin nylon her foot was warm. He held her instep in his palm for a moment longer than necessary before he gently released her. She didn't stir. He considered waking her for dinner, then discarded the idea. The darkness beneath her eyes told him that sleep was more necessary to her than food. But would she sleep, or would she be haunted by nightmares, residue of her earlier terror?

Sutter thought of lying down with Mandy and holding her against the nightmares he suspected would come. Maybe that would serve as an apology…his hard body pressed against her trembling one, his arms holding her, his mouth kissing away even the memory of her fear.

A hissed curse sizzled through the silence. Sutter came to his feet in a single motion and turned away from Mandy. Without looking back, he left the tent. As he strode down the path to get dinner, he cursed himself every step of the way. Miraculously he didn't get lost, but that owed more to the handful of people straggling toward the cafeteria than to any innate cleverness on his part.

The dining area was as spartan as the dive shop. There was a linoleum floor that was clean and old, perhaps twelve plastic-topped tables arranged at random, metal folding chairs, no curtains for the open windows. Dinner was served buffet-style and cooked by the college-age kids who vied for the privilege of spending time on Lady Elliot Island. Sutter lined up, accepted a lot of everything available and found an empty chair. It wasn't difficult. There looked to be no more than twenty guests camped at Lady Elliot's rustic resort.

The food itself was just what Sutter had expected— hearty, high calorie and plentiful. Perfect fare for divers who burned off thousands of calories every day simply keeping their bodies warm; for beneath the sun-heated surface of tropical waters lay the cool blue depths, where seventy degrees was considered quite warm, yet seventy was nearly thirty degrees below body temperature. Even in wet suits, diving used calories as fast as they could be replaced. As a group, scuba divers tended to be muscular and very hard, for all fat had long since been burned off.

By the time Sutter was halfway through dinner, Ray and two other divers had joined him. They told Sutter that beer and wine were available from the "bar," which boasted one of the two refrigerators on the island. Adding a can of Fosters beer to the menu perked it up considerably, Sutter discovered.

After dinner the men adjourned to the bar, which was about the size of a small bus. The decor consisted of six stools, a handful of tiny tables and the much-prized refrigerator, which cooled everything from beer to medicines to film. The spartan amenities were more than compensated for by the lively conversation and Australian beer, but an hour after the abrupt sunset, people began yawning and wandering off to their beds. Sunrise came early, and with it came the possibility of diving. That was what had lured everyone to the remote island—diving, not sleeping or fancy dining or hard drinking. On Lady Elliot Island the sea was the center of all conversations and actions; and as with all demanding mistresses, the sea required that the men who enjoyed her favors be strong, alert and skilled.

It was full dark with a lid of tropical clouds when Sutter

walked back to the tent. Heat lightning danced on the western horizon, but Sutter knew there would be no rain. Not yet. There would be a period of buildup before the clouds were released from their turmoil, days of waiting and seething and growing toward the glorious storm.

Wind rushed through the she-oaks, stirring their long, soft, needlelike leaves. The sound of breakers was very distant, almost lost beneath the wind, telling Sutter that the tide was at full ebb.

There was no light shining inside the tent.

"Mandy?"

Sutter's low query brought no answer. He hadn't really expected it to. He ducked into the tent, moved very quietly to the empty mattress and began patting along the side closest to the tent, searching for the "electric torch" Ray had assured him was there. The other tents all included a post with electrical outlets, but not Sutter's tent; it had been hastily erected in answer to hard pressure from the folks who owned Lady Elliot Island—the Australian government.

Sutter put his hand over the flashlight lens and turned it on. Red-toned light bloomed in the tent. He opened his fingers just a crack, allowing enough light to escape so that he could see the details of the tent's interior. Mandy hadn't moved. Her face was flushed; her breathing was regular and deep.

Even though Sutter suspected that he could have banged scuba tanks next to Mandy's ear without getting a response, he was careful to make as little noise as possible. As he played the light around the tent, he saw that someone had set Mandy's glitzy pink backpack just inside the doorway, alongside his own battered khaki model.

Suddenly the thought of getting out of his clothes became incredibly appealing to Sutter. He kicked off his canvas jungle boots, unbuttoned his short-sleeved bush shirt and stuffed it into the backpack pocket he reserved for dirty clothes. The khaki shorts followed, leaving him wearing nothing more than the narrow cotton jockstrap that was all he tolerated in tropical climates. He started to pull out a pair of cotton briefs and fresh khaki shorts, then stopped himself. If he had been alone he would have slept bare. He would wear the jockstrap for the sake of civilized sensibilities, but he'd be damned if he would wear shorts over it. Even now, in darkness with the wind blowing, the temperature in the tent was too close to eighty to bother with modesty. Surely a woman of Mandy's age and looks wouldn't faint at the sight of a man wearing a jockstrap.

The thought of fainting and clothes made Sutter glance over at Mandy again. She was wearing full office regalia, including suffocating nylon panty hose. After a few moments of wrestling with his conscience—and even Sutter couldn't have said which side of the question his conscience advocated—he stuffed the flashlight into a pillowcase. A soft glow filled the tent as the cloth muted the light's white glare. He knelt next to Mandy's mattress and began undressing her.

The skirt's zipper sounded loud in the tent's breathless silence. Mandy didn't stir even when Sutter eased one strong hand beneath her hips and lifted her so that the skirt and half-slip could slide freely off her body. Forcing himself to look away from the allure of her long, nylon-clad legs, Sutter went to work on the stubborn buttons on her navy-pinstriped blouse. When he finally lifted her upper body to peel away the cloth, she murmured protestingly.

He barely heard. In the muted light her skin gleamed tantalizingly through the openings in the bra's dark lace. Tiny drops of sweat glowed in the shadowed valley between her breasts. Sutter wanted nothing more than to lower his head and lick up each mesmerizing bit of moisture. He wanted that so fiercely that his lips almost brushed her skin before he prevented himself.

A throttled groan escaped Sutter. Fists clenched on his thighs, he fought to control the wild desire that was stabbing through him like heat lightning, telling of turbulence and need…but no release, no healing storm filled with passionate rain. Mandy was a woman for marriage. He was a man who had no belief in that particular institution.

Damn Anthea!

Sutter stared down at the sleeping Mandy. He knew he should remove her panty hose. Wearing that kind of suffocating underwear in tropic heat and humidity was asking for the most uncomfortable kind of rash. Yet he was reluctant to remove any more of Mandy's clothing. It wasn't concern for her modesty that slowed him down, for she was wearing bikini briefs of the same dark lace as her bra; but Sutter wasn't sure he trusted himself to touch Mandy again, even for her own good.

The realization shocked him. He was known for his self-control, for the steel will that drove him past the point where other men gave up and gave in. Nor had his own sexuality ever held him hostage, not even when he was a teenager angry at the world for giving him a mother who was a coward and a father who cared only for hard liquor and fast cars.

Sutter closed his eyes. Surely he could remove a sleeping woman's nylons without falling on her like a starving dog on a bone. Couldn't he? With an impatient curse, he opened his eyes, hooked his long fingers over the waistband of Mandy's panty hose and peeled them from her in a single continuous motion. When he was finished, he threw the filmy nylon aside as though it had burned him.

Because it had. The heat of her body was held in each gossamer strand. Moving swiftly, jaw set in a rigid line, Sutter lifted Mandy enough to allow him to pull down the top sheet of the bed. He eased her into the covers, lifted the sheet up to her waist and yanked back his hands.

A veil of hair had fallen across Mandy's cheek. Without stopping to think, Sutter reached out and smoothed the hair back from her face. With a sigh, Mandy turned toward the caress, her hands reaching. Sutter froze, then let out a long breath when she tucked one hand beneath her chin and let the other open limply on the sheet. He saw that her fingernails were very short.

Bitten off to the quick, I suppose. Damned little rabbit.

The partially sympathetic, mostly exasperated thought made Sutter's mouth turn down. Then he realized that her nails were broken off, not chewed, and his mouth became a grim line. Gently he picked up the hand that lay motionless on the sheet. A dark line of blood on two of the fingernails gave silent testimony to the force with which she had clenched her hands on her purse during the flight to the island. She had bent and broken off her nails below the quick, making them bleed.

She had been terrified, but she hadn't been without courage. The realization shook him. After his mother, Sutter expected very little from women in the way of fortitude. Yet everything he had seen of Mandy hinted that she fought to master her fears rather than to have them master her. And she fought with an intensity that transcended pain.

"Golden eyes," Sutter whispered as he very gently kissed Mandy's fingertips one by one. "I'm so sorry. If I had only known...."

There was no answer. Sutter hadn't expected one. His fingers had a fine trembling as he gently replaced Mandy's hand on the cool sheet. The back of his hand accidentally brushed the resilience of her breasts as he withdrew. The feminine softness made his gut wrench with desire.

An instant later Sutter was across the tent and stretched out full-length on top of his own mattress, carefully thinking of nothing at all, most particularly not of the silken allure of Mandy's breasts. Normally he would have been asleep as soon as his head met the pillow, but not tonight. He lay awake, restless, but it wasn't merely hunger that kept sleep at bay. The disturbance Sutter felt went beyond simple desire. He had undressed women before, but never had one been so defenseless. He couldn't forget how he had ignored her protests and stuffed her into the little plane, and how she had sat in a state of sustained terror throughout the flight. Yet she hadn't given in to fear. That kind of self-control was totally unexpected, especially for a woman like Mandy, who seemed to see life as a series of one-line jokes delivered on any and every subject that occurred to her.

How could the same woman who crooked her finger at me with a saucy, sexy smile in front of hundreds of people be in a state of stark terror over a half-hour flight in a small plane?

Sutter rolled over and looked at Mandy sleeping within arm's reach on the other side of the tent. In the cloth-filtered illumination of the flashlight, her body was all golden curves and black velvet shadows. The sight was so disturbing that he reached to turn off the flashlight. Before he touched the pillowcase his fingers hesitated and finally withdrew. If a nightmare awakened Mandy, she would need the comfort of light to orient herself.

With strong, impatient hands Sutter pushed his pillow into a more comfortable shape. As he lifted his fingers from the cloth he realized that they retained the faintest scent of Mandy's perfume. He rolled over abruptly, turning his back on the golden woman who slept in velvet shadows. For a long time he lay without moving, listening to the silky rush of air through the she-oak needles. Finally he fell into a deep sleep permeated by scented, elusive dreams.

Wind gently rocked the tent, making the enclosure expand and shrink as though breathing. Sun poured in a thick triangle of brilliant yellow light through the half-open front flap. Mandy stirred, stretched and smiled before she was fully awake. The soft sounds of wind and sea were a lullaby she hadn't heard for two years, soothing and renewing at the same time. Her stomach growled, disturbing her contentment. An instant later memories came—a long flight in a big plane, a shorter flight in a smaller plane and a timeless period of hell trapped in a tiny plane suspended over an endless sea.

Mandy sat upright, her heart pounding. The prosaic canvas ceiling assured her that she was no longer flying. Floor, walls, sheets, mattress. A tent. But where? Vaguely she remembered the auctioneer saying something about Sutter's Australian vacation not being a tour of luxury resorts. *You will be sleeping in a tent.*

Well, that explained it. She had finally arrived at her destination, whatever and wherever that might be. Now, was she supposed to cook and eat the tent as well as sleep in it? A single look at the faded canvas floor checked that particular flight of fancy. Perhaps the mattress....

As Mandy looked down to measure the mattress's potential edibility, she realized that she was wearing almost nothing. She couldn't remember undressing the previous night. In fact, now that she thought about it, she couldn't remember the previous night at all. Frowning, she tried to calculate how many hours she might have lost. The angle of the sunlight streaming into the tent suggested either midmorning or midafternoon. She looked at her wristwatch before she remembered it was set for California, not Australia. She had no idea how many time zones she had crossed. She did know that she had crossed the international date line, which meant she had flown into tomorrow. Or was it yesterday?

Sighing, Mandy decided that it didn't matter. She was on vacation, so she must be having a hell of a good time, if only she could remember it.

Think.

The last thing she remembered was gratefully getting off the plane at a place called Bundaberg, whose location in the greater Australian geographic scheme of things was still a mystery to her. She knew the town was close to the ocean, because the little plane had turned immediately on takeoff and had been out over the water very quickly.

Sudden sweat bathed Mandy's body as memories re-

turned. A little white plane waiting. Sutter's eyes green
and narrow and furious, totally indifferent to her terror.
His shocking strength as he boosted her into the plane and
strapped her down with the seat belt. A rush of ground, a
sickening leap into air, pure cold terror exploding. Waiting
to crash. Praying to die in the crash this time. Waiting.
Praying. And then a low, comforting voice, an encouraging
touch, Sutter's strong hands lifting her out of terror. Safe.
Finally safe, gentle strength and blessed darkness descending.

*Comforting voice? Encouraging touch? Gentle
strength? Sutter? Lord, I must have been hallucinating!*

And then the rest of the memories came. She had embarrassed herself in front of Sutter, revealing her weak-
nesses and carefully hidden fear of small planes, the sea,
boats. Humiliation swept through Mandy in a red tide that
went from her toenails to her scalp. Had she really told
Sutter to go to hell? And had he really said that she was
the one who would be comfortable there?

It's dry and there's not a pair of wings in sight.

Oh, yes. It definitely had happened.

Mandy put her flaming face in her hands. She wanted
to crawl beneath the sheet and hide forever. It was bad
enough to know that she was a coward; to have others
know it was unbearable. And to have Sutter know it was
unspeakable.

Her stomach growled again, insistently, informing her
that embarrassment was no reason to starve to death. People never died of humiliation—they just wished they had.
Lack of food, however, could definitely be lethal.

Too bad starving takes so long, Mandy thought wryly.
*No matter how much my stomach growls, I'll still be alive
and kicking wretchedly when Sutter comes back here to
sleep.*

The thought of Sutter sleeping within reach of her mattress made Mandy's stomach do an odd little flip. How
would she manage it in the small tent? How would she be

able to fall asleep listening to him breathe? How would she undress without bumping into him?

As a matter of fact, how had she managed to undress last night?

No matter how hard Mandy tried, she couldn't remember anything after an angry, disgusted Sutter had left her and strode off to who knows where. She had fallen asleep within moments, and she had been fully clothed at the time. She was sure of it. She couldn't remember awakening to undress herself, either. No matter how hard she tried, she couldn't remember awakening at all except for this morning.

If it was morning.

Mandy went over every instant that she remembered since being manhandled into the tiny plane. Gradually she was forced to acknowledge that Sutter must have undressed her after she had fallen asleep. The evidence of it was everywhere. Skirt and blouse set aside haphazardly, panty hose in a tangle on the floor, shoes kicked down to the end of the mattress. She wasn't the most tidy creature on earth, but she wasn't in the habit of shedding clothes at random and leaving them where they dropped.

With a sinking feeling Mandy looked down at the two bands of blue lace that were all that stood between her and complete nakedness. Staunchly she told herself there was no reason to be embarrassed; women all over the world went swimming in public with suits that covered less flesh than her underwear. Besides, it wasn't as though Sutter would have taken any pleasure in undressing her. His contempt for her couldn't have been clearer.

Locked up in a tent for three weeks with an amateur comedian who's afraid of her own shadow. And then, even worse, *With luck, you'll be safe in your little burrow at home before the last of the pills wear off.*

Her mouth turned down in a wry curve as she acknowledged the aptness of Sutter's description; she was a silly little rabbit afraid of its own shadow. It had been two years since the accident, yet all she could do was take shallow baths and fly on 747s. Well, not quite all. The second plane she had flown on had been about a quarter the size of the big jumbo jets, and she hadn't disgraced herself on that one. She hadn't panicked or screamed or wept or thrown up, and she had been fully capable of walking off the plane under her own power at the end of the flight.

When you got right down to it, she hadn't disgraced herself on the little plane, either; at least, not right away. She had shut down rather than come apart in hysterics, and if the effort of keeping herself together had exhausted her so much that she had fainted at Sutter's feet at the end of the flight, well, that could be endured. The bottom line was that she had flown in a small plane.

And she had survived it.

Mandy's breath came out in a long sigh. Despite all the fears and humiliations she had endured since she had left California on her totally unexpected vacation, she felt more at peace with herself than she had since the instant she had walked into a tent halfway around the world and had seen her husband topping off a sand bunny.

Smiling wryly, Mandy reached for the garish backpack, hoping Anthea had managed to pack some cool clothing for her most recent project. The first handful Mandy pulled out was promising—underwear of an extraordinary silky lace. Black, deep rose, cream, the underwear was as thin as a whisper and twice as soft. The second handful yielded two pairs of khaki shorts and several pairs of thick cotton socks. The third handful looked more like a pile of colored string than anything to wear. After a few moments, Mandy sorted everything into three bikini bottoms and six bikini tops. That answered the question of what she was expected to wear with the khaki shorts.

Further rummaging yielded several plain white blouses, a slinky sarong skirt and wrap top that would serve for covering up at the beach or for dressing up anywhere else, a pair of slip-on beach thongs and a pair of delicate leather sandals. Then there were various cosmetics, a hairbrush, toothbrush, comb, soap, heavy-duty sunscreen, feminine items and a small box of...

"Ohmygod."

For a moment of stark disbelief, Mandy stared at the trade name and happy couple that covered one side of the box. She opened it quickly, still unable to believe that the contents were as advertised. As small, neatly wrapped packets fell into her palm, she laughed helplessly. Anthea hadn't been joking when she had urged an affair with an Australian, and she had included just the thing to make sure Mandy would have an affair to remember rather than one to regret.

Almost afraid to continue, Mandy went back to emptying out the backpack. Nothing else unexpected turned up until the very bottom. There was an envelope with her name written across it in Anthea's clear, distinctive handwriting. Inside was six hundred dollars Australian, plus a note.

Mandy,
I sent your scuba gear ahead so you wouldn't have to worry about it. If something is missing or doesn't fit, buy a replacement with the enclosed. Otherwise, spend it all on something that makes you smile.

Diving gear?

For an instant Mandy was utterly motionless, torn in opposite directions, helpless. Part of her ached to know again the beauty and freedom of diving in the blue infinity of the sea. And part of her froze in terror at the thought. With hands that weren't quite steady, she began repacking the backpack, putting the damning little box in first. She could just imagine what Sutter would think of her if he saw it.

Mandy dressed quickly, stuffed a few of the Australian

bills in the pocket of her khaki shorts, grabbed the backpack and a frayed white towel that had been folded neatly at the end of her mattress and headed out of the tent. No matter how rudimentary the accommodations, she was certain they included some kind of bathroom.

Fifty yards away there was a scattering of tents. A hundred yards distant were several small cottages. Two larger buildings were somewhat closer. Mandy headed for them. A few minutes later she was enjoying a freshwater shower, soaping the residue of her trip from hair and skin, loving every instant of it. Feeling as though she had been reborn, she dried off, combed her hair, stepped into her new clothes and set off to find something that would end the rumbling complaints of her stomach.

Her luck held. The first building she tried contained the small bar. Ray was sitting there, flirting with the sun-streaked blonde who was handing him a beer.

"G'day, luv," Ray said, smiling when he saw Mandy. "Looks like a day's sleep was just the thing for you."

"A day?"

"Near as the same. The afternoon flight just left."

"Well, that explains my stomach. It's sure my throat has been cut."

Ray grinned. "We'll be serving in twenty minutes. I'll stand you a beer until then."

"Thanks, but I'd better not. I'm empty all the way to the soles of my feet."

Ray's blue glance moved from Mandy's sleek wet hair, past the well-filled black bikini top to the low-riding and very brief khaki shorts, down to the narrow feet clad in the plastic beach thongs that were practically part of the Australian national uniform.

"Empty? If all the Sheilas were empty like you, I'd die a young and very happy man."

Mandy smiled just enough to show Ray that she appreciated the compliment but not enough to encourage him to continue with more of the same. It was a smile she had honed to perfection on her way through school, when she had worked sixty hours a week to pay for her education. No time had been left for flirtations or socializing. That was why she had been so naive and so ripe for the attentions of one of the most famous men in her chosen field of oceanography.

Before Mandy could open her mouth to ask where the dining room was, the sound of a man's voice came clearly through the wall. It was Sutter's voice, deep and clipped and cold. He was talking about her, and he was mad as hell.

Chapter 6

"All in all, this is some vacation you planned for me," Sutter continued savagely, hoping that the radio phone was up to the task of carrying every nuance of his voice. He wanted Anthea to be in no doubt as to the extent of his anger at her manipulations. "I don't know about you, dearest aunt, but being stuck in a tent for three weeks with a basket case for a bunk mate isn't my idea of fun and relaxation!"

Angrily Mandy strode through the open door to the tiny combination office and gift shop. An instant later she was standing as though nailed to the floor, staring, unable to help herself. Sutter was wearing only a swimsuit, a black swath of cloth barely wider than her hand. The male strength that had startled her when she had been swept into the plane was very obvious now beneath the expanse of Sutter's smooth, tanned skin. Wide, well-muscled shoulders tapered to narrow, equally muscular hips. Long, powerful, covered with dark bronze hair, his legs were braced in a fighting stance, every muscle defined as he stood with one hand on his hip and listened impatiently to his aunt's explanations.

"You have no idea how reassured I am," Sutter said in

a sarcastic tone. "If she's so bloody damned efficient around the office, why didn't you keep her there!"

There was another pause before Sutter burst once more into clipped, furious speech.

"Give it a rest, Anthea. I know precisely what you had in mind when you shanghaied Mandy for this trip. Just forget it. When I need your dubious expertise in finding a sex partner, you'll be the first to know. Until then, stay the hell out of my private life." Sutter's tone was icy, flat, utterly without softness. "As for Mandy, if she's so hard up for a man, find her a nice pencil pusher whose idea of a hot time is watching wallpaper fade."

That galvanized Mandy. Without stopping to think, she snatched the phone from Sutter's hand.

"Anthea?" Mandy asked, her voice tight.

"Oh, dear, I'm so sorry you had a rough flight. If I had known, I would never have—"

"I understand," Mandy said, talking right over Anthea's unwanted apologies. "Don't worry about a thing. I'm firmly on the ground without a plane in sight. Everything's just hunky-dory."

"Good. Er, I understand that you don't care for water sports, either?" Anthea asked delicately.

"I'll survive. I'm sure there are other things I can do here besides going diving," Mandy added, ignoring Sutter's sardonic smile.

"I hope you hadn't planned on Sutter helping you, er, amuse yourself," Anthea said hesitantly. "That is, I'm sure he would be glad to help you learn how to dive, but—"

"No problem," Mandy interrupted, not wanting to hear another word. "If I want to dive, I know just how to go about doing it."

Sutter's smile flattened angrily. "If you think I'm going to teach—"

"Just shut up," Mandy interrupted, her eyes blazing, her voice vibrating with anger. "You've had your turn.

Now it's mine. No, not you, Anthea. Sutter is talking in my other ear.''

"Tell him to go away."

"Anthea says for you to go away," Mandy said, giving Sutter a killing look.

Sutter crossed his arms over his chest and stayed put. Mandy shrugged and went back to her conversation with Anthea.

"Don't worry, Anthea. I'm not counting on Sutter for one damn thing."

There was a long pause at the other end of the line before Anthea plunged ahead.

"When I said you needed a lover, I hadn't really considered Sutter. He's rather...too...too..."

"Much?" Mandy offered laconically.

"Well, not for the type of woman he's been with since his divorce. They must do fine with him, because they stand in line hoping for another chance. But you're a little too...too..."

"Ugly? Poor?"

"Heavens no! Sutter doesn't care about money and you're a striking woman, as every man who has ever been through the office has pointed out. It's just that Sutter doesn't really like women very well. His mother was a fragile little thing and his former wife was little better. You're too...well, inexperienced. You would walk starry-eyed into an affair with Sutter and walk out crying. You're much too nice, my dear. Sometimes my nephew can be very...er, that is..."

"Cold? Arrogant? Overbearing? Altogether insufferable?" Mandy offered, looking Sutter right in the eye.

Anthea sighed. "Oh dear, he *has* been difficult for you, hasn't he?"

"Yes," Mandy said, remembering how Sutter had casually forced her into the plane and strapped her in. Then she remembered how gentle he had been getting her off the plane. "No." But had that really happened, or had she just dreamed it? "Oh, hell, I don't know." Mandy sighed and shifted her weight. "Anthea, there's one thing I do know. If I ever decide to have an affair with a man, he'll have to feel something a lot warmer than contempt for me. My former husband gave me all of that any woman should have to take."

Sutter's eyes narrowed as he looked at the pale, determined set of Mandy's mouth. He wondered how her husband had burned her, and why, and how deeply, and if it had anything to do with her fear of water, of flying, of everything except staying locked within the safe walls of Anthea's office. Or perhaps it was those very same fears that had driven her husband away.

"Anthea," Mandy said soothingly, "everything is all right. Don't fret about a thing. I'm here, I've slept nearly a day and I'm so hungry I could eat a coral reef. In short, I'm fully recovered from my travels."

"But what about getting back home? Sutter said you were afraid of...er, that is, he mentioned that you didn't like boats, either."

"I'll charter a submarine," Mandy said wryly, forcing herself not to think about how in God's name she was going to get off the island. Three weeks was a long time. She'd spend every minute of her days and nights nerving herself up for the inevitable ride home. "Don't worry, Anthea. Really. It's my problem, not yours."

"Is there anything I can do to help?"

"No, but thanks for the thought."

"All right, dear. And do keep your eyes open for the right kind of man. Australia is reputed to be full of handsome knights in khaki armor. I want you to come back with a smile full of wonderful memories."

Mandy opened her mouth to say that she had no intention of cornering the first handsome Australian male she saw and asking him to try on the latest colors in American condoms. Then she remembered that sounds carried very clearly through the thin-walled building. She took a deep breath and controlled her too-agile tongue.

"Thank you, Anthea. Was there anything more that you wanted to say to Sutter?"

"Nothing he'll believe, I'm afraid. The poor boy is convinced that I'm meddling in his private affairs. But I ask you, is it my fault Sutter chose such a remote place to vacation that separate accommodations simply weren't to be had on such short notice? I couldn't very well demand that someone else's vacation be cut short or canceled just to accommodate Sutter, could I?"

The plaintive tone of Anthea's voice came through quite clearly. Mandy looked at the "poor boy" in question and decided that it was a clear case of mistaken identity. Sutter was neither poor nor a boy.

"No, you couldn't," Mandy sympathized. "I'm sure that point will occur to the 'poor boy' about the time hell freezes solid. He's nothing if not bullheaded."

Anthea laughed. "I can't argue with that. Say goodbye to my nephew for me. And don't worry. If you stay out of his way, I'm sure he'll take care of the rest. Good hunting, dear."

As Mandy replaced the receiver in its niche she turned to face Sutter. "Just in case you didn't catch the drift of what I told your aunt, I'll repeat it. I don't have designs on your vacation time, your masculine body or your vaunted expertise in the sack."

One of Sutter's bronze eyebrows climbed upward in arch query. "'Vaunted expertise'? Don't tell me my sainted aunt has descended to pandering."

"It wouldn't have done any good. I require more from a man than a fast wrestling match."

"How about a slow wrestling match?"

Sutter's knowing smile made Mandy wish she had kept her mouth shut on the subject of sex. "How about going to—"

"Dinner," Sutter interrupted smoothly. "If food doesn't

take the edge off that sharp tongue of yours, you'll never find yourself an Australian lover. Honey catches more flies than vinegar.''

"Really? And what makes you think I'm after flies?"

For a moment Sutter looked startled, then he smiled unwillingly. "Feeling feisty, are we?"

"Feeling condescending, are we?" she retorted. "Look, Sutter—"

"Damon," he interrupted coolly. "Since we're sleeping together, I figure you should at least know my first name. Don't you agree?" He looked past her stunned expression toward Ray, who had just walked into the office. "Hello, Ray. Chow time already?"

When Mandy realized that Ray had heard Sutter's outrageous remark, she blushed furiously. Sutter had deliberately made it sound as though she were the type of woman whose thighs were so loose they rattled when she walked.

"Demon," she said. "I'll remember that."

"Don't push it, honey. Sleeping together doesn't mean a thing these days."

"It doesn't mean a thing these *nights*, either."

"Disappointed?" Sutter retorted.

Seething, Mandy turned toward Ray. "What's the failure rate of your dive equipment along the reef?"

"No worries, luv. We haven't had an accident in years."

"What a pity. I was so looking forward to Sutter's last dive."

Mandy brushed past a startled Ray and followed the food smells to the other side of the building. She was early, but one of the girls loaded up a plate and handed it through the serving window to her. Meat, bread, pasta, canned vegetables and fruits, coffee and canned milk. It all tasted heavenly. Mandy cleaned her plate within minutes, unable to remember when she had had such a vital appetite.

Before any of the other diners arrived, Mandy was gone.

She hurried back to the office, pausing at the doorway long enough to listen for Sutter's voice. She heard only silence and decided that he must have gone somewhere with Ray. The bar, probably. It was part of the same building, just a thin partition away, as were the cafeteria and kitchen.

"G'day," said the girl behind the small counter.

"Hi," Mandy said. "Is this the gift shop, too?"

"Gift shop, radiophone, clinic, office. Everything but eating and diving. Did you want something?"

What Mandy really wanted was to know precisely where she was on the globe, but she could hardly ask the girl. The sound and smell of the sea, plus the pure, crushed coral pathways had told Mandy that she was somewhere within the coral belt of the South Pacific. But where?

"Er, do you have any pamphlets that can tell me more about this place?" Mandy asked innocently.

"This is the lot," the girl said, pulling out a faded ditto sheet and giving it to Mandy. "The postcards will tell you a bit, but the best thing is one of those books."

Mandy looked up from the sheet, which was entitled "Lady Elliot Island, Paradise Preserved." Her glance fell on a short shelf full of books at eye level behind the counter. "Yes, please."

"Which one?"

"All of them."

"Right."

Three of the books were of the oversize, four-color, glossy variety. Two others were definitely scholarly. The books covered the Pacific Ocean in general and the Great Barrier Reef in particular. One of them dealt exclusively with Lady Elliot Island. Another had detailed photos and information about the myriad species of coral and varieties of reef ecology. A single quick perusal of the stack told Mandy that she wasn't going to lack for reading material.

"I'll take them all." She reached into her pocket and pulled out a handful of crumpled bills. "Blast. Not enough," Mandy muttered as she counted. "I'll have to go back to the tent."

"No worries," the girl said, writing out a receipt for the cash. "Bring the rest by anytime we're open."

Mandy looked startled. The girl laughed.

"It's not like you're going anywhere, right?"

"Er, right." Mandy hesitated. "You don't happen to have a lantern of some kind, do you?"

"Did your lamp go out?"

"There wasn't one in the tent. Just a flashlight."

"Oh, right. You must be the Yank that Ray was in such a stew about. Finally awake, are you?"

"So far so good."

The girl laughed. "Hang on, luv. I've got a battery lantern in the back I can lend you." She vanished out a side door and returned within a few minutes. "Just bring it in every morning to recharge."

Mandy gathered up her books and the lantern and headed back for the tent, intent upon finding out the dimensions of her self-imposed coral prison. She read as late as she dared that night, then casually draped one of the extra—and wholly unnecessary—blankets over the books, concealing them from Sutter. The thought of what he would say if he found her cowering in the tent and reading about the reef when she could be out diving on it was enough to make her flush with shame.

Hastily she pulled out the sheer, lacy black nightgown and matching bikini briefs that had been part of Anthea's generosity. The wind had dropped steadily since sunset. Now the air was almost completely still. Warm, humid, smelling of salt and sun-bleached coral, the night closed around her like another layer of black silk. She didn't need the sheet for warmth, but she didn't kick it aside. The thought of Sutter seeing her in the provocative, hip-length black nightgown made her stomach do another of those odd little flips that were so disconcerting to her when she was around Sutter.

Mandy yanked the sheet up to her chin, closed her eyes and forced herself to think about something other than the vision Sutter had made standing in the office wearing nothing but a diver's brief swimsuit. She had expected to have trouble sleeping, but she didn't. The distant sound of the surf breaking on the reef unraveled her.

By the time Sutter came to the tent Mandy was deeply asleep, the sheet had been kicked aside, and she was lying in a pose of graceful abandon that made Sutter's whole body clench around a fierce shaft of desire. A long time later he fell asleep cursing women in general and his meddling aunt in particular.

For the next three days Mandy and Sutter managed to avoid each other. They spoke not at all. If one of them was eating at the cafeteria, the other was not. If one was awake, the other was asleep. If one was diving, the other was reading…and growing ever more restless.

Reading about the miraculous, intricate reef complex that lay within her reach made Mandy yearn to dive once more. In graduate school she had specialized in the ecology of coral reefs, working long hours with laboratory and computer simulations of reef conditions. But before now she had never had the opportunity to dive along a coral reef, to physically experience the gemlike beauty that stared up at her from the pages of the glossy books.

And now she was too cowardly to take advantage of the opportunity that lay within her grasp.

If I don't get my tail out of this tent I'll never be able to look myself in the mirror again. It should be about low tide, so I won't drown walking along the beach or even wading a little bit in the lagoon.

The bracing self-lecture brought Mandy to her feet. It also helped her to know that anyone who was going to dive had already gone long before and was now drifting down the reef's outer wall. In short, Sutter wouldn't be able to witness her fear. She slathered herself with sunscreen, rolled the bottle into the all-purpose towel that had come with the tent and went outside, determination in every line of her body.

There was just enough breeze that morning to ruffle the she-oaks' intricate, fine-leaved foliage and to give texture to the surface of the sea. As she had every day, Mandy went to the beach edge of the small grove, dropped her towel in the shade and stood staring out over the water that both tantalized and frightened her.

As always, the lagoon was exquisite. In its most shallow parts there was no color to the water, simply a polished, transparent surface that transformed sunshine into shimmering ripples of silver light. Farther out in the lagoon the water took on an aquamarine glow while still retaining its utter transparency. Here and there tiny pockets of deeper water shaded into pale emerald. Beyond the boundary of the lagoon the reef complex fell away into sapphire depths so pure they had to be experienced to be believed.

As Mandy looked out to the unbridled sea beyond the reef, she realized that her heart was pounding as though she had been running. She dragged her glance away from the open ocean's dangerous beauty and concentrated on the small white beach in front of her. As always, the composition of the ground came as a surprise. Though she understood intellectually that coral islands were different from the normal variety, Lady Elliot's lack of dirt or ordinary rocks was still new, still arresting. It was the same for the sparse vegetation. The island had no languid palms dipping down to white sand lagoons, or glorious bursts of jungle flowers, or fern-covered canyons filled with mist and silence. There was a flat island surface made up of the sun-bleached remains of billions of tiny corals, a few salt-tolerant plants and the small, dark green casuarina trees, which the Australians called she-oaks. The beach was the same composition as the land. The coarse sand wasn't ground-up rock at all but the wave-pummeled remains of once-living corals, corals that had been torn by storm and tide from the Great Barrier Reef itself.

Concentrating only on what was directly beneath her feet, Mandy edged closer to the water. Because the camp was on the lagoon side of the island, there were no waves breaking along the shore to threaten her. The full force of the Pacific combers hit the outer wall of the reef at the far side of the lagoon, perhaps a quarter-mile distant from the beach. The meeting of upthrust reef and sea was marked by a wide ribbon of flashing white water. The lagoon itself was serene, its crystalline presence untroubled by anything but the random stirring of the breeze.

At low tide the entire lagoon was reassuringly shallow. In fact, it was so shallow and so transparent that the water itself was nearly invisible. All across the lagoon to the outer reef beyond, blunt coral formations rose just above the surface of the water. Because the coral organisms couldn't live in air, the surface of the reef rose no more than a few inches beyond the reach of the low tide. Varieties of coral grew in profusion, looking like dark, many-hued shadows beneath the sheen of pure water.

The corals' incredible variations in shape fascinated Mandy. She edged closer, trying to get close enough to identify some of the many different species of coral. It was almost impossible to do from a distance; the corals often grew together, branching and intertwining until the original, distinctive shape was lost. Those corals closest to the beach were the most distorted, often dead, for constant exposure to sun with each change of tide killed the delicate organisms that built the reef.

Mandy shaded her eyes against the brilliant reflections and watched wistfully while several people walked and waded across the barely submerged inner reef toward the far boundary of the lagoon, where white water foamed and swirled over the outer reef. The people wore brief swimsuits and sneakers and carried stout reef sticks for testing the footing before trusting their weight to the sometimes-deceptive coral formations.

I could do that. The water is ankle-deep in most places

and barely above the knees in the rest. I could go out there and see at least a few of the extraordinary corals I've only known from books. And it's day, not night; warm, not cold. Surely I can do it.

Can't I?

Taking a deep breath, Mandy edged closer to the water. There was no point at which she could say that land stopped and the coral formations began. The island was itself coral from top to bottom. The interior of all reefs plus the dry areas above the waves were all composed of dead coral. The rest, the exterior of the reef that was washed by the ocean, was alive, billions of tiny plants and animals growing and breathing, building and rebuilding, reproducing and dying, leaving their microscopic skeletons behind; and in the process, creating the most massive structure ever built on earth by any living creature. Man's biggest cities paled in comparison to the vast, interlocking complexity of the Great Barrier Reef.

And a small fragment of that wondrous creation lay right at Mandy's feet.

At first she wasn't able to force herself to surrender more than her toes to the lagoon. The water itself was so warm that it barely registered on her senses. The thongs she wore protected the soles of her feet but tended to come off at the least excuse. If she was really going reef walking, she should be wearing sturdy sneakers. As it was, if she went into water that was more than ankle-deep, she would quickly find herself barefoot. That would be foolish. For all its beauty, coral was hardly defenseless. A few varieties were poisonous. Most of them could cut or abrade unwary, unprotected feet.

Moving slowly, Mandy paralleled the narrow margin where lagoon met beach, never getting in over the top of her feet, ignoring the too-rapid beating of her heart. She looked only at the area just around her toes, where the water was more shallow than the baths she had forced herself to endure in the past months.

As she concentrated on identifying the larger bits and pieces of coral debris scattered about, her heartbeat settled into more normal rhythms. For minutes at a time she forgot she was within reach of the deadly sea, closer than she had been at any time since her husband had died and she had finally drowned, only to wake up in agony in the bottom of a small, wave-tossed boat that smelled of dead fish.

"G'day. Are you the Yank that slept longer than Rip van Winkle?"

Mandy's head snapped up. Standing in front of her was a boy of about eight and his younger sister, who looked perhaps five. Both of the children were wiry, fit, tanned all over. Their swimsuits were the barest concession to modesty.

"Er, yes, I guess I am. My name is Mandy."

"I'm Clint and this runty little Sheila is my sister Di. Mum's diving. Pop's over in the shade asleep."

Di stuck out her tongue and took a poke at her brother's ribs. He fended her off with the ease of long practice. Mandy looked beyond the children, toward the fragile shade of the she-oaks fringing the beach. She caught a glimpse of a scarlet towel and a muscular body wearing little more than a deep tan. Like the children, the man had a thick mop of sun-and-salt-cured chestnut hair. Unlike the children, he was content to laze away the hours until the divers returned.

Mandy looked from the sleeping man to the lagoon. Though shallow, it was still deep enough in places for small children to get into big trouble, especially as the tide had turned and was slowly reclaiming the beach.

"Do you swim?" she asked.

Clint looked at Mandy as though she had just climbed out of a flying saucer.

"Too right we do! What do you think we are, Dubbos?"

Mandy suppressed a smile and decided that, for now, discretion would be the superior part of her valor; she wouldn't ask what a Dubbo was.

"Right," she said in her best Australian accent, making it sound like "roight." She smiled at Clint. "That was my silly question for the day. Your turn."

Long, flaxen eyelashes descended in a blink. Suddenly Clint smiled in comprehension. "Fair dinkum! You're not a blind Freddy after all. Want to feed the fish?"

"I don't know. Do I?"

Clint blinked again, then shook his head and smiled widely at the same time. "Let's get the bread."

Wondering what she had gotten herself into, Mandy followed Clint and the silent Di to the dining room. The door was closed, but the crusts and heels of bread leftover from breakfast had been put in a bowl outside the door. Clint grabbed the lot and distributed it almost evenly among the three of them. As soon as he turned his back to lead the way to the Fish Pond, Mandy slipped Di a few extra crusts and was rewarded with a shy, thousand-watt smile.

Despite its name, the Fish Pond wasn't a pond. It was simply a thirty-by-twenty-foot gap in the coral formations that otherwise carpeted the lagoon. At low tide the pool was only a few feet deep, which meant that the coral formations around the edge acted as a natural cage, confining whatever fish hadn't escaped before the tide fell. Visitors to Lady Elliot Island had gradually tamed the resident fish, feeding them crumbs, teaching the quick, wary little beggars to eat from a person's outstretched fingers.

Clint and Di waded out until they were waist-deep. Holding the bread aloft in one hand, feeding crumbs with the other, the children were soon the focus of a rippling, twisting blur of small fish. Mandy inched forward until the water came to midcalf. As she came down on a hidden bulb of coral, she lost one sandal and her balance at the same time. She nearly panicked. Pieces of bread went flying in all directions as her arms windmilled. Only the delighted laughter of the children as they fed fish kept Mandy from screaming her fear of falling in the water. Trembling, she backed up a few steps, leaving her rainbow-hued sandal behind.

Don't be ridiculous! she raged at herself as she stood on dry ground once more. *Even if you had fallen facedown you couldn't have drowned unless you were too stupid to brace your arms and keep your head above water. For God's sake, it wasn't even up to your knees! Now get back down there and pick up your sandal before you cut your foot.*

Mandy looked at the cheerful sandal lying in ten inches of water. She thought of bending down, putting her hand into the water, picking up the sandal and returning triumphantly to dry land.

Breath locked in her throat as her heart tried to hammer free of her body.

I can't.

Coward!

All right! I'm a coward! So what else is new?

Clenching her hands together, Mandy watched the tanned, laughing children stand waist-deep in the transparent lagoon while fish swirled around them like wind-driven silver leaves. Her dropped, forgotten crusts of bread absorbed water and then settled soddenly to the bottom of the lagoon only a few inches from the beach. Her body motionless, her fingers interlocked to keep them from trembling, Mandy stood, seeing nothing but the dark sea of her nightmares, hearing nothing but her own silent screams of terror.

Behind Mandy voices called back and forth from the direction of the dive shed. Carrying air tanks and wet suits, divers strode toward their tents, laughing and describing the wonders of the reef beyond as they walked. Mandy didn't hear. She was wrapped too tightly within her waking nightmare.

Sutter saw Mandy from a distance as he carried his equipment to the tent. He stopped suddenly, caught by something in her stance. As he watched, he realized that she was unnaturally still, the way she had been on the flight to the island, too terrified to move. No matter how carefully he looked, he could see no reason for her fear, yet there could be no doubt that she was afraid.

With a muttered curse Sutter turned off the path and headed toward the lagoon, which was only a few yards away. When he was within reach of Mandy he stopped. A single look at her deathly pallor and her white-knuckled grip on herself told him that she was once again in the grip of intense fear. But of what? There wasn't a plane in sight. All he could see was the Townehome kids feeding the lagoon fish.

Sutter spotted the bright colors of what looked like a rainbow beach thong dropped in the shallow water. He looked at Mandy's feet and realized that she was missing one sandal. Just when he was about to chew her out for risking an infection from a coral cut, Clint turned around and spotted Mandy.

"Don't you Yanks know anything?" Clint asked in a disgusted tone of voice. "You wasted your bread. You have to come out where the fish can swim up to you."

Dimly Mandy heard Clint's words and knew she must respond, must somehow shake off the paralyzing grip of her fear if only for a few moments.

"My mistake," she said in a strained voice.

Di turned and held out a crust of bread. "Here you go," she said softly. "I'll share."

Mandy suppressed a shudder at the thought of wading out into that clean, treacherous water once more. "That's okay, sugar. You go ahead and feed the fish. I'll watch and see how it's done."

"Nothing to it," Clint said, grabbing his sister's crust. "You rip off a piece, hold it underwater and the fish come swarming. Even a sleepy Yank like you can do it."

A little desperately, Mandy smiled. "I'll take your word for it."

From up the beach and behind Mandy, a woman's voice called out to the children.

"Now hear this! Now hear this! All 'roos fall in for tucker!"

Instantly Clint and Di splashed to shore, leaving a turmoil of disappointed fish behind. As Clint passed Mandy, he spotted her bare foot.

"Better get shod," he called over his shoulder. "Some of this coral is wicked."

"Took the words right out of my mouth," Sutter said.

Mandy flinched when she heard Sutter's voice behind her. Rather bitterly she wondered what else could go wrong that morning. Perhaps if she ignored Sutter he would go away.

"Mandy?"

And then again, maybe he wouldn't.

"Mandy," Sutter asked calmly, "what's your thong doing in the water instead of on your foot?"

"I—I was playing a silly game." She turned away from him and headed up the beach. "But I'm tired of playing it now."

"Mandy."

She froze.

"Don't you know better than to walk barefoot around here?"

"Yes!" she said savagely. "I know better!"

Before Sutter could say anything more, Mandy spun around and glared at the missing thong. It was less than five feet from shore, under no more than ten inches of water. She could either go and get the damn thing or she could spend the rest of her life hating herself for revealing to Sutter just what a blazing coward she really was—Sutter, a man who had been beaten, shot, stabbed, jailed and yet had never once flinched from doing what he believed had to be done.

In a rush Mandy took four steps into the lagoon, grabbed blindly and connected with the thong. She ripped it from the lagoon and raced back to the beach, where she stared at the dripping thong in delighted disbelief.

"I did it! Did you see that, Sutter? I waded out and picked up my sandal!"

Triumph radiated from Mandy, putting color back into her cheeks, taking fear away.

"Yes, I saw," he said softly.

Belatedly Mandy realized how she must have sounded to a man who had just returned from diving in the open sea. She bit her lip as she shoved her foot into the thong.

"It was just—just a silly game," she said.

Silently Sutter watched as Mandy ran up the beach and disappeared into the she-oaks. He didn't know what had been going on a moment before, but he was certain of one thing.

To Mandy, it hadn't been a silly game.

Chapter 7

"Is that the lot?"

Mandy smiled as she glanced from Clint's wide grin to shy little Di's hand held out trustingly to her.

"That's the lot," Mandy said, taking Di's hand and surrendering the bread crusts to Clint's eager grasp.

"You're sure you don't mind?" Ted asked.

"Not at all. After we feed the fish, we're going to walk around to the south end of the island and see if any turtles have come in to lay eggs."

"And then we're going to finish our coral castle," Clint added. "It's going to be bigger than you, Pop."

"Fair dinkum?" Ted said, ruffling his son's hair with a broad, blunt hand.

"Then it will be low tide and Mandy will show us how the starfish eat and what the sea squirts do and if there are any eggs floating around and..." Di's voice dwindled as she ran out of breath.

"Sounds like you have an exciting day planned," Ted said absently as he looked over his shoulder. "Gotta fly. The other blokes are waiting for me. Clint, you remember what I said about those fancy cone shells?"

"No worries. Mandy knows all about the ones that sting and the ones that don't."

Ted gave Mandy a quick, concerned look. "A lot of blokes are fooled or get careless. It doesn't matter so much for an adult, but for a joey…"

"I understand," Mandy said. "I've told the children not to touch any of the textile cone shells that have washed up until I've handled them first. If we go reef walking out far enough that there's a chance of seeing a live one, I know the difference between the siphon and the proboscis, and I'm well aware of the dangers of that particular mollusk's paralytic poison."

There was still a certain hesitation on Ted's part. Mandy knew why; she had told the Townehome parents she would be glad to watch the children as long as it was clearly understood that she was a nonswimmer. It was difficult for Ted to understand how someone who didn't swim at all could comprehend the ocean's many dangers.

"I spent years in school studying the ecology of coral reefs," Mandy said crisply, answering the unasked question. "If you have an hour to spare, I'll give you a list of every reef predator and whether that predator represents a danger to man, and if so, how the danger can be avoided or countered medically."

Ted couldn't conceal his surprise. "Coral reef ecology, eh? Then why don't you swim?"

"I choose not to," Mandy said in an even voice. "If that worries you, then perhaps you would feel better sleeping beneath the she-oaks while Clint and Di build their coral castle."

The father's grin told Mandy where Clint had gotten his casual masculine charm.

"Told me what's what, didn't she?" Ted said to his son.

"She's a mean 'un," Clint agreed, grinning.

When Ted turned back to Mandy, he was still smiling. "I'm not worried. A Sheila who can keep this lot under control can take care of the odd stonefish or poisonous snail."

Ted trotted off toward the other divers. Even from the corner of her eye, Mandy could see that Sutter had joined the adults—six days on the island had given his hair a pale, metallic sheen that was unmistakable, as was his rangy, well-muscled body. To her surprise, she had managed an unbroken exchange of civilities with him since she had made a fool of herself crowing over her sandal. She had expected Sutter to be caustic on the subject, but he had said nothing to her about it, then or later. He had simply appeared at dinner with a full plate in his hand and had sat down beside her.

Once Mandy had gotten accustomed to the frissons that chased through her every time Sutter was close, the two of them had passed an amicable half hour topping each other's Anthea stories. Sutter had offered to buy Mandy a beer after dinner. She had started to say how much she hated beer but hadn't wanted to end the unexpected truce. She had been shocked and delighted to discover that Australian beer was far superior to its American counterpart. In fact, she had a hard time believing that the two liquids shared anything in common but alcohol and a generic name.

"Your bloke's waving at you," Clint said.

Mandy didn't bother telling Clint again that Sutter wasn't her bloke and she wasn't his Sheila. She simply waved back at Sutter, then watched with unexpected yearning as the divers turned away and vanished into the she-oaks. The group was going to the opposite side of the tiny island, where the dive boat awaited them. It was a superb day for diving. The sea was calm, the air hot, the sun a burning brilliance overhead; and beneath the surface of the water it would be cool, silky, swirling with graceful fish and living corals sweeping up from the floor of the sea.

Suddenly Mandy wished she could see it all for herself, could feel the sea surrounding her, caressing her, freeing her from gravity until she came as close to unfettered flight as a human being could.

I can do it. I know I can. All I have to do is want it more than I fear it.

There was no answer for that bittersweet truth, not even in the deepest reaches of Mandy's silence. Quietly she followed the children to the Fish Pond, wading in as they did, feeling triumph as the water climbed above her ankles, her calves, her knees, partway up her thighs, then a few more inches, just a few more. She stopped when the water lapped at midthigh and forced herself to stand and endure the knowledge that she was partially within the sea's grasp once more.

The lagoon was warm, transparent and tasted far more salty on her fingertips than the Pacific Ocean off the coast of California. The air and water were so warm, so motionless, that when she closed her eyes, it was difficult to believe she was in the sea at all.

Fish swarmed just beneath the surface of the lagoon, bumping against Mandy's legs in their rush to get close to the crumbs, tasting her skin with tiny tickling touches. She broke off bits of bread crust, gingerly immersed her hand in the water and watched as the racing, flashing scraps of life vacuumed up every offering. Firmly she ignored her accelerated heartbeat and breathing, hoping that fear would pass as soon as her mind accepted that her body wasn't in danger. Finally, common sense won out over brutal memories. Her heartbeat slowly returned to normal and her hands became steady once more. Only then did she allow herself to retreat just a bit closer to shore, and then only for a few moments.

Meanwhile, Clint, who had wheedled a mask and snorkel from Ray, was lying facedown in the water with his feet pointing toward the outer reef. Sculling idly with his hands, he watched the fish dart about. He became so absorbed in watching that he drifted farther and farther out into the lagoon. Because the tide was partially up, the Fish

Pond wasn't completely bounded by coral formations. He could float right out over the wall of coral and into the rest of the shallow lagoon, where coral formations grew in an uninterrupted carpet and the water at that moment was very shallow.

Mandy glanced up from the greedy fish nibbling on her fingers and realized that Clint had drifted too far away. He was already out of the pond, floating in water that was barely eighteen inches deep. If he tried to kick his legs to propel himself back into deeper water, he would flail against coral rather than water.

"Stay here, Di," Mandy said.

Gingerly, ignoring the sudden race of her heart, Mandy waded deeper into the Fish Pond. From experience gained in the past few days, she knew where the most shallow parts were and where the bottom dipped down without warning. She made use of every high spot and skirted the low ones. It was barely twenty feet to the other side of the pond, but she felt as though it were miles. When she looked up she saw that Clint had discovered his difficulty. He was trying to scull forward with his hands but was succeeding only in pushing himself farther out over the corals lining the shallow lagoon.

"Just float," Mandy called. "I'll pull you in."

Clint's hands stopped churning. Mandy looked at the six feet of water separating her from the coral wall that marked the outer limit of the Fish Pond. She feared the water was at least waist-deep, perhaps more. On the other hand, Clint wasn't really in danger of more than a skinned knee if he kept his head and didn't thrash around too much.

I'm a great one to talk about someone keeping his head. I expect a child to do something I can't do myself!

Mandy bit her lip. Hard. Then she waded forward, welcoming the pain in her lip because it distracted her from the fear racing through her body, shortening her breath, making her body feel too brittle to move.

The warm water slid higher up Mandy's legs and then

higher still, despite the fact that she had resorted to balancing precariously on knobs of coral thrusting up from the bottom of the pond. Midthigh, then an inch more, then another inch. If she lost her balance and fell now, there would be no way to prevent her face from going under the surface, and she was trembling so much that a fall seemed inevitable.

Finally Mandy was able to reach out and grasp one of Clint's hands. Slowly, carefully, she towed him beyond the shallow area and into the deeper pool. With a cheerful wave of thanks he jackknifed his body and dove to the bottom for a closer inspection of the resident wildlife. Mandy just barely managed to stifle a scream as warm, very salty water splashed over her, compliments of Clint's windmilling feet. After that, it was several minutes before she could control her trembling enough so that she was able to retreat to the beach end of the pond.

It was with a great sense of relief that Mandy watched the final bread crusts shredded by busy little fingers and fed to even busier little fish. For her, the ordeal of the Fish Pond was over until lunch, after which more bread crusts would appear in the bowl outside the cafeteria. For now, however, Mandy was free to lure the Townehome kids up onto dry land.

"Candy bar for whoever spots the first turtle," Mandy called.

Instantly Clint's head popped out of the water. He and Di hit the beach running.

"Well, come on, don't be such a slow lot," Mandy teased as the children stormed past her.

Shouting and laughing, the Townehomes raced along the beach until they were even with the office. Then they slowed to a walk and lowered their voices to a whisper. Ever since Mandy had explained to them how important it was not to disturb the nesting terns, the children had all but tiptoed past the segment of beach that touched the birds' breeding colonies. Even so, sooty terns screamed and wheeled overhead constantly, not so much disturbed as simply being their normal, noisy, agitated selves. A few huge black frigate birds took flight, looking like shadows from a prehistoric time when birds were reptiles wearing more scales than feathers.

Farther up the beach, small gulls unique to the Great Barrier Reef perched in gray-and-white profusion on the wreckage of a ship whose captain had misjudged the depth of water over Lady Elliot's barrier reef. The shipwreck had occurred many years before. Now little more than the hull remained—curving timbers bleached by salt and sun and washed clean by sheets of tropical rain. Beyond the wreckage the lagoon ended. No coral formations rose to the surface of the sea, which meant that the island itself took the brunt of the ocean's ceaseless, sweeping waves. The beach became more narrow, steeper and of a white so pure it was almost blinding.

Clint and Di zigzagged through the coarse sand, picking up chunks of coral that had been ripped free by storm and wave and finally washed onto shore. A few of the pieces retained their original colors, rich scarlet or deep chestnut or, rarely, jet black. With time they faded to pale pink or antique gold or slate gray. In the end, all debris would be bleached to a dazzling absence of color, ground smaller by the waves and finally reduced to shimmering white sand.

Mandy walked slowly behind the children, forcing herself to look out over the restless, gleaming surface of the sea. The water looked less intensely blue than it had earlier and there were many subtle variations on the color gray. The change in color reflected the change in the sky itself. A sheer veil of clouds had covered the sun. The humidity, always high, had soared. If a wind didn't come up, the atmosphere would become oppressive. Clouds were piling up over the mainland in immense billows that even now were reaching toward the island. Tonight, chain lightning would coruscate through the vast, creamy towers in dazzling display.

A disappointed call from Di returned Mandy's attention to the beach. There were no odd, broad marks in the sand, as though a single caterpillar tread had gone from the sea to the warm sand above high tide line. The track of a green turtle was unmistakable—and unmistakably absent. None of the ancient reptiles had appeared mysteriously from the vast sea in order to haul themselves up the beach and lay their eggs in the warm sand. Nor could Clint or Di spot one of the big animals swimming through the sparkling clarity of the water. No dark bodies appeared against the flashing white of breaking waves. In the end even Clint gave up and joined Mandy and Di in building the coral castle to new heights.

As they worked, Mandy answered the children's endless questions about the creatures that had once inhabited the intricate coral skeletons and about the creatures that had no true skeleton at all. She described the difference between sponges and sea hares, snails and corals, fish and man, and she explained how the reef had been built of the same kinds of coral that they were using to build their own castle. With time, the reef corals became compressed by the weight of all the coral that had been built on above. As the reef bottom was slowly squeezed, it reacted with dissolved chemicals in the sea, transforming the millions upon millions of skeletons into a rock known as limestone. It was that fossilized reef structure that made up Lady Elliot Island.

"You mean like that shelf of rock on the other end of the island?" Clint asked.

"That's right. Limestone is all around us. If you dig down in the sand here you'll hit limestone very quickly."

"You mean that rock was once like this?" he persisted, holding up a handful of staghorn coral. "With patterns where the animals once were and tiny little holes and pretty branches and everything?"

Mandy nodded.

"Fair dinkum!" the boy said in astonishment.

Clint spent the time until lunch enthusiastically comparing every variety of coral he found with a slab of limestone that had been battered free from its island mooring during a storm and left high along the margin of the beach. No matter how carefully he looked, he found few traces of the limestone's previous life as a portion of the living reef.

"How did you learn all that?" he finally demanded of Mandy.

"School."

Clint muttered something Mandy wisely chose not to hear. Then he sighed.

"School, eh?"

"That's right," she said cheerfully.

"I want to go to a Yank school. All they teach in mine is the alphabet and little words and one plus one and smearing nasty colors on butcher paper."

Mandy hid her smile by turning toward the castle, which had grown until it was nearly as high as the Fish Pond was deep at low tide. The castle resembled an explosion in a pasta factory more than a stately building, but the children insisted that all things built upon a beach were castles, and this mess was no exception.

"I had to go through the gloppy painting," Mandy said. "Once you learn how to read—"

"I know how," Clint interrupted impatiently. "I've known since kindergarten."

"Then all you have to do is get your parents to take you to a library. You'll find books there about anything you can think of, and books are very good teachers, because they're so patient. Anytime you want to learn, there they are, waiting, just stuffed full of things to share with you."

Frowning, Clint looked from the coral in his hand to the limestone slab. "Wish there was a library here."

Mandy smiled. "Tell you what. After lunch, I'll bring

some of my books down to the beach and we can look at them together.''

Mollified, the young boy went to scavenging hunks of coral for the growing, teetering castle. After lunch Mandy surprised the kids with two brightly wrapped candy bars. As delighted as they were with the candy, they were even more fascinated by the glossy, full-color pictures in the books Mandy brought from her tent. To Mandy's surprise, Di was able to read almost as many of the words as her brother could. Mandy was kept very busy trying to translate Latin taxonomy into plain English—and repeating explanations as to why the names hadn't been in English in the first place.

For once neither child looked longingly toward the tents each time a scattering of adult voices indicated that the dive boat had shuttled in one group of tired divers and had taken off with a fresh batch. Even Clint, who was normally in a fever to go snorkeling with one of his parents, ignored everything but the books and the various chunks of coral he kept retrieving in the hope he would be able to stump Mandy.

Sutter, who had been standing motionless in the shade of the she-oaks since he had come in on an early dive boat, was watching with growing amazement as Mandy identified variety after variety of coral or shell from a piece of bleached remains.

''Bet you can't guess this 'un!'' Clint said triumphantly, waving a broken hunk of something beneath Mandy's nose.

She took the object from Clint and looked at it critically. ''Mollusk, not coral,'' she muttered.

''I know that,'' Di said instantly. ''There's no place for the little animals to poke out and feed.''

''What else do you see?'' Mandy asked.

''One side is real smooth.''

Mandy made an encouraging noise.

"And the lines here bend off in a...a...spiral? Is that the word?"

"That's exactly right, Di. Good for you."

"You mean good *on* you," Clint said.

"I do?"

"You want to learn to talk like a 'Straiyan, right?"

"Roight," Mandy said carefully.

"Good on you!" Clint and Di said together, laughing.

Smiling, motionless, Sutter enjoyed the easy give-and-take between Mandy and the kids as she taught them Latin taxonomy and they taught her Australian pronunciation, idioms and slang. The more he listened, the more he realized how little he knew about Mandy beyond the fact that she was intelligent, had an irrational fear of small planes and water, a quick tongue, surprising self-discipline for someone who was so timid...and a body that brought every masculine nerve in him sizzling to life.

It had also become obvious to Sutter that Mandy had a knowledge of coral that went beyond that of the books she had open around her on the overlapping beach towels. She didn't have to look up the corals and shells that were brought to her; she identified them on sight, talked about their place within the larger reef community, and only then did she turn to the index of one of the books to find on which page the creatures were pictured in their living state.

The chunk of shell Clint had just brought proved to be difficult. Di protested that there wasn't enough of the shell for Mandy to identify.

"It's bigger than some of the pieces of coral she named," Clint retorted.

"That's because coral animals are smaller than whatever made that silly bit of junk," Di said indignantly, standing up for her new friend. "An ant's an ant but you can't tell 'roo from goanna if the piece is only ant-sized!"

"Your sister has a point," Sutter said before Clint could argue.

Mandy's head snapped around. "What are you doing here? Is everything all right?" she demanded.

"Yes. Why?"

"You're back early," she said simply.

"I told the Townehomes I'd take Clint snorkeling so they could spend more time diving together. It's their last day here." Sutter paused, then looked into Mandy's golden-brown eyes. "Want to come snorkeling with us?"

"She doesn't swim," Clint said in disgust.

"Really? Then maybe I should stay here and make sure she doesn't get too close to the water," Sutter said calmly. "She could get hurt."

"She *can* swim," Di said in an earnest voice, defending Mandy once again. "She just *doesn't*."

One of Sutter's sun-bleached eyebrows climbed upward in silent query, but all he said was "I see." He stepped forward and sat cross-legged next to Mandy. "Since you won't go to the reef, I brought a bit of it to you."

Mandy looked down at Sutter's long-fingered, tanned hand. In the center of his palm was a perfectly formed, milk-white shell. It gleamed like the finest bone china against his skin. She made a sound of surprise and pleasure as she picked up the shell.

"A Malward's cowrie! Do you have any idea how rare they are?" she asked. "Did you find it while you were diving out on the reef?"

"Yes and yes," Sutter said, smiling at Mandy's pleasure and the reverent way she was handling the shell.

For an electric instant he wondered what it would be like to feel her slender fingers touching his body with half that much pleasure and sensitivity. Ruthlessly he shunted the sensual thought aside. Sitting as he was, wearing only a brief swimsuit, he had no choice but to keep his mind on shells rather than sex. He had no business wanting Mandy. She wasn't the kind of cool, free-living sex partner he preferred. He couldn't even honestly say that he liked her; he had spent a lifetime *dis*liking the kind of woman

who couldn't cope with even the luxurious reality of life
in one of the most stable, wealthy countries on earth. His
mother had been a prime example of a woman too weak
to survive without constant pampering. His former wife
had been another. It appeared that Mandy, with her host
of irrational fears, was yet another.

Now all he had to do was convince his body of what
his mind knew to be the truth: Mandy was not for D. M.
Sutter.

"Is the shell worth pots of money?" Clint asked eagerly.

With an effort, Sutter gathered his restless thoughts and
focused on Clint.

"Maybe one pot, to a collector," Sutter said. "But this
shell isn't going to be sold. I'm not even going to keep it
for myself or give it to Mandy, much as I'd like to. Lady
Elliot Island is a preserve, which means that all land and
sea life is protected."

"But the shell isn't alive," Clint objected.

"It once was part of a living animal. Have you ever
been to a curio shop or any place that sold shells?" Sutter
continued quickly, seeing Clint's bottled objections in the
boy's frowning expression.

Both children nodded.

"Did you ever think how those shells came to be in the
shop?" Sutter asked.

"Someone picked them up on the beach," Di said immediately.

"How many perfect shells do you find on the beach?"
Sutter asked. "And I mean perfect. No chips, no cracks,
no faded colors, no missing chunks."

"Oh," the little girl said, understanding. "They only
sell perfect shells, right? So where do they come from?"

"Divers find the living animal. The snail is killed and
the perfect shell remains. Those are the shells you find in
stores and collections."

Clint frowned. "But your shell was empty when you found it, right?"

"Yes."

"Then what's hurt if you keep it?"

"What's to keep someone from catching live cowries, killing them and then saying they found the shells on the beach?" Sutter countered. "That's why no one is allowed to take anything from Lady Elliot Island except pictures. We aren't even allowed to catch fish for dinner out on the reef."

Clint sighed and looked regretfully at the glistening cowrie shell. "Still, it seems a blood—er," he corrected hastily, "a terrible shame to throw such a pretty shell away."

Sutter smiled. "We'll keep it in the tent for two more weeks, then we'll give it back to the sea."

"Two weeks? You'll be here that long?" Di asked, turning to Mandy.

"Yes."

"We go home tomorrow," the girl said glumly. Then she sighed. "But at least I get the window seat this time, so I'll be able to see the island and the reefs and the cane fields and all."

"How nice," Mandy said in a faint voice, barely repressing a shudder. She had managed to keep the plane out of her mind very well so far, probably because she was much closer to another fearful object—the sea. Blankly she handed the cowrie back to Sutter and stared at the broken piece of shell Clint had brought to her. "Triton," she said.

"What?" Di asked.

"This is probably part of a triton shell. Like this one," Mandy said, picking up a shell that had been brought to her earlier.

The shell was long, fluted, wider than her hand. The shell's graceful lines were still intact, though the delicate interior colors had long since faded. There was a definite resemblance between both the vague pattern on Clint's piece of shell and the intact shell held by Mandy. Clint and Di promptly jumped to their feet and went off in search of another bit of debris for Mandy to identify.

"May I?" Sutter asked, reaching for the big shell balanced on Mandy's palm. He held the opening to his ear and murmured, "Still there."

"What is? The sea?"

He gave a rumble of agreement that was as low pitched as the voice of the distant breakers.

"You know it's just the sound of your own blood moving," Mandy said.

Smiling slightly, Sutter shook his head. "It's the sea. Listen."

With one hand he held the triton's flared opening against Mandy's ear. With the other he held her cheek, gently pinioning her between the shell and his own palm. Her eyes widened as she felt his fingers easing into her hair, seeking and finding the living warmth of her scalp. The sudden race of her heart was magnified by the shell held so gently, so immovably against her ear. Like distant storm surf, the sound beat rhythmically through her.

"Hear it?" Sutter murmured, watching the acceleration of Mandy's heart in the pulse beating beneath her neck.

"Yes," she said, her voice strained. She gasped when his thumb lightly caressed her lower lip.

"You cut yourself. How?" he asked.

"I—I bit it. In the Fish Pond."

"Does being in the water frighten you that badly?"

"Yes," Mandy said, closing her eyes, not wanting to see the contempt she was certain would be in Sutter's eyes when he heard her admission.

"Are you afraid of all water or just the sea?"

"All of it," she said harshly. "Even my damned bath!"

"Then why did you go into the pond?"

Sutter's voice was puzzled rather than rough or condemning, and his touch was reassuring, subtly caressing. Mandy opened her eyes. There was no contempt in his expression, simply an intense concentration that was almost tangible.

"I'm trying to get over it," Mandy said, her voice low. "I had worked up to my knees and even a few inches beyond, then Clint drifted out of the pond and over the coral knobs and I had to go get him or really hate myself for the coward I am so I just bit my lip and did it."

The rush of words took Sutter a moment to sort out. He remembered Mandy's puzzling elation at having retrieved her sandal from ankle-deep water. He looked from Mandy's golden eyes to the transparent glitter of the Fish Pond amid the dark brown carpet of coral that covered nearly all the lagoon. To him, there was absolutely nothing worth fearing there.

Yet there was no doubt Mandy's fear was real. There was also no doubt she had fought against it, forcing herself to go to Clint's aid. For a few moments Sutter tried to imagine how being in the small pool had felt to her, how much bigger fear had made the pool, how much deeper, her heart hammering, her teeth digging into her until blood flowed.

"Clint wasn't in any real danger, was he?" Sutter asked softly.

"No. Almost none of the coral is alive. Unless he panicked, the worst he would have done is skin his knees."

"But you went after him anyway."

Mandy took in a deep breath and let it out. "Yes."

Eyes as green and fathomless as gems watched her. "Why?"

"Because I have to live with myself," she said succinctly. "There was no more danger to me in the pond than if I had been walking across an empty road. My mind knew it. My body...didn't. How would you feel about yourself if you could have saved a child a bloodied knee just by walking across an empty road, but you were too big a coward to do it?"

There was silence and more intense scrutiny from Sutter's clear green eyes as he tried to understand Mandy. His mother had had many irrational fears but had never made any attempt to confront them. After his father had died in a drunken race through the Alps, his mother had retreated first to the country house, then to a single wing of the house, then to her room, to her bed, until all that was left was Valium. She had crawled into the pills, going away for weeks at a time. One day she hadn't come back.

His former wife had been afraid in a different way. She had been afraid of being alone. That fear had ruled her life and nearly ruined his. He had tried to adjust to always being in the center of a party or an outing. She had never tried to adjust to being with silence. Finally he had taken one trip too many for OCC and had come back to find that his wife was in Mexico, obtaining the fastest divorce available. She had remarried before she came back to the U.S. and had become a hostess known for the number and variety of her parties—and sycophants. Like his mother, his former wife had succumbed to fear rather than trying to overcome it.

But Mandy was fighting. If what had happened on the plane was any example, she was fighting with the kind of guts and sheer determination that he couldn't help but respond to. He, too, had known debilitating fear. He, too, had had to reach down deep in himself to go on despite fear, because there were things that simply had to be done no matter what the obstacles.

"You're tired of being afraid," Sutter said finally, softly.

Golden eyes widened in surprise as Mandy realized that what Sutter had said was the exact truth. She was very tired of being imprisoned within her own fears, cut off from the elemental mystery and beauty of the sea, cut off from the career she had loved, cut off from…herself.

"Yes," she whispered. "I am very, very tired of being afraid."

"And you risked wading across that pond for a child when you wouldn't risk it on your own behalf."

"Children are given to us to protect," Mandy said simply, "not to pay the price of our failures."

Sutter felt an instant of emotion so strong that it was nearly painful. Never had anyone put into words so clearly the reason he kept working for a better future despite the odds against success. He looked at Mandy as though she were a rare, perfect shell he had found unexpectedly, a gift from the sea.

Then he realized that it was sorrow as much as fear that haunted Mandy's golden eyes. He didn't know what had caused her sadness; he only knew that he wanted to ease it, to cherish her, telling her wordlessly that he would help her if he could, if she would allow him.

Sutter bent down to Mandy slowly, watching her eyes widen, feeling the warmth of her breath sigh over his mouth. The tip of his tongue slowly caressed the cut on her lip, drawing a small sound of surprise and pleasure from her. He very much wanted to deepen the kiss, to slide his hungry tongue into the heat and softness he knew waited within her mouth, but he heard the sound of the Townehome kids running back up the beach. He allowed himself one more light, gliding touch on her cut lip before he slowly released her.

"Thought you said he wasn't your bloke," Clint said slyly, watching Mandy's blush with great interest.

"Old American custom," Sutter said, hoping the child wouldn't understand the meaning of his suddenly husky voice. "It's called kissing a small hurt to make it better. Mandy cut her lip."

"Whatever you say, mate," Clint retorted dryly. He flopped down next to Mandy and opened his empty hands. "Couldn't find a ruddy thing."

Di stood nearby, her expression disconsolate.

"Di? Is something wrong, honey?" Mandy asked, wondering what had made the little girl so unhappy.

"Will you see us off tomorrow?" Di blurted out.

The last thing Mandy wanted to do was to get anywhere near the ghastly little plane that made twice-daily trips to the island. In fact, she usually made it a point to be in her tent when the plane appeared or disappeared. But Di was watching her so hopefully, her eyes clouded with the unhappiness of having to leave her new friend.

"Of course I'll see you off," Mandy said, forcing a smile.

"We both will," amended Sutter.

"Won't you be diving?" Mandy asked.

"Doubt it. Wind is forecast. I've been meaning to try my hand at a reef walk anyway. Will you give me a guided tour?"

Mandy started to refuse, hesitated, then said, "I'll do as much as I can."

Sutter brushed her cut lip with the pad of his thumb and lowered his hands, releasing her. "That's all anyone can ask, isn't it?"

Chapter 8

⟨⟨⟨⟨⟩⟩⟩⟩

Sutter's understanding and his kiss haunted Mandy for the rest of the day. She hadn't suspected that he was capable of such aching tenderness. The thought of being held and caressed and made love to with even a fraction of that gentle masculine care sent odd sensations glittering through the secret places of her body. She found herself watching every motion Sutter made, every breath he took, the sheen of light on his spun-gold hair and the satin allure of his skin stretched over hard muscle; and most of all she was caught by the obvious strength of his male body and the careful restraint of that strength while he played with the two children.

After dinner a strange restlessness claimed Mandy. She told herself it was the rising wind and the falling barometer, but she knew it was as simple and complex as Sutter's green eyes watching her watch him. When the divers adjourned to the bar for beer and tall tales, Mandy slipped outside, driven by a need to walk far and fast…for if she stayed, she wouldn't be able to keep herself from running her fingertip along Sutter's full lower lip, returning the caress he had given to her earlier that day.

Mandy walked to the end of the tiny island. Along one fifty-yard stretch of beach, the limestone understructure of the island pushed through the veneer of sand. Not even the hardy she-oaks grew there. A stone shelf sloped down to the lagoon. When the tide was out, there were pockets of sand here and there, long, pale ribbons filling troughs that currents had worn into the limestone. Mandy had discovered the previous day that the sand made a cushion to sit on and the water-smoothed, sun-warmed, slanting limestone shelf provided a comfortable backrest. But tonight the tide had already passed its lowest ebb and was well launched into its return. Soon the comfortable portions of the limestone shelf would be covered by water lapping over rock still warm from the sun.

Besides, Mandy was too restless to sit still. She walked on until she rounded the end of the island and headed back up the far side where waves beat in sunset-tinged ranks against Lady Elliot Island, the first obstacle the ocean had known in thousands upon thousands of watery miles. The wind blew steadily, making the eighty degrees of heat and equal percentage of humidity feel silky rather than suffocating, giving the brilliant carmine sky a cool polish.

Very swiftly light vanished into the velvet darkness of tropic night. Mandy made a complete circuit of the island, walking by the few small resort buildings without pausing. She needed no more illumination for her walk than that offered by the cloud-veiled moon and white coral sands. She encountered no one on her second circuit of the island; though the island was barely a mile long and a half mile wide, there were too few people around for there to be any danger of tripping over each other after dark.

The tent was deserted by the time Mandy had finally walked off the worst of her restlessness. She fell asleep quickly, only to dream of being caressed by a tender warmth that was both Sutter and the sea.

When dawn came, Mandy awoke in a rush. Just enough light filled the tent for her to see that Sutter was asleep on his back, one arm flung over his head, the other trailing onto the gritty canvas floor. The sheet had been kicked

Get 2

HOW TO GET YOUR
2 FREE BOOKS AND FREE GIFT

1. Peel off the 2 FREE BOOKS seal from the front cover. Place it in the space provided at right. This automatically entitles you to receive two free books and an exciting mystery gift.

2. Send back this card and you'll get 2 "The Best of the Best™" novels. These books have a combined cover price of $11.00 or more but they are yours keep absolutely FREE!

3. There's no catch. You're under no obligation to buy anything. We charge nothing – ZERO – for your first shipment. And you don't have to make any minimum number of purchases – not even one!

4. We call this line "The Best of the Best" because each month you'll receive the best books by the world's hottest authors. These authors show up time and time again on all the major bestseller lists and their books sell out as soon as they hit the stores. You'll love getting them conveniently delivered your home…and you'll love our discount prices!

5. We hope that after receiving your free books you'll want to remain a subscriber. But the choice is yours – to continue or cancel, anytime at all! why not take us up on our invitation, with no risk of any kind. You'll be gl you did!

6. And remember…we'll send you a mystery gift ABSOLUTELY FREE just for giving "The Best of the Best" a try!

SPECIAL FREE GIFT!

We'll send you a fabulous mystery gift, absolutely FREE, simply for accepting our no-risk offer!

MIRA®

© 1996 MIRA BOOKS

Books FREE!

DETACH AND MAIL CARD TODAY!

HURRY! Return this card promptly to get **2 FREE Books** and a **FREE Gift!**

YES! Please send me two free "The Best of the Best" novels. I understand that I am under no obligation to purchase anything further as explained on the opposite page. **Also send my free mystery gift!**

Affix
peel-off
2 FREE BOOKS
sticker here.

BB1-99
383 MDL CPQL   **183 MDL CPQM**

Name: _____
(PLEASE PRINT)

Address: _____ Apt. #: _____

City: _____

State/Prov.: _____ Postal Zip/Code: _____

STARLIGHT JOB 1   14 1/4"

The Best of the Best™—Here's How it Works

Accepting your 2 free books and gift places you under no obligation to buy anything. You may keep the books and gift and return the shipping statement marked "cancel." If you do not cancel, about a month later we will send you 3 additional novels and bill you just $4.24 each in the U.S., or $4.74 each in Canada, plus 25¢ delivery per book and applicable sales tax, if any.* That's the complete price, and — compared to cover prices of $5.50 each in the U.S. and $6.50 each in Canada — it's quite a bargain! You may cancel at any time, but if you choose to continue, every month we'll send you 3 more books, which you may either purchase at the discount price…or return to us and cancel your subscription.

*Terms and prices subject to change without notice. Sales tax applicable in N.Y. Canadian residents will be charged applicable provincial taxes and GST.

If offer card is missing write to: The Best of the Best, 3010 Walden Ave., P.O. Box 1867, Buffalo, NY 14240-1867

BUSINESS REPLY MAIL

FIRST-CLASS MAIL   PERMIT NO. 717   BUFFALO NY

POSTAGE WILL BE PAID BY ADDRESSEE

THE BEST OF THE BEST
3010 WALDEN AVE
PO BOX 1867
BUFFALO NY 14240-9952

NO POSTAGE
NECESSARY
IF MAILED
IN THE
UNITED STATES

aside by his long, powerful legs. His nearly nude body looked like a pagan sculpture, overwhelmingly male, each masculine line heightened by shadow and caressed by ruby light. The aura of barely leashed potency was emphasized by the stark white of the minimal jockstrap that stretched to contain him. Dark gold hair grew thickly across his chest, narrowed into a line down the center of his body and then fanned outward again, curling out from beneath the cloth pouch.

Sensations streaked through Mandy like hot rain as she watched Sutter. When she could bear it no more she rolled over and faced the tent wall, which glowed redly with the caress of the rising sun. Yet it was the image of Sutter's relaxed, beautifully male body that she saw. Certain she wouldn't sleep, she began to count the random places where light leaked through the canvas weave.

When Mandy awoke again she was alone in the tent. Though Sutter's mattress was empty, she couldn't look over there without seeing him as she had at dawn, fully aroused, fully male. Hands shaky, arms oddly weak, she changed into her island uniform—bikini and sandals. She grabbed her towel and knapsack and went to the shower. Half an hour later she emerged much cleaner and as restive as the tropic wind.

No sooner had she eaten breakfast than she heard the savage mechanical cry of the white plane swooping down for a landing. Memories surged up violently, threatening to immobilize her. She replaced them with the image of Sutter at dawn. After a few minutes she was able to climb down the cafeteria steps and walk toward the runway she had avoided since her first day on Lady Elliot Island. By the time she walked past the dive shed toward the runway, the plane had turned off the crushed coral strip and was taxiing toward the shed. Engine noise hammered rhythmically through the thick air.

Mandy slowed as memories rose like a cold, midnight sea, threatening to overwhelm her. Suddenly she felt a man's hand close around one of hers, lacing their fingers together securely.

"Ready?" Sutter asked.

Mandy's fingers tightened within his. She let out her breath slowly and nodded. Sutter squeezed her hand in return. Unconsciously she waited for him to gently prod her closer to the source of her fear. Nothing happened. Startled, she looked up into Sutter's calm green eyes. He smiled encouragingly but made no move forward. She realized that she would have to take the lead, confronting the plane by her own choice and in her own way. Sutter would neither force nor persuade her; he was simply there if she needed him. Her throat ached with sudden emotion.

"You understand," she whispered.

"What it is to fight fear?"

She nodded.

Sutter's lips curved in something that was too sad to pass for a smile. "Does that surprise you?"

"Yes."

"Everyone is afraid of something, golden eyes. The only difference is that some people fight and others go under without a struggle."

"What fear do you fight?"

"I'm afraid of being chained and beaten again," he said matter-of-factly, "of being helpless."

Mandy's breath came in with a harsh sound. She lifted Sutter's hand and smoothed it against her cheek, then pressed a kiss into his hard palm.

"Hey," he said, tilting her face up to his. "I didn't mean for you to feel sorry for me. Being beaten like that taught me fear. Up to a point, fear is a very healthy thing. It has saved my life more than once. I just have to make sure that fear doesn't *rule* my life."

Mandy couldn't speak. She simply watched Sutter with wide amber eyes, aching for all that he had suffered, not knowing why his past pain should matter so deeply to her, but knowing that it did.

"Damon," she whispered, "I..."

The sound of high, childish laughter drew closer as the Townehome kids raced each other to the plane. Slowly Mandy released Sutter's hand but was unable to keep herself from skimming one more kiss across his fingers before she turned toward Di and Clint and held out her arms. Instants later she was buried in exuberant hugs. Both children began talking at once, issuing explicit instructions for the continued construction of the coral castle. Finally the parents boosted their offspring into the plane, shaking hands all around and thanking Mandy for the extra dive time her baby-sitting had permitted.

Suddenly the engine of the plane ripped up the scale of sound as the pilot pulled back on the throttle. Instinctively Mandy reached for Sutter's hand. An instant later his fingers were interlaced with hers. He said nothing despite the painful tightness of her grip. The plane taxied down to the end of the runway, then accelerated hard up the crushed coral strip. The little aircraft leaped into the sky well short of the half of the runway that had been preempted by nesting terns. When the plane circled, gained altitude and vanished in the direction of the mainland, Mandy let out a long breath of relief.

"Have you always been afraid of flying?" Sutter asked casually as they turned away from the strip.

"I've never liked small planes," Mandy said in a flat tone.

Sutter sensed that Mandy's answer was only half the truth, and probably the less important half at that. He said nothing, however. He didn't blame her for not wanting to talk about her fear; he hadn't talked about his brutal experience in a South American jail since he had been debriefed at the American embassy after he had been freed. Even Anthea had been rather curtly told to satisfy her curiosity through the embassy report. In truth, Sutter was rather surprised that he had brought it up to Mandy. She hardly had the experience to comprehend what it meant to be beaten until you were held upright only by the same chains that had rendered you utterly helpless in the first place.

Yet Mandy had not only understood, she hadn't pitied him. She had been appalled that he had had to endure such an experience, but she hadn't made the mistake of trying to mother him as several of the women at the embassy had. Mandy had given him compassion, not pity. Empathy, not sympathy. She had offered no easy words because she had known there was nothing she could say to alleviate the brutality of his experience. There was no magic motherly act that would make it all better. He hadn't been a boy when he had been chained and beaten. He had been a man and he had suffered as a man, and no amount of mothering could change that. Mandy knew that and respected it.

"Thank you," Sutter said quietly.

Startled, Mandy looked up, only to be held captive by his clear green eyes.

"Some of the women at the embassy tried to mother me after I was freed," Sutter explained. "They meant well, I suppose, but they had the effect of reducing everything to the level of skinned knees on the rugby field. I was 'poor Damon' and 'dearie this' and 'sweetums that' until I blew up and told the women if they wanted to mother something so damned bad, there were thousands of orphans out in the streets who would benefit from it a hell of a lot more than I would." Sutter smiled ruefully. "I'm afraid I really put a high gloss on my reputation as an evil-tempered S.O.B. It was worth it, though. The women finally figured out that I wasn't a boy to be cuddled and petted and coaxed into giving mummy a tearful smile."

Mandy's own answering smile was almost sad. "Don't be too hard on them, Sutter. They were just trying to make a place for you in their world, a nice place where nothing happens that can't be cured by a mother's kiss and a red lollipop."

Sutter grunted. "I'm not a boy and I don't want to be one."

"A lot of men don't feel that way."

"Good. There are a lot of would-be mothers out there waiting to take the poor little dears to their maternal bosoms," Sutter retorted. "Why the hell women like that don't just have kids of their own…" He shrugged.

"Oh, sometimes they do. It's usually a disaster. The 'boy' they're married to has to grow up and share mummy with a squalling, helpless stranger who has first call on mummy's time and attention. How many boys do you know who like sharing the limelight?"

Sutter's teeth flashed in a sardonic smile. "Yeah, I suppose you're right." His smile gentled as he looked down at Mandy. "I'm glad you save your motherly instincts for kids like the Townehomes. You performed a small miracle with them, by the way. Both parents told me that Clint is a real handful."

"No disagreement here," Mandy said wryly. "He's also very, very bright. So is Di. When you get their attention, it's like being the focus of searchlights. Do the Townehomes know that both kids have taught themselves to read?"

"I made sure to pass on that tidbit, along with your suggestion about turning Clint loose in a library."

"Thanks. I was never with either parent long enough to find the right moment for telling them. For you, that was no problem."

"Are you hinting that I'm blunt?"

Mandy had only meant that Sutter had spent more time with the older Townehomes than she had. On the other hand, it was true that Sutter could be breathtakingly outspoken at times.

"How do you define blunt?" she asked blandly. "Is a baseball bat blunt? Is a torpedo blunt? Is a fifty-megaton—"

"That did it," Sutter interrupted, his threatening tone

belied by the humorous line of his mouth. He grabbed Mandy's bare shoulders and shook her very gently. "I always knew your smart mouth would get you into trouble someday. Well, golden eyes, this is the day."

"I'm terrified. I take it all back. Sutter, you're the very soul of subtlety," Mandy said dramatically, putting a hand over her heart to show her earnestness.

"Convince me," he murmured, flexing his fingers, enjoying the sleek feminine resilience of her flesh.

"No one," she said instantly, "and I mean no one, has ever curled his eyebrow, lip and index finger at me with such incredible arroga—er, deftness as you did at the auction. Finesse, even. Yes, finesse. It was a stellar display of fine coordination," she said, struggling not to smile.

"My lip, too?"

"Your lip most definitely!" she shot back.

Sutter laughed and wondered why he had been avoiding Mandy for the past week. The answer came in an unwelcome avalanche of common sense.

Because she feels too damn good between my hands, that's why! Because she isn't into casual love affairs and I don't want anything more, that's why! Because awake or asleep I dream about what it would be like to slide into her and watch those beautiful golden eyes get smoky with passion. Because right now I want to cherish her in a very special way, with my words and my hands and my mouth, with my body, all of it, so deep that neither one of us will ever be the same again, always joined no matter how far apart....

Very carefully Sutter lifted his hands from Mandy's smooth, too-tempting body.

"Accusing me of having lip is like the pot calling the kettle black," Sutter said, his voice husky with laughter and something much deeper, much hotter. "You've got enough lip for both of us."

When Mandy glanced into the green blaze of Sutter's eyes, her smile slipped. For an instant the look in his eyes went through her veins like chain lightning through night, a burst of sizzling brightness and many-tongued fire. She took a short, sharp breath and retreated behind her facade of humor once more.

"Are you calling me a duck?" Mandy asked.

"A duck?"

"As in having enough lip for two birds."

"Do birds have lips?"

"Only if ducks are birds. Then there's plenty of lip to go around."

"I think I'm going to cry foul."

"Roight," she said instantly, "but you have to cry real tears or it doesn't count."

Laughing, shaking his head, Sutter conceded defeat. "I begin to understand how you handled Clint. I, however, have a tactic that wasn't available to him. Brute strength." Sutter's arms snaked out and gently pinned Mandy against his body. He brushed his lips over her forehead before he hugged her. "You're good people, Mandy," he said against her ear. "It will be a long time before I forgive myself for chaining you into that damned airplane seat."

Mandy's smile vanished as she remembered what Sutter had said about his own past, his own worst fear—to be chained, helpless.

"It was a seat belt, not a chain," she pointed out.

"There's no difference when you're too terrified to open the buckle. I'm sorry, Mandy. I should have known you weren't joking. I should have seen your fear."

"Why? Do you come across my brand of cowardice often?"

"You're not a coward, honey."

"Don't," she said abruptly, twisting away from Sutter. "I may be afraid of my own shadow, as you pointed out a few days ago, but I'm not a child. I don't like being chucked under the chin and told fairy tales any better than you did at the embassy."

For an instant Sutter was tempted to grab Mandy and

show her just how little he considered her a child. He wanted to kiss her until she melted and ran over him in a hot rain of passion that wouldn't end until neither of them had enough strength left to lick their lips. Sweet, sizzling oblivion, to fall asleep with her taste in his mouth and her body slick and hot around him, caressing him even as he drove more deeply into her one last time.

Sutter expelled a sharp breath, wrenched his thoughts into another track and said evenly, ''I'm glad you don't want to be a child, because I sure as hell don't want to be your daddy. Now that we've got that settled, let's get some reef shoes. I promised Clint I'd find something you couldn't name if it took me the two weeks we've got left.''

Giving Mandy no time to answer or argue, Sutter turned away. She hesitated only momentarily before following him. The reef shoes were kept in ragged rows on the cafeteria steps, right next to the bowl that held crusts for feeding the fish. Sutter and Mandy sorted through the wet, scarred, sandy shoes, looking for a pair that fitted well enough for them to tolerate for a few hours, using thick cotton socks as a cushion. Sutter finally found shoes that were long enough for his feet. The shoes Mandy found were long enough but too wide. While Mandy rummaged hopefully for a better fit, Sutter trotted back to the tent through the blustery wind, retrieved an extra pair of socks and presented them to Mandy with a flourish.

By the time Mandy and Sutter got to the beach, seven other people had scattered over the reef, which was being unveiled by the dropping tide. Sutter declared Mandy the guide, letting her choose the way out through the coral maze. Most people gravitated toward the tiny pools and narrow cracks where water and reef life concentrated. Mandy avoided the areas where water gleamed among the blunt coral shapes, choosing to teeter and balance on un-even coral knobs rather than wade in the crystalline water and sandy patches that occurred in the shallowest parts of the lagoon.

The reef sticks Mandy and Sutter carried made her balancing act possible. Five feet long, two inches in diameter, the sturdy reef sticks probed for weak patches of coral and braced people for whom two legs just weren't enough for the demands of reef walking. Even with the stick, a timely hand from Sutter saved Mandy more than once, and vice versa. Slowly, randomly, they zigzagged over the coral floor of the draining lagoon.

Whenever Sutter spotted a new shape of coral, he required Mandy to name the creature that had created it. Every time she replied quickly, effortlessly, unintentionally revealing to him how utterly familiar she was with the denizens of the reef. Yet at the same time, her small sounds of delight and surprise at seeing the living animals told him that experiencing the reef was very new to her. The paradox baffled Sutter, but he was reluctant to question her. He didn't want to replace her wonder and delight with hesitation and withdrawal.

"Oh, look!" Mandy said, her voice ringing with excitement. "I've heard about this and seen pictures, but it's unbelievably beautiful in its natural habitat."

Mandy crouched down, bracing herself with one hand on the reef stick and dipping into a small coral pool with the other. Carefully she pried up a starfish. The animal was a sapphire blue so brilliant it looked unreal.

"What's that?" Sutter asked.

"Starfish," Mandy said absently, turning over the animal to appreciate the alien beauty of myriad tiny, slender "feet" rippling like grass in a slow wind.

"Really?" he said dryly. "You're sure? Maybe you should count the arms again."

"Five."

"What's its name?"

Mandy gave Sutter a sideways, impish smile. "I know just enough of the Latin name to fake you out the way I've been doing for the last hour."

"Aha! Thought so. I didn't think there was such a thing as a *Roseate vucuumupi*."

Mandy snickered.

"But you can redeem yourself by telling me why the beast is so blue," Sutter offered generously. "And if you say it's blue because it's unhappy I'll make you walk back barefoot."

"Would I say such a rank untruth? Never! This little beastie is happy because it isn't seasick."

The words were spoken with such casual certainty that it took a moment for their meaning to sink in.

"It isn't seasick," Sutter repeated carefully, trying not to smile.

"Roight. If it were seasick, it would be—"

"Green," Sutter interrupted, groaning.

"Good on you," Mandy said, laughing, her eyes brilliant with enjoyment.

Sutter's warm, salty fingertips brushed over her cheek. He whispered her name once, then again, knowing that he had never seen a woman quite so beautiful to him as Mandy was at that moment.

"I'd like to bottle you and take you out when I'm in some place so poor and remote that sunlight has to be piped in," Sutter said softly. "At the end of the day I'd pour you into my hands and bathe my senses in you until finally I'd fall asleep smiling, dreaming of all the colors of your laughter."

Mandy blinked back sudden, stinging tears as she thought of how often Sutter must have been tired and hungry and alone at the end of the day.

"I'd like that," she said huskily. "I'd like to give you warmth when you're cold, laughter when you're alone."

With an odd, almost sad smile, Sutter caressed Mandy's cheek again and then turned away abruptly, not trusting himself to touch her anymore.

The humid wind gusted over Sutter, lifting his hair, making him restless. Mandy's golden eyes watched him, wondering what he was thinking, what she had done to make him turn away so abruptly, why he affected her so deeply.

He had always affected her, from the first day she had walked into Anthea's office and seen Sutter's intense green eyes and go-to-hell smile staring at her from a picture frame. In the background had been empty grassland and a low tree where a leopard lay asleep in kingly ease. Sutter had been photographing the big cat when another photographer had called out. Sutter had turned, seen the camera, smiled challengingly…and the result had been the arresting snapshot that had been enlarged and framed for Anthea's office.

The picture had haunted Mandy. Every time she heard of another one of Sutter's close escapes, another diplomatic coup, another reluctant government talked into allotting more money for education and less for ostentation, her admiration had increased.

And with each of Sutter's adventures, Mandy had become more uneasy at being around him on the few occasions when he came into the office. She had been certain that a man of such proven courage would have nothing but contempt for her cowardice. So she had kept him at bay in the same way that she had kept the rest of the world from coming close enough to hurt her again; she had turned aside every potentially serious moment with a quip and a flashing smile.

But she couldn't smile when she was in the grip of her private terror. Sutter had seen her terrified, yet ultimately he had come to respect rather than to sneer at the depth of her fear. He was too much a man to fatten his own sense of self-worth by being contemptuous of people less strong than he was. Instead of lecturing her on her fear or self-righteously dragging her into the water—for her own good, of course—he had simply accepted her as she had come to him.

Quite imperfect.

Yet despite her imperfections he had wanted to bathe his senses in her, to dream of all the colors of her laughter. She wanted that, too. She wanted to know she could bring him ease when the rest of the world brought him only pain. She wanted that with an intensity that shook her.

My God. I'm falling in love with him.

"Hey, careful!" Sutter said, catching Mandy as she stumbled without warning on the coral. "You okay?"

Mandy looked at the green eyes so close to hers and trembled. "I—I was thinking of something else."

"You're shaking. Are you sure you're all right?"

She nodded. "I just scared myself, I guess. You know me. Afraid of my own shadow."

Strong fingers closed more tightly around Mandy's arms in silent rebuke. "But that's just it," he said flatly. "The better I get to know you, the more I realize you aren't a coward. If you were, you wouldn't fight your fear with the last breath in your body." His hands gentled on her arms. "Come on. The tide has turned. We'd better head back."

Mandy looked toward the outer reef. Her eyes widened. Instead of standing dark and rugged above the surface of the sea, the reef had once again succumbed to the ocean's irresistible embrace. By the time Sutter and Mandy had crossed half the lagoon toward the beach, she was wading through the low, sandy points by choice, because it was so much faster and safer than balancing on the slippery, water-smoothed corals. The presence of water didn't disturb her in the way that it had just a few days before. She was even able to stop in a long, narrow slit where water came to midthigh and enjoy the astonishing beauty of a piece of frilled sea life unfurled to its maximum scarlet glory, looking for all the world like a spiral chrysanthemum as it filtered the returning seawater for food.

"Wonder what a fish would make of that," Sutter said.

"It would never bite twice on one. I think that's a stinging variety of tubeworm."

"Ugly name for such a pretty thing."

"You know how it is in the ocean," Mandy said. "The more brightly colored the object, the better the chance that it's no good to eat."

"Mother Nature's little joke on man."

"More like Mother Nature's way of saying 'Look but don't touch.'"

Sutter gave Mandy a sideways look, wondering if Mother Nature knew she had utterly failed to warn off predators in Mandy's case—golden eyes and black hair, skin tanned to a honey brown by the tropic sun, laughter and grace and the promise of sensual heat in every move she made. He was having one hell of a time looking and not touching. As he followed her back to shore he admired her elegant back, her long legs and the inverted heart shape of her bottom, and he found himself hoping she would lose her footing and give him an excuse to grab her and run his hands over her just once. Then he wondered how he would make himself let go of her.

Damn Anthea anyway....

Yet even as Sutter mentally cursed Anthea, he was watching Mandy, remembering her laughter, and his curse lacked its usual force. Even so, he knew he would be a fool if he succumbed to the womanly temptation of her. The fact that he had come to like Mandy and to respect her attempts to control her fear rather than be controlled by it was simply one more reason for not succumbing to raw desire and seducing her. She wasn't a woman for casual sex. She felt too much, too deeply. He would hate himself if he took advantage of that.

But unless he stayed away from her, he didn't know how he'd manage to keep himself from reaching out and taking all that golden sensuality and secret fire for himself, and to hell with his civilized scruples.

"Blackjack," Mandy said, turning over the ace and lining it up next to the king of spades she had just been dealt.

Ray and Tommy groaned.

"That's three in a row," Ray grumbled, pushing four pennies toward Mandy. "If I weren't dealing, I'd wonder...."

"Isn't it time for you to feed the fish?" Tommy asked, tossing his two cards at Ray while looking at Mandy.

"Nope. Tide's too high."

Tommy muttered, "Bet it isn't more than four feet deep in the pond." He took the cards from Ray. "I'll deal for a while. Sally, you want in on this round?"

"Sure."

Sally, who had been tending bar, looked at the other customers. Two of them were elderly teachers from France, who could make a single beer last for an hour between them. The other five were divers who, like Ray and Tommy, were very restless after three days of enforced time on land. The men had tried to get out diving that afternoon by walking out over the reef at low tide, but the surf had been too violent. The divers had returned grumbling and had been drinking beer and playing cards and listening to the wind ever since. An hour ago the wind had died as suddenly as it had come up, but it was too close to sunset to do the divers any good.

"What about you lot?" Tommy asked, looking toward the other disappointed divers. "You want to help me take this Sheila to the laundry?"

"Sounds like that's as close to water as we're going to get today," said one of the men. The others muttered agreement.

Moments later the tables had been pushed together, beers had been ordered all around, pennies were thrown into the pot and cards were dealt.

"Where's the big Yank?" Sally asked.

"Sutter?" Mandy asked, peeking at her hole card.

"He's the biggest Yank on the island," Tommy said. "Bloody good diver, too. Never makes a careless move."

"He's going over his scuba gear," Mandy said, hoping that she was keeping her disappointment out of her voice.

She had no right to expect Sutter to entertain her. Her presence on his vacation had been unexpected, to say the least. All in all, he had been a very good sport about it. He had gone reef walking with her several times, fed the tiny fish, made circuits of the island looking for turtle tracks, eaten meals with her and had always tactfully withdrawn from the tent at night until she had fallen asleep. What more could she ask?

A little less tact, she admitted to herself ruefully.

"Hit me," Mandy said.

"Don't tempt me, luv," Tommy said, giving her a flashing smile and the card she had requested.

Mandy smiled in return, remembering Anthea's advice about finding an Australian lover. With a cross between amusement and exasperation she looked over her cards at the expanse of bare, muscular male chests and sexy grins surrounding her. She had yet to see an Australian male who wasn't tall, well built, tanned, easygoing and good-looking. She had no doubt that Ray or Tommy or one of the tourist divers would be more than happy to accommodate her with a sandy fling, especially when the wind was blowing too hard for the dive boat to get out. Sally and the other girls who worked on the island certainly never lacked male attention.

So why didn't Mandy take Anthea's advice and snaffle one of these engaging Australian males?

Because they aren't Sutter, she admitted to herself.

"I'm good," Mandy said absently, frowning at her own thoughts.

Tommy's smile changed indefinably. His blue glance shifted from the cards in his hands as he made a leisurely, thorough appraisal of the womanly flesh that filled out the black bikini top Mandy wore.

"I'll just bet you are, luv," he said, winking at her.

Mandy blinked, then laughed, shaking her head. Even if she never so much as kissed one of these Australian males, they were good for her ego.

"Hit me," Ray said.

Indolently Tommy flicked him a card.

"Again."

Another card fell.

"Busted," Ray said in disgust, turning his other card faceup. The three cards totaled twenty-two.

Tommy went around the tables until no one remained but himself. He turned over a ten to match his nine.

"Pay twenty."

"That's me," Mandy said promptly, showing a jack and a queen.

"You keep that up and I'm going to feed you to the fishes," Ray said in disgust.

"I'd poison them."

"A sweet little Sheila like you?" Ray said. "Not a prayer, luv. Not a single prayer."

On the next deal Mandy got a blackjack. It was the same on the following deal. When she turned over a blackjack for the third time in a row, everyone threw in the cards in disgust.

"That's it," Ray proclaimed loudly. "To the fishes with her!"

Laughing, Mandy tried to divide her modest mound of pennies among the losers so that the game could continue. The divers were having none of it.

"The door, Sally," Ray said, reaching for Mandy with a gleam in his eyes.

"Right," Sally said, grinning.

Suddenly Mandy found herself out of her chair and hanging upside down over Ray's shoulder. She didn't believe what was happening until the door slammed shut behind the laughing, rowdy divers who were urging Ray on. A few feet beneath her nose the coral path sped by.

"Beer!" Mandy called out, thinking fast. "Drinks are on me, guys, but only if I stay dry!"

The other divers didn't bite on the offer. They had been

drinking beer most of the afternoon. Dunking Mandy promised more diversion than one more round of brew.

The upside-down world went by Mandy with dizzying speed. Most men would have had the wind taken out of their sails just by carrying her halfway to the Fish Pond, but not Ray. His diving career had given him both strength and endurance. He wasn't even breathing hard.

Damn these muscle-bound Aussie men! Mandy thought as she struggled to free herself.

It was futile. Short of biting, she could make no dent in Ray's strength. She wasn't ready to resort to her teeth before she had tried reasoning with the men.

"Ray? Ray, put me down," Mandy pleaded, shouting over the raucous encouragement of the other divers. "I promise I won't play cards anymore."

"Too late, luv," he said cheerfully. "I warned you."

The path gave way to the beach. Blue water flashed beneath the heat-misted tropical sky.

"Ray! Please! I don't like water!" Mandy shouted, her voice high. "Please! Listen to me! This isn't funny anymore! I—I'm afraid of water! Don't drop me in! Please!"

Shouts of laughter and pure disbelief greeted Mandy's frantic cries.

"Sure you are, luv," Ray said, laughing. "That's why you spent a pot of money to come to this little bit of nothing in the middle of the biggest ocean on God's earth. Afraid of water? That's rich, luv, really rich. All right, you lot. Make way for the fish food. Give us a hand, Tommy, there's a good lad."

Suddenly the world flipped over and Mandy found herself even more helpless than she had been before, unable even to bite or claw or kick, her feet held securely in Ray's grasp and her wrists in Tommy's while the rest of the divers called outrageous suggestions as to the best way of launching the fish feast.

"One," chanted the divers as Ray and Tommy swung

Mandy between them, her hips skimming the surface of the water. "Two."

Suddenly Mandy screamed and twisted frantically in the grip of the two divers. It was no use. She was utterly helpless to free herself. With that realization came both terror and despair. She screamed again, a single raw sound that was Sutter's name.

"Three!"

There was a giddy time of flight and then the Fish Pond splashed up and over Mandy just as she was taking another breath to scream again. Instantly she choked and panicked. She thrashed around futilely, unable even to get to her feet in the shallow water. She opened her mouth again but there was only water surrounding her, engulfing her, drowning her.

Chapter 9

Suddenly Mandy was pulled free of the water and held in a man's powerful arms. She knew it was Sutter who had rescued her even before she heard his deep, icy voice flaying Ray and Tommy in measured phrases of contempt. Knowing that she was safe, she wrapped her arms around Sutter and hung on while he walked to shore. Her body convulsed with sobs and coughs as she cleared her lungs of the lagoon's salty water.

"I heard her pleading with you all the way over at the dive shed," Sutter continued, his green eyes narrowed as he watched understanding dawn on the divers. "How in God's name could you do it? Are you as deaf as you are cruel?"

"Bloody hell," Ray said softly, looking from Mandy's shaking body to Sutter's barely contained rage. "She meant it, didn't she? She's really afraid of water!"

"Your mental acuity leaves me breathless," Sutter said, anger vibrating in every word.

"How was I to know? Bloody hell, mate, people who are afraid of water don't come *here*. It makes no sense! When I found out I had no stomach for heights, you can bet your arse I never went rock climbing in the Snowy Mountains again!"

Ray had a point and Sutter knew it, but he was far too angry at the moment to be reasonable. His arms closed protectively around Mandy when she sagged against him, her body shuddering with the strength of her sobs as she tried to speak. He couldn't understand what she was trying to say. He bent until his ear was next to her mouth. She was repeating two words over and over again, the syllables broken by sobs: *The baby, the baby.*

"It's all right, golden eyes," Sutter murmured soothingly, stroking her gently. "You're safe." He continued holding and caressing her, speaking reassurances over and over again until he sensed that she finally had heard him. "That's it. Hold tight to me. You're safe, darling. You're safe." He smoothed his cheek over the wet, tangled hair, kissed her salty cheek and held her even closer, wishing he could understand what she was trying to say. Maybe then he would be able to ease the terrible sobs shaking her.

"Mandy," Ray said softly, his voice as troubled as his blue eyes. He touched her shoulder. "I'm sorry."

The words were repeated many times as the other divers apologized.

Mandy didn't hear anything but her own wild grief.

"Mandy...?" Ray asked.

"Give it a rest," Sutter said, pinning the young diver with a hard green glance, then moving on to look at the others. "All of you. Clear out."

Sutter had faced down armed men with a similar look. The divers wasted no time in finding somewhere else to be. Neither did Sutter. There were people all over that part of the beach—reef walkers chased to shore by the rising tide, swimmers who enjoyed a lazy paddle in the Fish Pond as it deepened with the tide, and other people who simply liked to stretch out on the sand and dream while the sun descended into a sea stained purple by the end of day.

With long strides Sutter walked down the beach, away from the office and cabins and other people. He ignored the tent set apart from others. It would be stifling in there. There was no wind stirring now, nothing to ease the intense, sultry heat of the tropics. Clouds had formed in the absence of the wind, holding the hot air close to the earth. Light flickered oddly within the clouds, heat lightning made almost visible by the descending sun.

As he walked, Sutter felt the shudders that took Mandy's body without warning, heard her tearing breaths, felt the scalding touch of her tears against his chest. With every step he took he raged at himself for not reaching the Fish Pond a few seconds sooner—and for having left her alone in the first place. He should have guessed what kind of horseplay a bunch of young, bored divers would find appealing. He should have stayed in the bar and kept the lid on things.

But it was his own self-control he had been worried about, not that of the divers. It had been driving him slowly wild to sit next to Mandy, to feel the occasional brush of her bare leg against his when she shifted position, to sense her smooth feminine warmth so close to him that all he would have had to do was to move his hand a few inches and it would have lain in the soft, shadowed darkness between her thighs.

He had taken it as long as he could, and then he had fled to the dive shed to check equipment that didn't need checking.

The sand beneath Sutter's feet changed to a pea gravel made of tiny hunks of coral. A hundred feet farther down the beach the gravel gave way to a limestone slope striped with random small troughs of sand. The sand cushions were barely inches above the incoming tide, but that would be enough for now. There was no one else at this end of the island. Mandy could hold on to him and cry in privacy, working out the last residue of her fear.

Sutter lowered himself until he was sitting with his back braced against the smooth limestone. Gently he arranged Mandy across his lap. In silence he held her against his chest, smoothing her hair and her back with slow sweeps of his hand. After a long time she was quiet, with only random trembling to mark the aftermath of her panic. She took in a deep, shaky breath and then simply leaned against Sutter, absorbing his undemanding presence. Slowly her breath evened out.

"I'm sorry," Sutter murmured, brushing Mandy's forehead comfortingly with his lips. "I should have known they would make the same mistake with you that I made. Not believing until it was too late."

Wearily Mandy shook her head. "My fault," she whispered. "I should have told everyone that I was afraid of planes and boats and water on the first day." Her mouth turned down in self-contempt. "Like you said—afraid of my own damned shadow."

"Don't," Sutter said, putting his fingers gently across her mouth. "I was tired, jet-lagged and wrong from the first word I said about you."

Mandy simply shook her head and tried to sit up, but Sutter's arms were too tight. When she persisted, he turned her shoulder blades to his chest, opened his legs and settled her on the sand between his thighs.

"Use me for a backrest," he offered. "I may not be much smarter than limestone but I'm a hell of a lot more comfortable."

At first Mandy resisted the temptation of Sutter's offer. She sat awkwardly upright, feeling chilled despite the heat trapped in the sand and air and ocean around her. But after a few minutes the lure of Sutter's living warmth was too great to deny. Mandy sighed raggedly and leaned back. Big, gentle hands stroked down her arms, silently reassuring her, warming her.

In silence Sutter and Mandy watched the sun complete the last of its fiery arc before being consumed by the restless, incandescent sea. When the molten rays of light vanished into a surreal gloaming, Sutter began talking about sunset on the African veld, about projects that had worked

and those that had not, about the animals and the men and
the laughing, black-eyed children whose future well-being
depended on the generosity of tyrants.

Mandy listened in a dreamy, suspended silence, feeling
Sutter's deep voice vibrate subtly through her body, seep-
ing into her soul. Only gradually did she become aware of
the water that had risen slowly, flowing across the reef,
flooding the lagoon, the ocean licking softly at her outstretched feet. There was no coolness, no hint of chill in
the water, simply a tidal exhalation of warmth lapping
slowly closer.

Distantly Mandy knew that she should move, retreat up
the beach, get away from the devouring sea...but she was
held suspended in the warm and gentle moment, Sutter's
hands smoothing her arms, his breath feathering against
her cheek. She didn't want the time of peace to end. If
that meant enduring the sea's blind caress, then she would
do so as long as she could. The water was barely three
inches deep, no threat to her.

And Sutter was so close, his living warmth radiating into
her body, sinking into her very soul.

Sighing, Mandy shifted her weight slightly, a matter
more of relaxing utterly against Sutter's chest than of any
real movement on her part. He felt the subtle increase of
her weight against him and closed his eyes for an instant
in reflexive response to the emotion twisting through him.
Mandy's wordless declaration of trust in the face of the
rising tide moved him as nothing else could have. Gently
he brushed his cheek against her hair. The strands were
damp, scented with the sea, infused with the warmth of
her body.

Overhead, the sky was half glittering stars, half towering
clouds, where chain lightning silently danced through velvet darkness. The moon was a distant, tilted smile, as
though approving the sequined shimmer of lightning so far
below. The surface of the sea reflected darkness and light,

becoming both, breathing warmth into the air and the land alike.

Mandy smiled back at the moon as she drifted within the timeless moment of peace, suspended between the warmth of the sea and Sutter alike, feeling as though she were in a different reality, a world where Sutter's words were intangible caresses, phrases murmuring through her flesh and bones, whispering deeply to her soul. She murmured in return, sound without meaning, soft echoes of her serenity.

Sutter heard and understood Mandy's wordless message. With subtle movements of his body, he gathered her closer against himself. Closing his eyes, he held her, wishing that he had the power to turn back the rising tide so that Mandy could always stay as she was, relaxed in his arms, allowing him to ease the icy terror of past helplessness with the healing warmth of present companionship.

But no man could hold back the hushed silver glide of the sea. When it lapped almost over Mandy's calves, she brought her feet in close to her hips, raising her knees and most of her legs above the water. Reluctantly Sutter shifted position, as well. He didn't want Mandy to get up, for then the time of peace and intimacy would end. He wasn't ready for that. There had been nothing in his experience quite like these languid moments when he had been suspended with Mandy between warm limestone and the swelling tide.

Finally the rising water dissolved Mandy's peace.

"Sutter, have you ever heard the phrase, 'caught between a demon and the deep blue sea'?"

He laughed softly. "Getting too wet? Try this."

Sutter lifted Mandy, turning her until she straddled his lap facing him. In that position the sea claimed her only from the knees down.

"Better?" he asked.

Mandy was so close to Sutter that she could see the flash and gleam of distant lightning reflected in his eyes. His smile was like his hands, like his body, like his words, warmly reassuring, demanding nothing of her.

"I was wrong," she whispered. "You're not a devil at all."

"Does that mean we can stay out here for a while?"

She nodded.

"Good. I don't want to leave. Not yet. Not until we have to."

When Mandy realized that Sutter was enjoying the gentle intimacy as much as she was, a fragile shimmer of warmth unfurled deep within her. She lowered herself very slowly against Sutter's chest, feeling her breath unravel as his living heat touched her from her forehead to her thighs. Sensations shivered through her body at random, sweetness dancing like distant, silver lightning over her nerves.

Sutter smoothed his hand down Mandy's back in a gesture that was meant to be soothing and reassuring but somehow fell short of its intended goal...or far surpassed it. With a sigh, Mandy tucked her cheek against his shoulder and turned her face into his neck. For an instant he thought he felt the lightest brush of her lips against his throat.

Suddenly he became aware of far more than the relaxed trust of Mandy's body lying against his. He felt the soft weight of her breasts behind the bikini top's scant confinement. The cloth was damp and vaguely cool, her skin satin and warm. Every time he took a breath his skin brushed hers, sending heat through him, heat gathering from the pit of his stomach to his thighs, heat changing him with each quickening heartbeat.

For a few moments Sutter fought the urgent surge of his body; then he succumbed with a mental shrug. He could get as hard as the limestone shelf and it wouldn't make any difference. He wasn't a boy to lose control of himself at the first rush of desire, and Mandy wasn't an inexperienced girl to be embarrassed by a man's aroused body. Besides, they were hardly in a position to do anything

more than savor the unexpected rewards of peace and companionship. Peace, not passion, because at any moment
someone might come walking up the beach. It wasn't particularly likely, but it was still possible.

The thought didn't prevent Sutter from enjoying the
sweet weight of Mandy lying along his chest. Nor did it
make him turn away from the warmth of her lips against
his neck. Instead, he closed his eyes the better to savor the
sensation of a gliding, butterfly kiss breathed onto his skin.
Slowly, inevitably, he turned toward her, intending to do
no more than brush his lips across her cheek as he had
done before.

Somehow it was Mandy's lips Sutter touched, not her
cheek. There was an instant of brushing contact, then another, then another and yet another until finally his mouth
was rocking very gently over hers. By the time he fully
realized what he was doing, it was too late.

Mandy sighed, sending a wave of sweetness and warmth
over Sutter's lips. She returned his kiss so delicately that
he held his breath at the unexpected beauty of the caress.
Never had he guessed there could be such exquisite, pierc-
ing pleasure in a chaste kiss.

Nor had Mandy. With a tiny sound that could barely be
heard above Sutter's own heartbeat, she nestled once more
against his neck, warming his throat with her breath.
Slowly his hand came up to her face. Fingertips traced her
forehead and the line of her cheek, the curve of her chin
and the warmth of her lips. She shivered delicately, feeling
as though she were being licked by tender fire. Turning
her face into his hand, she returned the pleasure he was
giving to her. The warm caress she breathed into his palm
became another kind of kiss as he tilted her face up to his.
Their lips met again, rocked softly again, separated for the
space of a breath, then met once more, clinging gently,
repeatedly.

Mandy's hands crept up Sutter's chest until she could
hold his face between her palms. The holding was as gentle

as the kiss, as soft as the glide of his hands down her back. She felt suspended once more, only this time she was being gilded with sensual pleasure, quivering with the beauty of it. Never had she imagined that a man could be so exquisitely restrained with his caresses.

The touch of Mandy's hands and lips on Sutter's face sent pleasure shimmering through his flesh, through his bones, through his mind. Part of him was astonished that such a simple caress could so ravish his senses, and part of him cared only that the heated, oddly fragile touching not stop. Suspended amid passion and tenderness and sweet surprise, he held himself very still, focusing himself entirely in the moment, wanting that moment never to end.

When Mandy's gentle mouth finally lifted, Sutter let out a long breath and captured her hands. Holding them cupped before his face, he turned his head slowly from side to side, causing her hands to slide caressingly over his face while he kissed her palms and fingertips and the softness of her inner wrists. Her breath caught as she remembered what he had said while they were walking on the reef...*I'd take you out and bathe my senses in you.*

That was what Mandy would like to do, as well, to bathe in Sutter's warmth and masculine textures, savoring each instant, immersing herself in him.

When Sutter lifted his head from Mandy's cupped hands, moonlight washed over his face, giving his eyes a haunting intensity. He looked at her as though he had never seen her before and was afraid he might never see her again. He memorized her with his eyes and his sensitive fingertips tracing every bit of her face. Her eyelids fluttered down as pleasure radiated through her body, bringing warmth in its wake. The instant before his lips touched her cheek she felt the heat of his breath. Very slowly she turned her head from side to side, offering herself to his mouth as he caressed her. With a low, husky sound he accepted her gift, brushing kisses over her face until only her lips remained untouched, aching.

"Damon," Mandy whispered, not even knowing that she spoke. "Please...."

By slow degrees Sutter's fingers worked into Mandy's hair. He flexed his hands very slightly, but she was so sensitized to his every movement that she tilted her head back, giving herself to his hands as he had silently requested. His mouth feathered the hollow of her throat with heat, and the tiny probings of his tongue called a broken sigh from her. Lips that were both gentle and firm traced the tendons in her neck. The curving line of her jaw knew his touch next, soft kisses and the heat of his tongue tasting her lightly. She trembled between his hands, wanting to speak, trying to tell him that he was unraveling her so slowly, so completely...but she had no words, only the soft unfurling of warmth deep within, pleasure radiating through her body.

When the tip of Sutter's tongue outlined Mandy's lips, she moaned very softly. The sound sent a shiver through him. He lifted his head and looked at her lips glistening from his caress. The sight sent another ripple of emotion through his powerful body. By increments he lowered his head once more until he could taste the curve of her smile. She breathed his name again, parting her lips, sending a rush of warmth over him. The tender penetration of his tongue drew a low sound from her throat. She caressed his tongue with her own, tasting him, trembling.

It was the same for Sutter, his senses spinning slowly, revolving around the woman who came to him so softly, so completely. When he finally raised his head again, he couldn't bear to be without Mandy's taste on his tongue for more than an instant before he bent to her once more. Her lips opened for him willingly, letting him dip repeatedly into her mouth, probing her softness while she caressed him in turn.

When Sutter's mouth lifted again, Mandy made a husky sound of protest that became a sigh of pleasure as he caught her lower lip between his teeth and taught her how exquisitely gentle a love bite could be. She murmured his name wonderingly, feeling as though she were being held captive by a loving fire, and the world had begun to spin slowly around captor and captive alike.

Sutter's big hands tightened in Mandy's hair when he heard the throaty cry that was his name. Her head tilted back even more, offering the smooth curve of her throat to his mouth. Slowly one of his hands slid from Mandy's hair. The remaining hand tightened, holding her arched and aching for the feel of his mouth once again. As he bent to kiss the pulse beating in her throat, his fingertips stroked her spine from nape to hips, untying the two strands of cloth that interrupted the elegant length of her back.

Mandy felt only the caresses, the sliding warmth of Sutter's fingers, the shivers of sensation chasing down her spine; and she moved always toward his touch, his warmth, his taste. Feeling her instant, uninhibited response to his lightest touch made Sutter almost dizzy with unaccustomed emotion. Holding Mandy in his arms was like spinning slowly through soft flames, tongues of heat licking everywhere over his big body, teaching him how sensitive every bit of his skin could be.

His hand moved again, this time tracing the delicate curves of her ear, touching the pulse beating at the base of her throat, gliding down the center line of her body to her navel, circling the sensitive dimple until she shivered. Breath held, Mandy waited for the next caress, the next touch that would teach her that her body was made of silken heat and dizzying sensations. When the touch didn't come, she opened her eyes.

Sutter was motionless but for the heavy beat of blood at his temple. His eyes were half-closed, glittering, and he was looking at the creamy flesh he had uncovered. Mandy knew an instant of surprise that she was no longer wearing her bikini top, but that didn't matter nearly so much as the pleasure Sutter clearly took from looking at her bare breasts.

"Mandy?" he asked softly.

"Yes," she whispered, sliding her fingers deeply into Sutter's thick hair, caressing him even as he bent to her.

As he had once done with Mandy's cupped hands, Sutter turned his face slowly from side to side, caressing her breasts, being caressed by them in turn. His tongue traced the lower curve of both breasts, touching her with fire. She closed her eyes and went very still, living entirely in the instant, knowing only the gliding heat of his tongue outlining her. Lips kissed each warm curve as he nuzzled against her softness, yet somehow he avoided the dark crowns that awaited him, drawn tight with anticipation and need.

Mandy's fingers worked through Sutter's hair, caressing and silently pleading at the same time. When his breath washed over one nipple she made a soft sound at the back of her throat. When his tongue licked a velvet crown, her breath came out in a sighing rush. A small, hoarse groan was pulled from him as he felt her change even more with each stroke of his tongue, her nipple drawing tighter and tighter until he could not hold back from suckling her in the same primal rhythm that was pulsing through his aroused body. Her fragmented whimpers of pleasure sank into him, urging him to feed deeply on her softness, making the world spin more quickly around them with each tiny cry.

Slowly Sutter pulled Mandy up his body until she was kneeling astride him, her back arched, her hands gripping his shoulders, her head tilted back as his mouth drew rippling sounds of surprise and pleasure from her. Sutter heard and shuddered in response, never lifting his head, drawing her ever more deeply into his mouth, wanting to become a part of her and at the same time to consume her as gently, as completely as the sea was consuming the lagoon.

As though at a distance Mandy heard soft, glittering cries of pleasure. Dimly she realized that she had made them, was making them even now, but the realization had no meaning to her. Nothing had meaning but the exquisitely restrained strength of the man who was caressing her, making pleasure tremble and burst sweetly, secretly inside her, sensations she had never before known, never dreamed, never imagined. His hands stroked languidly down her back, caressed her waist, sent expanding rings of pleasure from her navel, smoothed over her hips and slid down her thighs. When his hands returned, they eased up her inner thighs until he brushed against the feminine mound between her legs, rocking gently against the narrow triangle of cloth that was infused with more than the heat and dampness of the sea.

Knowing he should stop, unable to deny himself just one gliding caress, Sutter eased his finger beneath the cloth, heard and savored the ragged intake of Mandy's breath. Slowly he touched her, his fingertip as delicate as his tongue had been, and he felt the quivering of her response all the way to the soles of his feet. He eased more deeply into her, savoring her fire and softness and the heat of the satin flesh that clung to him, wanting him.

"Oh, love," Sutter groaned, retreating slowly from Mandy, feeling her soft flesh tighten around him, trying to hold him within her. "We've got to stop," he said, but even as he spoke he was sliding into her once more, probing tenderly, trembling as her response washed over him. "At first I thought I could just hold you, and then I thought I could just kiss you, and then I told myself that I could look at your breasts, no more, just that. But you're so beautiful," he said hoarsely, "so responsive. Your nipples tightened with a look, and when my tongue touched you…"

Sutter closed his eyes, unable to bear the exquisite torture of her breasts so close to his lips, so sweet. He shouldn't touch her anymore. He knew he shouldn't.

And he knew he must.

"Just once more," he said, his voice hoarse.

Mandy murmured dreamy pleasure while Sutter's lips and tongue caressed first one breast, then the other, then the first yet again. Each sultry, changing pressure of his mouth sent streamers of fire licking through her. It was the same for him. When his palm rubbed lightly over the cloth between her legs, he remembered how it had felt to be held within her incredible satin heat.

"Just once..." he whispered, slipping a long finger beneath the triangle of cloth, caressing her even as he slid within.

Mandy's body arched as sweet lightning shimmered through her. With a strange, rippling sigh she began to move in slow motion, rocking against Sutter's hand, wanting only to know more of the caress that was making her melt in rhythmic waves of pleasure.

Sutter felt both the tightness of Mandy and the sleek ease with which she accepted his touch. He whispered her name as he redoubled the caress, stretching her gently, feeling the immediate heat of her response. Instinctively he tried to deepen the touch, wanting to feel her pleasure all around him, to taste it, to bathe his senses in her and then to slide deeply into her, bringing her ecstasy.

But he had to stop.

"Mandy," he said huskily, trying to withdraw his touch once more.

It wasn't possible. She felt too good, wanted his caresses too much. And her hand was over his, holding him inside her deepest warmth. He kissed the smooth skin of her belly, then probed her navel with his tongue as he probed her feminine secrets with his hand.

"Help me to stop," Sutter said in a hoarse voice, turning his cheek against the warm, resilient flesh below Mandy's navel.

Her answer came in the smooth glide of her hips, a motion that caught him deeply within her once more.

"Mandy, we..."

Her fingers slid down Sutter's body and beneath the

warm surface of the sea until she cupped the hard, aching flesh between his legs. Whatever he had been going to say was lost in a husky cry of pleasure when she caressed him with slow sweeps of her hand.

"Love, you're killing me," he said raggedly, unable to keep his hips from moving in counterpoint to her hand.

Mandy's only answer was a sweet, broken cry of pleasure as his thumb found and teased the hard bud in the midst of her softness. The sound made Sutter smile despite the urgent ache of his flesh. He moved his thumb again, felt her tighten around his fingers and wanted to laugh with the deep sensual heat of her response. Then suddenly her hand was inside his swimming trunks, naked skin moving over naked skin, and their mutual cries of discovery and pleasure sent shudders through his powerful body.

With the last of his self-control, Sutter prevented himself from pulling on the strings that fastened the maddening triangle of cloth in place between Mandy's legs. He told himself he could pleasure her and know the bittersweet heat of partial release. Slowly he turned his head and caught first one of her nipples and then the other in his mouth, gently sucking on the hard, velvet flesh, feeling his whole body clench with her instant response.

Without thinking, Sutter moved his hand to the strings that were fastened precisely in the crease where thigh met body. The feel of cloth instead of hot, soft skin warned him of what he was doing. Abruptly Sutter knew he couldn't trust himself anymore. He turned his mouth aside from Mandy's too-tempting body, but when he would have withdrawn his touch from her soft heat, her own hand prevented him.

"Mandy, no," Sutter whispered, kissing the small hand that was holding him within her. He felt her other hand caress him one last time, withdraw, and he bit back his helpless sound of protest. Then he saw Mandy's fingers catch the end of a bikini string and pull slowly, unraveling the bow, and he groaned. "Mandy, we can't."

"Why?"

"I came to the island to dive, not to have an affair," Sutter said huskily. "I have no way to protect you from an unwanted pregnancy."

Mandy looked into Sutter's eyes and felt a shaft of pure pleasure arrow through her at the thought of conceiving and bearing his child. Two years ago the sea had taken more from her than she had to give…and tonight, with the warm tide lapping higher and higher between her thighs, the sea could return it all to her again.

"I'm sorry, golden eyes. I never should have let it go this far," Sutter said. "I thought I could just pleasure you, but I don't trust myself anymore. Not with you. You're…different. With you it's…too good."

Even as he spoke, Sutter's hand moved slowly between Mandy's legs, caressingly, because feeling her response to his touch was a pleasure more intense than he had believed possible. She smiled and moved with him. The bikini strings separated beneath her hand. She reached across herself to tug on the other bow.

"Mandy. Don't. If you take off that bit of cloth… Haven't you been listening to me? I can't protect you!"

She tried to tell Sutter that there could be no such thing as an unwanted pregnancy with his child, but no words came through the waves of sensation that had begun rippling through her at the thought of holding Sutter deeply within her body, feeling him shudder and cry out as he poured his seed into her. Finally she bent down and kissed his mouth very gently, stopping his protests.

"I don't need protecting," she murmured against his lips.

Sutter felt the warm triangle of bikini cloth give way, allowing him the absolute freedom of Mandy's body. With aching slowness he caressed her taut hips and the sultry heat between her legs. Kneeling, she swayed with his touch, wholly lost.

"Are you sure?" he asked huskily, nuzzling the soft,

dark tangle of hair that lay revealed at the apex of her thighs.

"Yes," she whispered. "Oh, yes."

The last words came from Mandy's lips in a broken cry as Sutter's hot tongue sought and found her in a caress that was utterly unexpected. Her eyes closed and lightning splintered delicately through her body, setting off tiny, satin contractions deep inside.

Slowly Sutter increased the pressure of his fingers within her, smiling at the sleek heat of her, wanting to feel all of that heat closing around him in the rhythms of ecstasy, wanting to catch her most sensitive flesh very gently between his teeth, holding her captive for an exquisite kind of loving. Yet even as he moved to follow his desire, Mandy sank bonelessly back onto his legs, too weak to support herself any longer and hungry to caress his masculine flesh once more.

Her hands slid from his shoulders down his back to his lean waist and then to his hips. Slender fingers eased inside the strip of black cloth that was all Sutter wore. Gently she freed him, smiling to see the instant, hard rise of his erect flesh above the water's reach.

Seeing Mandy's smile, Sutter felt as though he had been dipped in loving fire. His fingers sank luxuriantly into the creamy flesh of Mandy's hips, urging her closer. Then his hands slid forward, caressing and pressing against her silky inner thighs, separating them until she was poised just above his rigid flesh, her feminine heat utterly open to him. He held her that way for long, shivering moments, brushing her with the same fiery flesh that ached to be within her. When he could stand no more of the sensual teasing, he gently began to part the soft, hot folds between her thighs.

Mandy moaned as she felt Sutter coming to her. She convulsed delicately around him while he moved slowly into her, so slowly, taking her by sensuous increments, savoring the sweet, repeated shivering of her climax at the satin penetration, hearing her breath catch again and again at the ecstasy pulsing through her.

Her response dragged a deep groan from Sutter. He wanted to drive hard and deep into her, but once he sheathed himself fully in her, he knew it would be impossible for him to hold back his own climax. He didn't want it to end so soon, before he had even begun to plumb the depths of her response, or his own. He had never taken a woman like this before, never before felt so perfectly the shimmering pulses of feminine release, never felt himself so full and hard, so much a man, pressing into sultry heat and shivering ecstasy, sliding deeper and deeper and then deeper still, until finally he was fully sheathed and time stopped and his flesh pulsed with hers, he was joined to her, giving himself to her again and again until he thought he would die of the endless release he had found within her.

Chapter 10

For a long time Mandy was aware of nothing but a silky lassitude claiming her in the aftermath of a pleasure so intense that she still trembled with almost every breath. Gradually small elements of reality condensed around her once more. She realized she was naked and Sutter was naked and their bodies were still joined beneath the silver glinting of the sea...a sea that was even now lapping gently higher up her bare hips. She knew the slowly deepening water should bother her, but she felt too supremely cherished at the moment to be frightened. With a contented sigh she closed her eyes.

Sutter felt the stirring of Mandy's body over his and guessed that she must be uneasy about the increasing depth of the water lapping at the limestone ledge. For an instant his arms tightened around her, holding her in place. He didn't want the moment of intimacy to end. It was too new, too unexpected. He felt renewed, reborn, everything utterly right...except for the tide, licking higher with each instant. He didn't want the boneless relaxation of Mandy's body to change into tight fear.

Reluctantly Sutter loosened his embrace. Even if Mandy wasn't afraid of the water at the moment, there was another problem. No matter how warm the sea seemed in the heat of mutual passion, he knew the water was slowly but surely sapping their body heat. Gently he ran one hand down Mandy's lovely back and nuzzled against her face, which was tucked against his chest.

"Wake up, golden eyes."

Mandy murmured and kissed the corner of Sutter's mouth. He smiled and brushed his lips over hers. From the distance came the sound of laughter, a door closing and someone calling across the velvet darkness. A moment later an answer came, sound without meaning.

"Time to get up, you lovely, lazy wench," Sutter whispered, caressing the warm curve of Mandy's hip.

"After you," she said, kissing his neck.

He laughed softly. "That's not how it works, darling. You're on top. You have to get up first."

"Oh." Then, "Sutter?"

"Mmm?"

"You haven't encountered my bikini lately, by any chance?"

There was silence followed by tiny splashing sounds. After a few moments Sutter's hand appeared above the water. Odds and ends of clothing hung limply from between his fingers, shedding thin streamers of water.

"This what you're missing?" he asked.

Mandy looked, looked again and said, "Actually, I think it's what *you're* missing."

Sutter examined the fistful of cloth in the moonlight. "I think you're right. Wait a sec." He fished around in the water for a few more moments before emerging triumphantly with other pieces of cloth. "Got it."

Reluctantly Mandy began to separate herself from Sutter in order to get dressed. Before she could do more than register her intention with a slight shift in her weight, she felt his arms close snugly around her, holding her around him while he sat fully upright. He tied the neck strings of her bikini top in place, then began to pull the tiny triangles of cloth into place over her nipples. The temptation of her breasts was too great to entirely ignore. He nuzzled the cloth aside and kissed her slowly, tasting the sea on her skin, licking salt from her nipples. Finally, very reluctantly, he eased the two triangles into place.

"These things should be outlawed," Sutter said huskily, looking at Mandy's tight, erect nipples pressing against the bits of cloth as he tied the strings behind her back.

"That would upset a lot of babies."

"What?" Then Sutter laughed softly, understanding. "Not these," he murmured, bending his head to bite her nipples lovingly. "The two little scraps of cloth. Makes a man want to run his tongue around the edges and then slide it underneath to sample the goodies."

Mandy laughed but couldn't conceal the shiver that went through her at the thought of Sutter's tongue gliding beneath the bikini top to caress her nipples. He felt her telltale trembling and knew an instant, hot response that surprised him. He had just taken her, he was still inside her, he shouldn't want her so urgently; and he knew it would be all he could do to withdraw from her body long enough to drag her to the tent before he buried himself deeply in her once more.

"You're a witch," Sutter said thickly, closing his eyes in an involuntary reaction to the vital hardening of his body. His hands closed around Mandy's waist, lifting her from him as slowly as he had entered her, then allowing her to slide back down, then lifting her slowly again. "If you sit in my lap for another instant I'm going to…ah, love, help me," he groaned, "you feel too damned good."

Only the sound of voices coming closer up the beach permitted Mandy to move the final fraction of an inch that separated her completely from Sutter. Even so, she had to bite back a tiny cry as his hardening flesh caressed her in the act of leaving her. Blindly she took her bikini bottom from his hand and untangled the strings by feel alone. Her fingers were trembling so that by the time she worked over the second hip tie Sutter had already pulled his suit into place and stood up next to her. The realization that his swimsuit was fighting a losing battle to cover his burgeoning masculinity did nothing to calm Mandy.

Still kneeling, Mandy looked up and saw Sutter watching the small triangle fastened at the apex of her legs. She knew suddenly that he wanted to slide his tongue beneath the edges of the cloth until he found the secret, responsive flesh beneath. The thought of such intimacy sent a rush of fire through her that made her weak.

"Damon," she said, her voice shaking.

"Don't say my name like that," he whispered.

"Like what?"

"Like you're reading my mind…and loving it."

"But I am…loving it."

"God," he groaned, "I'm going to be lucky to get you back to the tent!"

Mandy looked at Sutter's powerful body heightened by shadows, silvered by water and the moon and so very male it made anticipation tingle through her.

"We'd better not meet anyone on the way," she said in a throaty voice.

Sutter followed Mandy's glance to his swimsuit. The contest had definitely been lost. Before he could rearrange himself in a semblance of modesty, Mandy was there. Gently, almost possessively, she eased his erect flesh back within the confines of the wet cloth. When he was covered to her satisfaction, she trailed a fingertip lightly along his hard length.

"There. All done," she murmured.

Torn between humor and raw desire, Sutter lifted Mandy to her feet.

"What you need is a cold shower," he said thickly, biting her neck just hard enough to leave tiny marks.

"Is that what you call it?" she whispered, boldly moving her hips against him, savoring the hard thrust of his arousal. "I thought that was called a—"

Sutter kissed her hard and deep, shutting off the teasing

words. Finally he lifted his head. "You have a saucy mouth, woman."

Mandy's smile slipped. "Isn't that—is that all right?"

For a moment Sutter thought she was still teasing him. Then he saw her stillness and realized that she was uncertain of his response. He caught her face between his hands, tilting it up to his lips.

"I love your saucy mouth," Sutter said, biting Mandy's lips gently. "I love feeling your hands on me, and I love your smile when you see what you do to me. You're the sweetest, sauciest, sexiest woman I've ever had the privilege of touching. And that's just what I want to do right now. Touch you. All over. Everywhere. I feel like a boy with his first woman. Everything I do with you is new and I want to do everything at once and yet I want to do it all slowly, perfectly, because I'm afraid nothing will ever be this good again."

Tears magnified Mandy's eyes for a moment. Smiling, blinking, she clung to Sutter. "Yes," she whispered. "That's how it is for me, too."

For several long, electric moments they simply held each other in warm silence. Then Sutter moved his hips against Mandy once, very slowly, caressing her with his hard, aroused flesh.

"And for your information," he murmured, "that's called a—"

"Sutter!" Mandy said threateningly, covering his mouth with her hand.

His tongue probed between her fingers, tickling and teasing her until she couldn't bear it and lifted her hand so that she could kiss him. The taste and heat and textures of her mouth tempted him into a long, intimate exploration that did nothing to improve the fit of his swimsuit. After too long a time, he lifted his head.

"Rooster," he murmured lovingly against her lips.

For an instant there was silence, then Mandy's silvery laughter surrounded Sutter like another, richer color of moonlight. His smile became a wicked grin and then he was laughing, too, enjoying the combination of passion and humor that was uniquely Mandy, the intelligence that made her as unpredictable and fascinating as the chain lightning pulsing across the far horizon.

Smiling, Sutter took Mandy's hand and walked out of the warm lagoon. After a few steps she lagged behind noticeably. He turned questioningly and realized that her feet were bare. Instants later he lifted her into his arms.

"You should have said something," Sutter whispered, brushing his mouth over Mandy's hair.

"It's not far enough to the tent to matter," she said.

"You've never had a coral cut, have you?"

Mandy shook her head.

"Come to think of it," Sutter said, smiling to himself in anticipation, "I'd better check you over completely. You might have picked up some scrapes in the Fish Pond."

Mandy's body stiffened at the memory of being helpless and then being tossed into the very sea she feared so much.

"I didn't thank you for pulling me out," she said, turning her face into the strong, warm neck that was so close to her lips. "Thank you, D. M. Sutter. That's one more rescue to your credit."

"You would have found your feet without me," Sutter said, kissing her forehead.

Mandy's arms tightened around his neck but she said nothing. She wanted to believe she wouldn't have been too frightened to stand up and save herself from drowning in shallow water, but she wasn't sure. When she had felt the ocean close over her face she had panicked in a way that she hadn't even during the horrible flight to the island.

Win some, lose some, she told herself.

The thought didn't cheer Mandy. Sutter had been quite right about her emotions. She was very tired of her prison of fears.

"Trees ahead. Hide your face," Sutter warned softly.

Mandy buried her face in Sutter's neck and felt his shoulder muscles bunch as he bent and turned sideways, avoiding the graceful she-oak branches in the grove that surrounded their tent. A flap of canvas trailed over her back as Sutter ducked into the tent and carefully set her on her feet before he released her. It was much darker inside the tent than it had been on the beach.

Soft illumination bloomed suddenly, revealing Sutter bent over the flashlight. He wrapped the cloth one more time around the lens, muting the illumination to a golden glow that suffused everything it touched with riches. After he braced the flashlight in a corner, he shook out his beach towel, threw it over his bed and turned to Mandy.

"Lie down, darling. I want to check your feet."

"My feet?" she asked skeptically, giving him an amused, sideways kind of look.

Sutter smiled in a way that made Mandy's knees weak. "Of course. What else?"

Mandy blushed, feeling suddenly shy. It had been one thing to make love with Sutter in the silver and shadow of a moonlit lagoon. It was quite another to see him in the clear, golden illumination that filled the tent. The thought of her boldness in the lagoon was embarrassing to her now. She was more than happy to sink down on the mattress and turn her flushed face away from the too-revealing light.

Sutter noticed Mandy's sudden shyness but said nothing. As soon as she was settled, he picked up her right foot matter-of-factly, brushed off a few particles of shell and crushed coral, touched every bit of suddenly sensitive skin and pronounced her whole. Mandy felt his long, strong, fingers pick up her other foot, hesitate and then probe gently.

"Hurt?" he asked.

"No."

Sutter made an approving sound and resumed checking her. Mandy's curiosity overcame her embarrassment. Lying on her back, propped half-upright on her elbows, she looked down the length of her body at her foot held in Sutter's large, strong hands. While she watched, he brushed every bit of her foot carefully, almost caressingly. She thought she saw a smile just beneath his calm expression as his finger rubbed tenderly between her toes, removing each particle of shell or coral no matter how small.

"Sutter?"

"Mmm?"

"I thought that a cut from living coral was the only kind you had to worry about."

Absently Sutter nodded, only half-listening, caught up in tracing the high arch of Mandy's foot with his index finger.

She didn't really notice what Sutter had said or not said. She was too fascinated by the picture he made sitting nearly naked at her feet, touching her as though she were made of spun crystal and dreams. In the muted light his eyes were a green so intense it was nearly black. His hair was molten gold, catching and holding the light with every motion of his head. Dense, long eyelashes cast feathery shadows across his tanned skin. His wide, high cheekbones and blunt, masculine jawline fully suited the strong tendons in his neck and the muscular width of his shoulders. The damp, curling hair on his chest was a rich amber color. The dusky, wedge-shaped pelt emphasized the smoothness of Sutter's skin and the supple male strength that was so much a part of him.

"Sutter?"

Mandy's voice was husky, barely a breath in the silence as she watched him with eyes that were as warm and clear as the golden light. There was no shyness in her now, only a very female appreciation of the man who was cherishing her with his hands.

"Mmm?"

"There isn't any living coral on the beach, and probably none between the tide lines, as well."

"Probably," he agreed.

Mandy's breath caught as Sutter kissed the most sensitive area of her arch with unerring accuracy. Involuntarily her toes curled. Sutter smiled and touched her arch with the tip of his tongue, drawing a small sound from her lips.

"Sutter?"

"Mmm," he said, biting Mandy's sensitive skin very carefully, feeling her foot flex in helpless response, "I'm beginning to think the foot fetishists have a point."

Smiling, feeling laughter and desire shimmering through her body, Mandy watched light and shadow flow over Sutter as he caressed her foot.

"Of course," he murmured, circling her slender ankle with one hand, "ankle fetishists aren't all crazy, either."

Strong teeth closed just above Mandy's heel, making her gasp at the unexpected sensations rushing up her leg. Sutter kissed the tiny indentations his teeth had left, caressed her with his tongue and fingertips and moved farther up her leg.

"Have you ever heard of a calf fetishist?" Sutter asked, kneading the resilient muscle in question with his strong hands.

"No," admitted Mandy, sighing with pleasure, "but don't let that stop you."

He smiled and bent lower, rubbing his cheek against her calf. Involuntarily she closed her eyes, caught by the sensuous feel of his cheek's sandpaper masculinity against her soft skin. When the tip of his tongue found and traced the sensitive nerve that went down her shin, she drew in her breath with a soft, rushing sound. When he retraced the passage with his teeth, she felt as though she were coming unraveled.

"Knees..." Sutter began in a husky voice.

"Are ticklish!" Mandy gasped.

"Sensitive," he amended, caressing her with a touch firm enough not to tickle. "Very sensitive," he added, "especially here."

A soft, ragged sound was Mandy's only answer. Until that moment she hadn't guessed that the back of her knee had so many nerve endings, and that they were connected to so many interesting places on her body.

"But," Sutter continued in his deep voice, "I've never known of a knee fetishist, have you?"

Mandy tried to answer, felt the sultry heat of Sutter's tongue behind her other knee and flexed her leg in sensual response.

"Probably no man is really into knees," Sutter said, running the back of his fingers over the soft flesh he had just kissed, "because by the time a man gets up to a woman's knees, he's so close to some truly beguiling territory that he can't help skimping the knees and going on to higher things. Such as…"

Mandy half closed her eyes and shivered visibly as Sutter trailed his fingertips up her inner thighs. Her quickening breaths were a soft, almost secret sound in the tent's intimate silence. Hearing the sensual catches and quivers in her breathing with each of his caresses made Sutter want to shout in masculine triumph and at the same time to cherish Mandy with utmost tenderness. Watching his touch take her from blushing shyness to uninhibited lover aroused him fiercely. Slowly he bent his head and kissed the warm skin his fingertips had been stroking.

Mandy's eyelids closed as she simultaneously felt the heat of Sutter's mouth on the inside of one thigh and the silky brush of his hair against the other. He rubbed his cheek over the inside of each thigh, letting her feel the soft, exciting rasp of beard stubble, then soothed her with his tongue, teased with his teeth, feasted on her warmth while her soft cries lapped around him like the rising, moon-drawn sea.

After a time Sutter's teeth closed on Mandy not quite gently and his mouth sucked hard on her tender flesh for an instant; yet the cry that was torn from her lips came from a lightning stroke of pleasure rather than from pain.

He turned his head and gave another measured, fierce caress to her other thigh, smiling as he heard her pleasure and felt it in the heat of her skin. He smoothed his hands repeatedly over her slender, rounded thighs from inner knee to the sea-damp warmth of the bikini between her legs and back again.

"Yes," Sutter murmured, looking at the long, shapely legs and the alluring shadow between, stroking Mandy's thighs with a subtle pressure that spread them farther apart. "It's easy to understand why a man would become a thigh fetishist. Especially with you. You have such lovely legs, darling. But they're only the beginning...."

With a sense of spinning anticipation, Mandy waited to feel Sutter's gentle hands caressing the softness that ached for his touch. When she felt nothing more between her legs than the tropic warmth of the air in the tent, she opened her eyes slowly. Sutter was watching her, sharing her anticipation, smiling in a way that made sensual lightning shimmer in the pit of her stomach.

"Sutter?" she whispered.

"Read my mind, golden eyes," he said huskily, bending down to her.

Sutter's tongue probed teasingly beneath the tie on one hip, then traced the edge of the damp cloth across the top of the triangle that lay between her legs. At the same time his hands caressed her legs, holding her captive as though he were afraid that her shyness would suddenly return.

Shyness was the last thing in Mandy's mind. After the first glittering instant she was lost. Every hot, wet glide of his tongue over her skin, the hard edges of his teeth biting through cloth, his breath mingling with her own warmth, everything about the moment combined to hold her in delicious captivity, enthralled by a slow, heated sensuality that dissolved her bones, leaving her wholly at the mercy of the man who so clearly was enjoying her.

With a final, loving rake of his teeth over cloth, Sutter became impatient with even the bikini's minimal restrictions. Long fingers unfastened both bows and slowly peeled the damp cloth away from her, leaving nothing between Mandy and himself but the hot rush of his breath as he bent down to her once more. The first touch of his tongue surprised a ragged cry from Mandy's lips, a cry that soon fragmented into whimpers as he pursued the sweet secrets he had uncovered, his big hands holding her for his slow, sultry explorations. When he lovingly teased the sensitive nub he had aroused, her back arched helplessly. Heat flushed through her suddenly, almost frighteningly.

"*Damon.*"

His answer was the exquisite restraint of his teeth holding Mandy captive for the kind of loving he had never given and she had never imagined. She shivered repeatedly, echoing the lightning strokes of pleasure stabbing through her, each stroke hotter and brighter, driving her higher, heat and pleasure so intense she would have screamed if Sutter's elemental male sensuality hadn't taken from her even the ability to breathe. Something burst deep inside her, dragging a hoarse cry from her throat in the instant before ecstasy convulsed her, waves of molten pleasure sleeting through her with each of his hot, consuming caresses until she could take no more.

Reluctantly Sutter lifted his head slightly, releasing Mandy's violently sensitive flesh. He whispered soft, loving words as he brushed his cheek against the musky triangle of her hair, trembling even as she did in the aftermath of her sensual storm, whispering her name, holding her hips between his strong hands, nuzzling her incredibly delicate flesh, giving her slow, gentle caresses until he felt tension rising in her again.

Smiling, shuddering with the leashed wildness of his own body, Sutter bent to Mandy once more, stroking her, loving her with a gentle intensity that drew sweet shivers from her. With each of his sultry caresses her breathing and heartbeat quickened, sending heat streaming out from the pit of her stomach once more, giving her skin the sheen and taste of passion. His hands flexed until his fingertips sank into her thighs, holding her utterly captive. He felt her fingers thrusting into his hair, her nails flexing against his scalp as she shivered within his loving grasp.

The thought of thrusting himself into the center of Mandy's gathering storm dragged a thick groan from Sutter. He was on fire for her, hard and thick to the point of agony, needing her until it was tearing him apart; but he didn't want to take her just yet. The consuming sensuality he had discovered within her and himself was too new, too hot, too elemental for him to bring to an end. There had been no woman for him like Mandy, and he sensed at some deep level of his mind that there never would be one like her for him again. Whatever he didn't know or do or feel or be with her right now might never happen for him at all.

Mandy moaned as she felt the shivering forerunners of intense consummation surge through her again and again, drawn by Sutter's exquisite caresses. She called his name in a broken sigh and was answered by the hot perfection of his mouth and the sweet power of his hands holding her helpless. A wave of pleasure ripped through her, followed by another and then another, matching the primal masculine sensuality of the lover who was bringing her closer and closer to the kind of passionate discovery she wasn't sure she could survive.

"Stop," Mandy cried finally, her voice hoarse, low, shattered. "It's too much...I can't bear any more!"

"Not even this?" Sutter murmured, caressing the velvet bud of her passion.

Her answer was a tiny, ecstatic convulsion that stripped away his restraint. With a thick cry he knelt between her legs and fitted himself to her, feeling the hot, slick perfection of her cling to him as he sank deeply into her. He held himself utterly still, every muscle in his body rigid with restraint as he absorbed the wild shivering of her body, heard the breathless cries of her ecstasy, drank the sensations of her climax into himself, feeding on her satin fire.

And then, when the last of her cries faded, he began to move within her.

Mandy's eyes opened, dazed, golden. Disbelief and searing pleasure exploded through her violently sensitized body. The sweet friction of Sutter within her brought with it a ravishing heat that grew greater with every motion of the man who filled her so completely, so perfectly.

Sutter's eyes were a blaze of green, watching her as he moved, his body advancing and retreating in ancient, always new rhythms. Looking at him, utterly lost to him, she moaned and convulsed softly around him with each measured penetration, each slow withdrawal, each motion a new revelation as her body learned that rapture had no beginning and no end, existing beyond place, beyond time. She was in the fiery, luminous center of ecstasy and it was in her very core, and there was nothing left of reality but the man whose body had become part of her own.

"Damon?" she gasped, frightened.

"Love me, Mandy," he said hoarsely, bending down to join their mouths as deeply as he had joined their bodies. *"Love me."*

Mandy tasted herself and the sea and Sutter all at once, felt him driving into her even as her hips strained upward to claim him, to hold him fiercely inside her, all of him. He arched into her again and again, each time harder, deeper, and he felt the sweet violence take her, racking her with pleasure at each powerful stroke of his body until she wept and called out his name with every broken breath. Suddenly she gave a raw cry and went rigid, transfixed by unbearable pleasure. Her satin convulsions ripped the world away from Sutter. He knew nothing but the hot, intense pulses of completion pouring endlessly from him until he could bear no more...and then he tasted her tears and his own while chain lightning pulsed between their joined bodies once again, a rapture so fierce he had no choice but to give himself to it and to the woman who had become part of him in the free-fall through fiery oblivion.

Chapter 11

Morning had filled the tent with a soundless tide of light, illuminating every shadowed corner. Sutter looked across the tent at Mandy's relaxed, sleeping body concealed by the sheet he had pulled over her a few minutes before to prevent himself from stroking her into wakefulness and passion once again. With a silent, searing curse he looked away from her and pulled on his clammy swimsuit. He had been awake for half an hour, cursing Anthea's meddling and his own baffling lack of self-control, wishing that he could change what he had done, knowing that he couldn't, wondering how he would prevent himself from making the same mistake all over again as long as Mandy was within reach.

Sutter knew that no decent man would have taken advantage of a frightened woman who had turned to him for help, and that knowledge sent self-contempt twisting within him. But nothing was as painful as the visceral certainty that he would do it all again if he were offered the least excuse. In the bleak light of day he knew he would have killed or died to be inside her once again. She was a sweet, honeyed fire and he was a man who had discovered yesterday that he had lived his life in darkness and bitter cold.

He didn't know how long he would feel as he did about Mandy; he only knew that while he felt this way he must have her. Yet she wasn't the type of woman who slept with a man casually. He had known that before he touched her, yet he had seduced her anyway. Being the kind of woman she was, she would have to call what had happened between them last night "love," and then he would feel an even more ruthless predator than he already did.

Mandy stirred, seeking the powerful body of the man who had held her through the long night, coming to her for the last time just before dawn set the sky ablaze. Her moving hand met only emptiness. There was no one next to her on the single mattress.

"Love?" she asked sleepily. "Where are you?"

Sutter closed his eyes against the pain of the first word she spoke.

"Mandy," he said, "we've got to talk."

She woke up instantly. Sutter's voice was too low, too tight, almost harsh. It belonged to a different man than the one who had taught her the torrid, consuming, unspeakably beautiful ecstasy a man and a woman could share with each other. There was no teasing lilt in Sutter's tone that morning, no husky hunger, no hoarse delight, nothing but…anger?

Mandy's eyes focused on Sutter. His mouth was tight, flat, and his eyes were opaque. He looked even more angry than he sounded.

"Do you always wake up in a good mood," she asked, "or is this a special effort on my behalf?"

Sutter shot Mandy a sideways glance out of bleak green eyes as he kicked into his sandals.

"Will coffee improve your mood?" she continued.

"Mandy——" he began grimly, wanting to get it over with.

"I thought so," she interrupted, sighing. "Waking up vicious is genetic, you know."

"Like stupidity?" he retorted. "Like doing my part and

then some when it comes to paving the road to hell with good intentions?''

Mandy closed her eyes, knowing she wasn't going to like what would happen next, and knowing that didn't matter; it would happen, willy-nilly, whether her eyes were closed or wide open. Her long lashes lifted as she rolled onto her side to confront Sutter, the man she had stupidly fallen in love with.

The man who clearly wasn't thrilled to have become her lover.

''I can't vouch for my intentions,'' Mandy said neutrally, ''but when it comes to sheer stupidity, I can hold up my end of any paving operation.''

As Sutter looked into Mandy's luminous golden eyes he felt a shaft of regret and something much stronger, much deeper, raw need twisting through his guts. The realization that he wanted her again both baffled and angered him. He shouldn't want a woman at all. Not after last night. He had barely been able to drag himself out of bed a few minutes ago. Yet when he looked at Mandy's slender, bare shoulders and the black bikini bottom thrown carelessly onto the floor of the tent, he felt passion's white-hot claws raking his loins into readiness, torrents of blood pouring through him, hardening him in a single wild rush.

''I came to Lady Elliot Island to go scuba diving, not to seduce a frightened innocent,'' Sutter said harshly, as much to himself as to Mandy.

''Congratulations. You've achieved the first and avoided the second.''

''Mandy—''

''So relax,'' she continued, ignoring Sutter's attempt to speak. ''Divorcées are hardly classified among the world's innocents, and the fact that my husband died before I could divorce him is a mere technicality.''

Sutter's head snapped up. He hadn't known that Mandy's husband was dead. He wanted to say something, to ask questions, to find out more about the woman who destroyed his steel self-control with such baffling ease. But she was talking quickly, not allowing him to speak, as though she were afraid of what he would say.

"As for diving, have at it," Mandy continued. "I don't expect you to drop everything and build shell castles on the beach with me just because we're lovers. I can amuse myself quite nicely during the day. I've been doing it for years."

"So have I. At night, as well as during the day."

Mandy flinched, telling Sutter of her vulnerability. He swore explosively, knowing he was making a hash of what should have been a simple, adult explanation of what had happened last night and why it couldn't happen again.

"Look, Mandy, I'm sorry about last night. I only meant to calm you down and give you a little comfort after Ray scared you, but once I started touching you…" Sutter made an oddly helpless gesture with one big hand. "It's my fault. I lost control, I took advantage of you, and I feel guilty as hell about it. It never should have happened. It won't happen again."

Mandy's mouth drew into a thin line as she understood what Sutter was saying: he had made love to her out of pity not desire, and now he regretted it.

"Save your guilt for one of your many worthy causes," she said in a voice that was too calm. "We aren't the first adults in creation to have a one-night stand and we won't be the last."

"That wasn't a one-night stand and you know it!"

"You're so right," she retorted. "We did it every way *but* standing."

Even as Mandy spoke she was swamped beneath a flood of sensual memories—Sutter's eyes a passionate green blaze, his hands and mouth and body touching her exquisitely, drawing from her depths an untamed sensuality she had never imagined to be part of her, showing her an ecstasy whose sweet aftershocks still echoed through her memories.

With memories came the realization that no matter why Sutter had made love to her, he had given far more than he had taken. He deserved better from her than the cutting edge of her dismay that he had found less to enjoy than she had.

After a moment Mandy found the strength to turn back toward Sutter. Her barb had indeed gone into its target; the bleak lines on Sutter's face were deeper and his mouth had flattened as though he were in pain. He hissed a curse between his clenched teeth when he met her eyes.

"Sorry," Mandy said, keeping her voice neutral as she lay back and closed her eyes. "I guess I'm not at my best in the morning, either. In any case, there's not a damn thing for you to feel guilty about. Before last night I often wondered what all the hoopla between the sexes was about. Now I know. So accept my profound gratitude, forget your guilt and go diving with a squeaky-clean conscience."

For a long moment Sutter stared at Mandy, silently willing her to explain what she meant; but she neither spoke nor opened her eyes. She looked tired, fragile, far too tightly strung. Guilt coiled coldly in his stomach. He should never have touched her. She had needed reassurance last night, not sex.

We did it every way but standing.

Sutter winced as Mandy's words echoed painfully in his mind. "Please don't think less of yourself," he said, his voice gentling. "What happened was my fault, not yours. You were too frightened to act rationally. I wasn't."

"Hold it. Let me get this straight," Mandy said, trying to curb her tongue and her rising anger at the same time. She doubted that she was being successful. The knowledge that her night of love had been Sutter's night of pity was simply too bitter to wholly conceal or absorb. "Are you saying that last night I was in the same category as one of the children you're saving the world for?"

"If you had been a child, last night never would have

gone beyond comfort,'' Sutter said keeping his voice calm with an effort.

"Comfort," Mandy repeated bleakly. "Ah, Sutter, what a diplomat you've become. The word you're too polite to say is pity."

"That's not what I meant and you know it," he retorted, feeling his uncertain grip on his temper slipping away.

"Wrong. It was precisely what you meant."

Sutter closed his eyes, unable to watch Mandy's unhappiness any longer, knowing that his own lack of control had caused it. "What I meant was simply that I knew you weren't a woman for casual affairs but I took you anyway. My fault, not yours. I knew what I was doing. You didn't.''

Mandy flinched again. "Sorry my technique wasn't up to yours.''

"Damn it!" exploded Sutter. "Stop taking my words and twisting them! All I'm trying to say is that I don't think any less of you for what happened last night and you shouldn't think any less of yourself, either!''

"Save your pity for the children of the world. They need it. All I need is a few hours of sleep."

"Mandy—"

She interrupted without hesitation. "You'd better hurry, Sutter, or you'll miss the dive boat."

"Mandy, listen to me. It wasn't your—"

"No! You listen to me, D. M. Sutter," she said, slicing across his words as she came up on one elbow to confront him, ignoring the sheet that slid off her bare breasts. "I don't want your pity. I had one hell of a good time last night. I'm sorry you didn't, but when it comes to sex, one out of two ain't bad. It's sure better than my husband and I ever managed!''

"What the hell are you talking about?"

"Read my lips. You have nothing to feel guilty about. Not…one…thing.''

"Oh, sure," Sutter agreed caustically, his fists clenched

on his lean hips. "I carry a hysterical woman off into the night and seduce her repeatedly, but I have nothing to feel guilty about the next morning when she wants to talk about love and I know there's not a damn thing to talk about but white-hot sex!"

A moment of quivering silence was followed by another and then another.

Finally Mandy spoke very softly. "There's a whole ocean waiting out there for you, Sutter. Go soak your white-hot rooster in it."

It was several hours before Mandy got out of bed. Sutter hadn't returned. Nor had she expected him to. She pulled on a white bikini and left the tent. Someone had found her sandals and placed them neatly next to the path. She kicked into them and went to the shower.

By the time she emerged she felt more in control of herself. At least she wasn't blushing every time she saw the faint bruises on her thighs and remembered how she had gotten the loving marks. Now if she could just stop her breath from unraveling and her bones from going soft every time images from last night surfaced in her memory, she might be able to get through today. As for tonight...

One thing at a time. Right now it's food. Then it's the Fish Pond. Then it's...

One thing at a time.

Mandy kept lecturing herself because it was preferable to having her mind revolve around what had happened the previous night. Every time she thought of what it had been like to be Sutter's lover she would stumble or drop something or stand as still as a coral lump in the lagoon. The only thing that saved her from embarrassing herself was the fact that nearly everyone else was out diving on the reef, trying to beat the storm that was surely brewing within the towering clouds.

With a determined set to her mouth, Mandy walked up to the Fish Pond. Crusts of bread stuck out every which way from her clenched fingers. The fish, which had been on short rations since the Townehome kids had left, came to meet her in a glittering wave. Deliberately she walked into the water up to her knees before she knelt down and thrust her fists beneath the surface of the warm lagoon.

"All right, you little beggars. Come and get it."

Mandy's voice was strained almost to breaking and her heart was hammering much too hard, shaking her, adrenaline pouring through her in a tidal wave of irrational fright. The warm, crystalline water just barely reached her hips. She knew that all she had to do was stand up and the water would only reach to her knees once more. She was as safe as though she were standing on the beach.

And that was where she desperately wanted to be.

But first you feed the fish, Mandy told herself, clenching her teeth until her jaw ached. *What are you afraid of, anyway? You were in deeper than this with Sutter last night and you barely noticed. Hell, you were in way over your head with Sutter and fear was the last thing that crossed your tiny little mind.*

Little fish darted and feinted, but few came to eat from Mandy's hands. She might have fooled herself about the depth of the water by kneeling, but the fish knew that the lagoon where Mandy waited was far too shallow to protect them from feathered predators. When Mandy finally admitted to herself what was holding back the fish, she came to her feet and walked forward until the water slid up her thighs to her hips and then beyond, not stopping until she was waist-deep in the lagoon's liquid embrace.

For the first few minutes her hands were so tightly clenched that no bread oozed out between her fingers. Fish swept around her in flashing clouds, secure in the deeper water and driven wild by the scent of withheld food. When her initial burst of fear finally ebbed, Mandy drew a slow, ragged breath and forced her fingers to relax. She was rewarded by a swirling, nibbling mass of reef fish skimming over her fingers. Within moments her hands were empty of all but the tactile memory of tiny mouths vacuuming her palms.

Watching intently, Mandy stood motionless while the clouds of fish thinned into individual bodies shining in shades of silver and unexpected jeweled flashes of color. As the fish sorted themselves into species and went about their usual business in the Fish Pond's small world, Mandy realized that, while she might not be able to go out and over the edge of the reef, she could see at least some of its life-forms in a natural habitat.

Eagerly Mandy watched the various fish. She knew from past study that none of their motions was random; each movement was in some way related to fish survival, whether it be eating, hiding, courting or defending a particular patch of coral as their very own. The skimming of wind over the surface of the lagoon hampered her observations by ruffling the water's surface, making it opaque to a land dweller's eyes. With a sudden stab of yearning Mandy remembered what it had been like to swim beneath the sea, her vision enhanced by a watertight mask. She had been in ocean water from Alaska to Scammon Lagoon in Mexico, but never had she gone diving in anything as clear as the sea surrounding Lady Elliot Island. If she had been wearing a mask, the water would have inhibited her sight barely more than air.

Brilliant observation, Dr. Samantha Blythe-Cameron, she congratulated herself, underlining her sarcasm by using the name she had signed on her academic papers, *but just how do you propose getting your face into the drink long enough to enjoy all that rare marine visibility?*

Suddenly Mandy had an idea of how she might see beneath the surface without getting wet. She was still congratulating herself on the idea's brilliance when she returned from the cafeteria carrying two colorless water glasses. At first she simply waded in thigh-deep and poked the bottom of the glasses into the lagoon. Instantly a clear circle of vision appeared in the wind-ruffled water. All she had to do was stand around until something interesting swam into the narrow circle of focus formed by the bottom of the glass.

The fish weren't feeling cooperative. Gingerly Mandy inched around the shallow end of the Fish Pond, holding the glasses partially submerged, trying to look through the clear circles without bending down or getting her face any closer to the lagoon's liquid surface. She caught just enough tantalizing glimpses of marine life to keep her trying to see more. As the tide dropped she waded out farther, until finally she was waist-deep once more, utterly enthralled by her small windows into the warm world of the lagoon.

Finally voices seeped into Mandy's awareness, the calls and laughter of the first wave of divers returning from the outer reef. She knew Sutter wouldn't be with them. He would still be out in the shimmering blue world of the sea...weightless, soaring, watched by fish that were living jewels.

Mandy would have given her soul to be with him, free and unafraid, no longer the object of unwanted masculine pity.

Slowly she turned and waded ashore, reluctant to end her contact with even the brief flashes she had seen of the life beneath the warm sea. But she hadn't eaten breakfast, and unless she wanted to face Sutter over lunch she had to eat with the divers who had just returned. So she traded her two wet glasses for a dry one at the cafeteria, ate hurriedly and then went to the dive shed before her courage deserted her.

Ray was there refilling tanks with Tommy's help. Both men looked up at the same instant.

"G'day, luv," Ray said. "Are you...is everything all right?"

"Fine," Mandy said quickly.

"I'm sorry as bloody—" began Tommy.

"It wasn't your fault," she said, cutting across

Tommy's unwanted apology. "I should have told everyone right away that I have a problem with water. I was just too ashamed."

"No reason to be," Ray said matter-of-factly. "Some people just don't like water or heights or dark nights. Hold it steady, Tommy, or we'll be squirting air all over the bleeding island."

Mandy watched until the two men finished with the tank before she said, "Ray?"

He looked up.

"Is there an extra snorkeling mask around?" she asked.

"Sure thing, luv, but why don't you just take your own?"

Mandy blinked. "Mine?"

"It's got your name on it, just like those two tanks, that wet suit, the fins, all that lot," he said, pointing toward a corner of the dive shed. "Came to Lady on your ticket."

"Oh." Mandy looked at the new, beautifully made diving gear, mentally added up the cost and wondered how she would ever repay Anthea. "Well, in that case, I'll take the mask."

Ray handed it to her with a curious sidelong look but said nothing.

"Thanks," she muttered.

Before either man could ask what a woman who was terrified of water was going to do with a diving mask, Mandy had turned and quickly walked away, her fingers tightly wrapped around the familiar shape and texture of a diving mask with snorkel attached. She made a brief detour at the bread bowl just outside the cafeteria, but she didn't hang around to listen to the divers talk about angelfish and sharks and anemones as big as soccer balls. She wouldn't be seeing anything that spectacular where she was going.

But she would put her face in the water if it was the last thing she did on earth.

"Thanks, Ray," Sutter said, shrugging off the weight of the scuba tank and passing it over to the other diver.

"Sure you have time?"

"No worries, mate. I'm here to keep the paying blokes happy," Ray said, grinning as he took the tank and set it up to be refilled for an afternoon dive. "Besides, it's a pat on the back."

"What is?"

"Letting me take care of your equipment."

Sutter paused, then grinned in return. He usually didn't trust other people enough to let them take care of all those little items on which his own life could depend during a dive. But Ray had proven to be as meticulous as Sutter himself.

"And here I thought I was just getting lazy in my old age," Sutter said.

"Not you, mate. You're like one of those deep-water sharks. No frills, no noise, no racing about, just muscle and confidence." Ray hesitated. "Your Sheila was in just a bit ago. Wanted her mask. You taking her snorkeling?"

Sutter's eyes narrowed. He had spent most of the time since waking trying to keep Mandy out of his mind. He hadn't been successful. "Did she say I was?"

"No."

"Did she take her fins?"

Ray shook his head.

The breeze freshened suddenly, rippling through the low vegetation surrounding the dive shed and landing field.

"Squall line coming through," Ray said, breathing in, tasting the difference in the air as he scanned the changes in the sky. "Be raining soon."

"Wind?"

"Too right," Ray said, sighing. "Maybe we can walk out on the reef again and dive off the wall. Depends on the swell."

"Her mask, huh? Anything else?" Sutter asked, unable to keep his mind off Mandy.

"Just a smile and a white bikini."

Involuntarily Sutter's expression changed as he thought of Mandy's sweet body and of how little of that sweetness would be covered by a bikini.

Ray saw Sutter's annoyance and smiled. "No worries, mate. There's more cover in her bikini than in most around here."

Sutter grunted and walked off toward the cafeteria. He had hoped a morning of particularly demanding diving would defuse the sexual tension that had had him in its grip since his first look at Mandy after dawn. Diving, however, hadn't done the job. Although his body definitely knew that it had spent a physical morning—and an even more physical night—there was no decline in his baffling, prowling sexuality.

A swift look down the beach told Sutter that Mandy was wading in the Fish Pond, apparently oblivious to the comings and goings of the people on the beach. She was wearing the big mask pushed up on her forehead in the manner of a diver who had just come from the water, yet it was obvious that her hair and upper body were dry.

Sutter stood and watched for a few moments, screened by the she-oaks that grew up to the edge of the beach. Mandy was doing nothing but standing up to her hips in the lagoon, stirring her hands through the warm water, stroking it as though it were a lover. The thought of having her fingers stroking him in the same way sent sudden, white-hot desire spearing through Sutter, a need so fierce that it almost drove him to his knees. He closed his eyes against the sight of Mandy's long, graceful back, her golden-brown skin curving in to a slender waist and her high breasts filling the bikini top as they had once filled his hands.

But closing his eyes didn't banish Mandy from Sutter's mind. Memories of the night before condensed, Mandy's body glistening with moonlight and sensual heat, her hips sinuous, graceful, moving in slow, sexy rhythms until tiny cries rippled from her lips, cries that matched the rippling heat deep within her body.

Abruptly Sutter turned away from the beach, determined to put Mandy out of his mind. After a shower, a huge lunch and a desultory beer, he turned down an offer of cards. He was too restless to put up with penny-ante poker. A single look at the combers booming over the reef even at low tide told him that diving was out of the question. He turned his back on the beach leading to the Fish Pond, choosing instead the path that went in the opposite direction, skirting the noisy bird colony.

In the hot, sultry afternoon, the sky was a turmoil of wind-shredded clouds. The sea seethed and churned in shades of stormy gray.

Before Sutter was halfway around the island, rain began to fall. The drops were as warm as the air, as hot as his body. They gathered in his hair and ran down his cheeks like tears. He barely noticed. He simply walked on until he rounded the far end of the island to complete his circuit, striding along the section where waves were held at bay by the inner reef. A few hundred yards farther up the beach brought him to the sloping limestone shelf where he had first comforted, then wanted and finally seduced Mandy. He stood and looked at the small ribbons of sand caught in limestone troughs and fought not to remember how it had been to push into Mandy's tight satin depths, to feel her clench in pleasure around him.

With a wild curse Sutter turned away from the rain-washed stone and strode up the beach. There was no one around to distract or disturb him. The weather had driven everyone into tents or cabins or to the card games and conversations in the tiny bar. Sutter walked on, oblivious to the wind and sheets of rain, until he suddenly realized that he wasn't alone on the beach. Mandy had stayed in the Fish Pond, sitting so still that he hadn't noticed her until he was within ten yards.

Without stopping to think, Sutter faded back into the

she-oaks that fringed the beach. Motionless he watched while Mandy stared at the water that was barely up to her rib cage even though she was sitting down. The diving mask had been pulled into place and the attached snorkel was held between her lips as though she were going to push off and float facedown in the rain-swept lagoon. But she didn't move.

At first Sutter couldn't figure out what Mandy was doing. She would bend forward a fraction of an inch at a time, then jerk back and sit utterly still for several minutes. Then she would begin leaning forward again, slowly, slowly, slowly, only to jerk upright once more and sit motionless for a time.

After watching the sequence several times Sutter suddenly understood that Mandy was trying to force herself to put her face in the water. Chills roughened his skin at the realization. He had known that Mandy was afraid of water. He had heard the panic in her scream, seen it in her face, felt it in her thrashing body when he had pulled her from the Fish Pond; but he hadn't truly understood just how great her fear was until this moment. She approached the surface of the lagoon as though it were molten metal that would burn her to the bone…or a prison where she would be chained, beaten, tortured. The certainty of her own destruction was written in every trembling line of her body.

Yet Mandy leaned closer to the water's surface anyway, closer and then closer still—visibly, physically torn between the opposite demands of her fear and her determination to overcome that fear.

Why? Why is she so afraid? Why is she so determined? And where in God's name does someone who is afraid of so many things get the courage to confront fear?

There were no answers to Sutter's silent, almost anguished questions. There was nothing but rain pouring down in warm sheets, Mandy bending closer, closer, closer to the water while minutes sped by and he held his breath and prayed that this time she would make it…this time…this time, *please, God, let it be this time, let her torment end!*

Mandy jerked back from the water.

Sutter's breath hissed out through gritted teeth. His hands ached from being clenched into hard fists. His whole body was drawn with a tension almost equal to Mandy's as she tilted her head toward the rain-churned sea and began to lean forward once more.

Sutter was halfway to Mandy before he realized what he intended to do: he was going to drag her out of the water, ending her torment.

She's not in any danger and you know it. So why interfere? What's wrong with you? he asked himself savagely.

The answer was as simple as it was baffling.

I can't bear to watch her pain.

So don't watch.

I can't bear that, either.

In the end Sutter remained where he was, fighting the nearly overwhelming need to end Mandy's self-imposed ordeal. Yet, as much as he wanted it to end, he couldn't help admiring the sheer grit Mandy displayed each time she forced herself to begin all over again.

Suddenly Mandy bent at the waist and fairly rushed the water, sending it splashing over her face and hair. Instantly she yanked herself upright again. Sutter felt waves of triumph and relief so great they made him light-headed. Finally it was over. She had done it. Now she could get up and get out of the water she so clearly hated and feared. Now he wouldn't have to watch, feeling savage and helpless because there was nothing he could do to affect the outcome of Mandy's ordeal, nothing he could do to take away pain or to give her strength or comfort. He was helpless. But no longer. It was over. Now he could take a deep breath and…

Slowly, Mandy began to bend toward the water once more.

"Mandy," Sutter whispered, appalled, wanting to hold her, to cherish her, to restrain her, to do anything but stand helplessly on the beach watching her. "Don't, love. Don't."

Sutter was speaking far too softly for Mandy to hear him above the rain. Not that it made any difference. He knew she would have ignored him just as he had once ignored all the well-meant advice never to go back into the primitive country whose government had chained and then beaten him, teaching him the meaning of helplessness and fear. But he had gone back because he couldn't give in to fear and still respect himself.

It was the same choice Mandy faced, and his heart turned over for what she was going through.

Slowly Sutter withdrew to the cover of the she-oaks once more. From there he watched Mandy try to push back her dripping hair from her face but her hands were shaking too hard. She flipped her head, slinging her hair away from her face. Ten minutes and three tries later, she was able to bring her face into contact once again with the water's warm surface. And once again, she jerked back.

Sutter waited and prayed. When Mandy began bending slowly forward once more, it took all his self-discipline not to walk into the lagoon and drag her back to land. He lost track of time while he stood and watched, hands clenched, guts knotted, his face grim, sharing her ordeal in the only way that he could. When she finally held her face in the water for three seconds before she jerked upright again, Sutter wondered if she felt half the elation he did.

Without warning Mandy stood up and pushed back her mask with the easy motion of someone who had used diving gear countless times. Sutter remembered that it had been the same when she had flipped back her wet hair—the gesture spoke of long familiarity with water. But that didn't make sense. Someone who was as terrified of water as Mandy was wouldn't be a swimmer, much less a diver.

Mandy stepped out of the lagoon and removed her mask with a single quick movement of her hand. Again, the ease and economy of the motion betrayed expertise with diving gear. Most novices grappled with the awkward mask-and-snorkel combination, tangling their fingers and their hair, grimacing and struggling to master the stubborn equipment without ripping out every hair on their head.

Where did Mandy learn to use the equipment?

And then Sutter realized that wasn't the important question.

What taught her to fear the water she once must have loved?

There was no answer in the falling rain, none in the warm lagoon, none in the drenched she-oaks screening Sutter from the beach. Yet Sutter knew he must have an answer. He needed it with an urgency that transcended the driving sexual heat Mandy called from his body.

Determination in every hard line of his body, Sutter left the she-oaks and went to find Mandy. Behind him, delicate foliage shivered quietly, caressed by the warm rain.

Chapter 12

"G'day, luv. Dry off while I get you a beer," Ray said, tossing a towel toward Mandy.

"Thanks."

Mandy caught the towel one-handed and blotted up the worst of the rain. The small bar area was steamy, filled to overflowing with divers who, being unable to dive, were doing the next best thing—talking about diving. When she looked up from drying herself Tommy caught her eye, hooked his foot under Ray's empty chair and dragged it closer to the ragged circle surrounding his table.

"Here you go, luv," Tommy said.

"What about Ray?"

"Ray who?"

After a brief hesitation Mandy smiled and took the chair. She was too wrung out from her hours in the Fish Pond to refuse the chance to sit on something dry. Ray didn't object to the loss of his chair. He simply snagged a stool from behind the bar, grabbed a beer so cold that the can sweated icy drops, and put the stool next to Mandy.

"Wrap your throat around this," he said, handing her the beer.

With a sigh she took a swallow of the mellow, lively beer and smoothed the cold can over her forehead and cheeks. The diving mask she had slung over her wrist banged against the table when she took another drink. Ray removed the mask and set it on the bar.

"Go on, Tommy," Ray said, opening his own beer, "tell us about the hammerhead as big as a house trailer that followed you last summer."

Tommy finished the shark story, which had been interrupted by Mandy's entrance. She listened, smiling in appreciation and gentle disbelief, and drank the incredibly refreshing beer. Very quickly the contents of the can disappeared. Ray held up his hand. The girl who was tending bar leaned over the counter and slapped another Fosters into Ray's palm. He opened the can and substituted it for the empty one in Mandy's hand. She gave him a startled look, received a beguiling smile and decided that one more delicious Australian beer wouldn't hurt.

Sipping at the heady, frothy brew, Mandy listened while each diver in turn around the table volunteered a story about the biggest chunk of marine life he had ever encountered. For one man it had been a manta ray as big as the bar. For another it had been a sixteen-foot shark. By the time it was Mandy's turn, her second beer was fizzing softly through her blood and a third was in her hand. She spoke without stopping to think, wanting only to share a special moment in diving with the people who would most appreciate it—other divers.

"I once swam with the gray whales in Scammon Lagoon, on the west coast of Baja California," Mandy said softly, remembering the eerie, enchanted experience. "The visibility was thirty, maybe forty feet. Whales would just kind of condense out of the sea at the edge of your vision, blue on blue, huge shadows moving with the kind of massive grace that made you think of God."

"Grays? Aren't they the ones that migrate from Alaska to Mexico and back each year?" Tommy asked.

Mandy nodded.

"Tell us about it, luv," Ray said as other divers added

their encouragement. "None of us blokes have ever been close to a whale."

She took another swallow of beer, then continued talking, encouraged by the enthusiasm of the men and relaxed by the two beers she had drunk.

"One female was especially curious," Mandy said. "She condensed out of the blue and came toward me, and just kept getting bigger, swimming straight for me, and I thought she would never end. She was so big I couldn't see all of her at once in the murky water. She had to have been more than thirty-five feet long, which meant that at least thirty-five tons of curiosity and intelligence and power were cruising to a stop less than a foot away from me. I hung there like a fly on a blue wall, my heart hammering. It was exhilaration, not fear. Grays are as gentle as they are huge."

Slowly Mandy rubbed the cold beer can over her cheek as she continued to talk. "She looked at me out of one black eye, then turned her whole body to put her other eye on me. Each time she moved it was like I was caught in a wave, water rushing everywhere, displaced by that huge body. I was so close I could make out the smallest detail of the barnacles that clustered on her skin. I held out my hand very slowly to see what she would do." Mandy laughed with delight, remembering. "She turned and presented her nose for a good rubbing!"

"Fair dinkum!" Ray said, shaking his head in wonder, laughing.

"It's true," Mandy said, smiling around another sip of beer. "I found out later she was one of the whales that followed scientists and tourists everywhere in the lagoon. She'd surface by boats and let people touch her or even scrub her with soft brushes. Guess the barnacles made her skin itch, and she had figured out real fast that the tiny and otherwise useless humans littering the lagoon made excellent ladies' maids."

Another shout of laughter went up, followed by a spate

of questions about diving off the west coast of the Northern Hemisphere, a place as alien and exotic to the Australians as the Great Barrier Reef was to Mandy.

"Well, I know you're proud of the taste of your Morton Bay bugs," Mandy said "but have you ever eaten fresh California abalone? It's like eating the most delicately flavored crab crossed with a truly succulent Maine lobster. And like anything tasty, abalone aren't very easy to get to. Today you have to go down so far that the water is black and the chill eats into your wet suit long before your air is gone, and you have to carry a crowbar to pry the animals loose from the rocks. But it's worth it. If you don't believe me, ask a sea otter."

"You've seen them?" Tommy asked eagerly. "I'd give my right arm to dive with otters."

"They'd take you up on it," Mandy said dryly. "They're every bit as mischievous as they look, and they can outswim silver salmon from a standing start. Otters love to play, to hunt, to eat, and they are among the most tender mothers I've ever seen in the animal world."

The men murmured and leaned closer eagerly, encouraging Mandy to continue.

"When the babies aren't old enough to hunt with the adults," Mandy said, "the mothers take the cubs to the surface of the kelp forest, wrap them carefully in the fronds and then dive deep into the forest in search of dinner, confident that their cubs will stay safely cradled." Mandy paused for a moment, remembering, and then added softly, "The months I spent diving with the otters were extraordinary. Otters are so vividly alive. Sometimes, in my dreams, I'm back with the otters, playing hide-and-seek through amber kelp forests eight stories tall...."

Ray and Tommy exchanged sidelong glances, each silently urging the other to ask the question that burned between them. But it wasn't the Australians who spoke first. It was Sutter.

"Why did you give up diving?"

The reality of the present returned to Mandy like a blow. Color and laughter went out of her between one breath and the next. Slowly she set her beer can on the table and pushed back her chair. Without looking at anyone she turned and went to the door.

"Mandy," Sutter said as she passed.

His voice was hard, urgent, as was his hand on her arm. She opened the door without looking at him and stood watching the silver veils of rain.

"There was an accident," Mandy said finally, her voice lifeless. "People died."

Sutter waited, but she said no more. So he asked another question, one whose answer he suspected he already knew. "Was your husband one of them?"

"Yes. And I was another, Sutter. I died, too."

Mandy slipped from his grasp and stepped out into the rain, shutting the door behind her. She walked quickly to the tent, only to realize while she was drying herself that she couldn't bear to be within the sultry confines of the canvas. With a low sound of distress she rushed back out into the rain, still carrying the towel.

The first surge of her restlessness took her to the tiny airstrip. She crossed it and went into the she-oaks beyond, passing a tiny lighthouse before turning toward the beach, where huge combers boiled up onto crushed coral that was as white as the sea foam being torn from the waves. Standing beneath the rain-tossed casuarina trees, she watched the ocean and thought about the extraordinary seascape that lay so close at hand, yet had never been farther away. Desperately she wished she had come to the Great Barrier Reef before she had learned to fear the sea.

But she hadn't, and it was too late now to do anything but clench her teeth and hate the coward she had become.

"What are you thinking about?"

Sutter's voice wasn't unexpected to Mandy. She had known he would follow her. That knowledge had driven her from the confines of the tent.

"Cowardice," Mandy said flatly. "Mine."

"You listen to me!" Sutter said savagely, cutting Mandy off and spinning her toward him so quickly that she lost her grip on the towel. "I know what a coward is, lady. A coward is a woman like my mother, who couldn't take a less-than-perfect life so she took Valium instead, until finally she took enough and died, leaving a bitter, confused son behind. A coward is a woman like my ex-wife, who couldn't face her own emptiness, so she filled every instant of every day with parties and sycophants."

Sutter's hands gentled suddenly, stroking Mandy's arms. "You're not a coward, Mandy. I know that as surely as I know you're alive. I stood and watched you this afternoon. You were fighting, not running. You were trying, not denying that anything was wrong. Again and again you fought to bring your face down to the lagoon and—"

"Lost," Mandy hissed across Sutter's words. "Over and over and over again. Because I'm a coward."

"No! You won, Mandy! I saw it! It tore me apart to watch, but I saw every instant of it. You forced your face into the water three times. That's victory, not failure, Mandy. Victory!"

"Three times in as many hours, for maybe five seconds total," Mandy said bitterly. "That's not victory, that's a bloody rout!"

"But—"

"But nothing," she interrupted, her voice tight, her eyes almost wild. "Three-quarters of the world is water, and I'm cut off from it because of my own cowardice! For you, diving is a hobby. For me it was everything. All that I had wanted since childhood, all that I'd studied and worked for, a career that I loved, *all that is gone because I'm a coward.*"

"Mandy," Sutter whispered helplessly, stroking her cheeks where tears and rain mingled. "What happened, golden eyes?"

Mandy shuddered suddenly but couldn't prevent the

words from spilling out of her, the past welling up like a dark current, drowning her but for Sutter's strong, warm hands holding her afloat in the present.

"Andrew was an oceanographer," Mandy said. "I was first his student and then his wife. Marriage wasn't all that I'd hoped it would be, but then, what is? I was a virgin. Andrew was used to experienced women who were quick off the mark." Mandy laughed abruptly. "In bed we were a bad match. We should have made up for it professionally, because our strengths in oceanography were complementary. But Andrew wanted children, not a co-researcher, and he wanted the children the same way he wanted sex— instantly. He had turned forty, you see, and I was his second wife. There were no children from the first marriage. He told me he didn't want to grow old and die knowing that nothing of himself lived on."

Slowly Mandy shook her head, not realizing that she did it. "As soon as I could wrap up my research on sea otter habitats, I went off the pill. It took a long time to conceive. Too long. Andrew got more and more depressed, more angry, more difficult. When I finally got pregnant I was thrilled. It was our anniversary and Andrew's forty-third birthday. I took the ferry out to Catalina, where Andrew was camping and diving. He didn't expect me that early. I was going to surprise him."

Mandy felt Sutter's hands tightening on her arms again and smiled crookedly. "Yeah, you guessed it. He was having sex with some neoprene bunny when I walked into the tent. When he finished explaining how it was all my fault because I was such a lump in bed, we went to the airport. Did I mention that he was a pilot and owned a small plane?"

"No," Sutter said softly.

"Well, he was. I'd never liked flying. It was something I tolerated because it was the most efficient way to get from point A to point B. And that's what I wanted that night. Efficiency. We took off. It was dark. It felt like it had always been dark. Somewhere over the ocean, something went wrong. Heart attack. Stroke. No one knows because his body was never found.''

The pupils in Sutter's eyes expanded suddenly. "Mandy?" he whispered, his voice raw.

"Oh, yes," she said, shuddering. "I was with him. All the way. The plane went in and floated but not long enough. I dragged at Andrew and dragged at him and kicked out the window but he was too big and the ocean was too cold and it was pouring in the window and we went down and down and down and my lungs ached and burned and burst and I breathed icy water and I...I drowned," she said, her voice broken.

Sutter's arms closed around Mandy in a crushing hug as he tried to convince her and himself that she was alive. The thought of what she had been through was agonizing. The realization that he had forced her to relive her terror during the flight to the island was a knife of regret turning in his guts.

And then he remembered her incoherent words after he had pulled her from the Fish Pond's shallow waters: *The baby, the baby.*

"Oh, God, Mandy," Sutter said, his voice raw. "No...."

But she was still talking, still telling him things that were too painful to bear. Yet they had happened. They must be borne.

"I woke up at dawn in the bottom of a tiny boat that bounced all over the sea. I was dead but it still hurt. It still hurt! It was...hell. I was sure of it." Mandy took a deep, tearing breath. "Somehow the fisherman got me to the hospital before cold finished what the sea had begun. But.." her voice faltered and then went on, a sound as ragged as her breathing "it was too late for the baby. I could have lived with failing Andrew, but not my child. The child I was going to teach to dive and to laugh and to love...my child died before it even had a chance to live.

I should have died, too." She shuddered. "Sometimes...sometimes I think I did."

Sutter whispered Mandy's name again and again, gathering her even closer, holding on to her with fierce strength, as though he were afraid the sea was going to sweep up and claim the woman who had evaded drowning two years ago.

"You're alive," Sutter said in a low, intense voice. "Do you hear me, Mandy? You're alive, more alive than any woman I've ever known!"

"Am I?" she whispered, pulling back until she could look at him with shadowed golden eyes.

"*Yes.*"

"I felt alive last night, with you. Alive as I never have been. But in the morning you...walked away."

Sutter closed his eyes against the pain in Mandy's voice. "You're not a woman for affairs. You would want more. You sure as hell deserve more, and I know it, just as I know I'm not the man to give it to you. I learn from my mistakes, Mandy. And that's what marriage was for me. A mistake. But I wanted you so damned bad I stopped thinking!"

"Two years ago you would have been right about me and affairs," Mandy said. "But not now, Sutter. Not now. Like you, I've learned. Now I want what I had last night. I want to be alive, to feel you inside me, to be so close to you I can't tell where I end and you begin. That's all I'm asking. I don't expect pretty words or deathless promises or anything but you, body to body, breath to breath, heat against heat, hard against soft. Come inside me, Sutter," she whispered, running her hands over his bare, rain-wet chest. "Please."

"Mandy," Sutter whispered, shuddering with the onslaught of desire, a cataract of heat pouring through him, gathering between his legs, making him so full and rigid that he groaned. "No."

But Mandy wasn't listening to anything except the

pounding of storm surf and the rain and her own blood matching the hammering of Sutter's heart beneath her hand.

"Don't worry, Sutter," she continued, words tumbling out in a torrent, pushed by her own tearing need to make Sutter understand. "I won't expect you to change your diving schedule or your meals or anything else about your vacation. I just want a little of your time when you aren't diving, that's all. I don't expect to be your lover back home. I don't expect you to acknowledge me in any way. It ends when we leave the island. No fuss, no muss, no tears or recriminations. Just a vacation affair between two consenting adults."

Mandy took a broken breath and looked into the blazing green of Sutter's eyes and the warm rain washing over his body. She wanted to be like that rain, bathing him in heat. She stood on tiptoe and whispered against his mouth, kissing and biting and tasting him between words.

"Teach me what you want, how to please you, how to make you feel as though you've been dropped into the hot center of life," Mandy said while her hands slid down Sutter's lean body and inside his swimsuit, pushing it down and away in a single twisting stroke, freeing him for her touch. The size and heat of him transformed her, suffusing her with an answering readiness, preparing her for the presence within her body of the very male flesh that pulsed so urgently between her hands. "I know I'm not much as a lover," she continued, "but I'll do any—"

Sutter's tongue thrust between Mandy's teeth, cutting off her words as he ravished her mouth, pinning her in his arms, pressing their aroused bodies together while silver rain poured over their hot skin. She made a shivering sound of desire and sucked on his tongue, pulling him even deeper into her mouth, not even realizing what she did, knowing only that she must have more of him or die.

He ate her mouth hungrily while his splayed fingers slid down her wet stomach to push inside her bikini, spearing through the musky dampness of her hair, probing until he found her slick readiness bathing him more hotly than any rain. His other hand raked down her back, tearing away her bikini in two powerful jerks even as he kicked aside his own suit. With a thick, hungry sound he sank his fingers into her thighs, spreading them and at the same time lifting her, plunging into her until he could go no deeper for he was completely, tightly sheathed in her wild heat.

The sudden thrust and hard pressure of Sutter within Mandy ripped reality away. Arms wrapped around his powerful neck, body quivering, Mandy hung on to Sutter, knowing only him, feeling only his potency filling her and ecstasy convulsing her. Her body clenched and stroked and clenched around him again, pulling him in even more deeply, her consummation streaming over him in a torrid rain until he stood transfixed, pouring himself into her in return, his breath coming out in an extended, broken cry.

For long moments Mandy and Sutter held on to each other, oblivious to the weather, the waves, to everything but the shivering aftermath of intense pleasure. Slowly their breathing returned to normal. Even more slowly Sutter lifted Mandy, separating himself from her, allowing her legs to slide down his until she stood on her own feet once more. After the steamy heat of her body, the air felt cold on his still-aroused flesh.

"Are you all right?" Sutter asked, his voice uneven as he hugged her.

She made a sound of contentment against his chest.

"I didn't hurt you?" he pressed.

"What?" she asked, looking up at him with puzzled golden eyes.

"I was very…aroused."

Mandy smiled. "Yes. I liked that, Sutter. I liked it very much."

She ran her fingertips down the center line of his body until she found the blunt, partially aroused flesh nested in a dense thicket of amber hair. She heard Sutter's breathing change as she traced the growing length of him before she went on to cup the twin weights suspended just below. With curiosity and gentle care she stroked the different, very male textures.

"Do you like that?" she murmured.

Sutter heard the catch in Mandy's voice, saw the sensual shiver that claimed her and felt his blood rushing heavily once more.

" 'Like' isn't the word for what I feel right now," Sutter said huskily, putting his hands over Mandy's, guiding her in the ways of pleasuring him.

She was a very fast learner. Sutter's breath caught in his throat as he stifled a groan. He knew he should stop her, walk her back to the tent, get out of the open so that there would be no chance of someone stumbling across them. But the beach was utterly deserted and the casuarina grove partially shielded them and the rain was falling in sensuous silver veils. He decided that next time he would take her to the cloistered shelter of the canvas walls and lie between her legs for a long, deep loving. But not this time. This time he wanted to lie in the open with her, licking the hot rain from her body in a loving as wild and free as the storm sweeping over the island.

Mandy closed her eyes, caressing Sutter as she absently tasted the rain on her lips with the tip of her tongue.

"Let me," he said huskily.

"What?"

Sutter's answer was the warm, velvet rasp of his tongue over Mandy's lips. She shivered and held his responsive flesh in her hands, caressing him, loving him. He was smooth and hard and flushed with heat, his skin stretched as tight as a satin drum, slick with passion and rain.

"Love?" he asked.

"Mmm?" she murmured, eyes closed, lips parted.

"What happened to that towel you had?"

"I think I'm standing on it."

Sutter's lips curved in amusement despite the heavy beat

of desire in his blood. He reached down and slowly, gently caught Mandy's erect nipples between his fingers, rolling the tight buds, tugging at them. Her breath broke and her knees sagged.

"You have the same effect on me," he said, caressing her breasts with rain-wet hands before he released her. "This time I want to lie between your legs, Mandy. I want...*you*."

She sank to her knees and fumbled with the drenched towel, spreading it over the crushed coral and fallen she-oak leaves. Her task wasn't made any easier when Sutter distracted her by kneeling behind her. He rubbed his long fingers down her spine to the shadow cleft of her bottom and then lower still. She gasped when she felt him spear sweetly into her warmth. Heat rippled out from the pit of her stomach with a force that made her dizzy.

"Sutter?" she whispered, unable to speak aloud.

Mandy looked over her shoulder at Sutter just as his tanned, powerful thigh eased between her legs, pressing them apart, rubbing rain-slick skin over her bottom, unraveling her with the unexpected intimacy. The pressure increased, pushing her thighs apart until she swayed on her knees.

"What do you want me to do?" she asked raggedly.

Sutter bent and gently bit the nape of her neck and whispered, "Rain on me, Mandy."

His left arm came around her just beneath her breasts, holding her shoulder blades against his chest while his leg opened her thighs to the ravishment of his palm sliding over her swollen, heat-flushed flesh, retreating and sliding and retreating until she swayed with his caresses. His long fingers teased the velvet bud of her passion, making her tremble with need. His teeth closed deliberately on the nape of her neck at the same instant that his finger penetrated the slick, hungry core of her. He felt the tiny convulsions deep within her, the hot rain of her pleasure over him.

"I love touching you," Sutter said hoarsely, biting Mandy again, caressing her even more deeply. Feeling her steamy, shivering reaction, he groaned and closed his hand possessively on her hot flesh.

"Sutter," she moaned. "Stop. I want to hold you...."

"I can't stop," he admitted, rubbing his hand slowly between her thighs. "You're so damned responsive you make me lose control."

Mandy made a broken sound that could have been laughter or passion or both. "But I'm not," she said, then moaned at the sweet, involuntary shuddering of her body as he caressed her again.

"Tell me all about it," Sutter said huskily, sucking drops of rain from Mandy's spine with hard pressures of his mouth, sending wild bursts of pleasure through her. He laughed thickly, sucking hard on her soft skin, thrusting deeply, feeling himself drenched with her passion. "Yes," he murmured, "*Yes*. Tell me how unresponsive you are while you come apart in my hands."

Mandy tried to speak, but Sutter's fingers had captured one of her erect nipples and he was tugging at it with the same slow, sensuous rhythms of his hand moving between her legs. The twin assault was too much. She swayed like a slender casuarina caught in a storm, letting the warm rain wash through her to her lover. Sutter closed his eyes and caressed Mandy gently until the storm passed and she could speak once more. Then he turned her and lowered her to the towel, where he kissed her flushed lips with a sensual thoroughness that soon had her shivering again.

"Do you want me?" he asked.

"Yes," she whispered, "oh, yes."

"How?" he murmured, spreading her legs apart, stroking her hot, delicate skin. "Gentle? Fast? Slow? How do you want me, Mandy? *Tell me*."

"Deep," she whispered. "So deep it never ends."

"Oh, love," Sutter said, shuddering in a vise of need, "that's how I want it, too."

Mandy's eyes opened when she felt her legs pulled first around Sutter's waist, then up over his shoulders until her hips were lifted clear of the towel.

"Tell me if I hurt you," Sutter said, his voice husky with need. "You're so sweet, so tight, and you make me so hard...."

She started to answer, to tell him that she wanted him, all of him, but her voice unraveled into a husky moan as he pushed slowly into her. She saw his face become oddly flattened, his eyes slitted, his lips thinned with the force of his passion and the self-control that held him in check. Slowly he gave her more of his weight, more of his power, more of the potent flesh that was filling her until she was sure she could hold no more...and then he taught her how little she had known about her capacity to receive and his to give. The pressure was fierce, burning and so delicious she trembled helplessly and rocked against him, wanting more. He gave it to her with a smooth thrust of his hips, embedding himself completely in her, hearing her shattered cry. He shuddered and held himself savagely still.

"Mandy?" he asked hoarsely. "Mandy?"

Her eyes opened. Her pupils were so dilated that only a tiny rim of molten gold remained. She could feel Sutter from the back of her knees to the small of her back and she wanted only to measure him again and again and again until she died of it, but she could think of no way to tell him what she so desperately needed. Her slender hands pulled his head down until her lips were against his ear. As her teeth closed on him, she whispered a hot, dark command that ripped away his control.

Sutter's powerful body flexed and he began driving into Mandy, plumbing every last bit of her softness as she cried out in wild pleasure and urgent demand. Her hands raked down to his buttocks, clenched, then instinctively gentled as she followed the cleft and discovered the exciting male flesh below, twin spheres drawn tight with excruciating need. At the first soft caress of her palm Sutter threw back his head and bared his teeth in an agony of pleasure. Her hand moved again, shaping him, loving him, making him explode. She felt it happening for him, the tiny convulsions and the long, shattering release, the secret dance of life in her cupped hand; and then heat burst from the pit of her stomach, burning through her, stripping away the world, leaving her impaled on ecstasy even as she was sheltered within her lover's arms.

Chapter 13

The island days took on a new pattern for Mandy and Sutter. Each morning they awoke as they had slept, body to body, warmth to warmth, breath to breath. While Sutter dove out in the open sea, Mandy went to the Fish Pond. Each time she went she was able to endure having her face in the water for a few minutes longer and then a few minutes beyond that, until finally she was able to enter the water at high tide and float on her back or patrol the pond with a languid breaststroke that kept her face clear of the water.

When Sutter returned from his dives, they would eat and she would listen to his descriptions of the Great Barrier Reef. He would see the yearning in Mandy and feel it in himself; he would have given his soul to share the exotic beauty of the sea with her. But the reef was not his to give. All he could bring to her was his touch, his smile, his body locked deeply within hers as they explored together the sensual sea they had discovered in one another.

Both Sutter and Mandy tried not to count the days remaining to them on the island. Both failed. The morning before they were due to fly out, Sutter left Mandy in the Fish Pond and called his aunt instead of going off to the dive boat.

"Anthea?"

"Sutter! I had almost abandoned hope of ever hearing from you again. Is everything all right?"

"Everything's fine, except my vacation is too short."

"A common problem."

"I have an uncommon solution. You're going to give us two more weeks."

"Us?"

"Mandy needs more time, too."

There was a long pause from Anthea's end, followed by a sigh.

"Damon? Is there something I should know?"

"Two years ago Mandy and her husband crashed at sea in a small plane. He died. She was sucked down with the plane and damn near drowned, and she lost the baby she was carrying."

"Dear God," Anthea said in an appalled voice.

"Since then Mandy's been terrified of small planes and any water deeper than a sidewalk puddle. But she doesn't want to be afraid anymore. She got to Lady Elliot Island on sheer guts, and now she's at the point where she can put her face in the water and even swim around the lagoon a little. If she had more time, she'd be able to dive along the Great Barrier Reef. I'm sure of it. I want her to have that chance."

"Damon, my dearest boy, that's an enormous amount to ask of Mandy. Learning to dive would be hard enough, but learning to dive when you're terrified of water—and for excellent reason!—is too much to ask of anyone."

"Learning won't be a problem for Mandy. She's been scuba diving from Alaska to Mexico. She has a Ph.D. in marine biology, with a specialty in the ecology of coral reefs. Before the accident the ocean was her life. I want her to have that life again."

There was another long pause.

"Is that what Mandy wants?" Anthea asked finally.

"If you heard her talk about the ocean, you wouldn't

have to ask,'' Sutter said, smiling almost sadly. "Anthea, remember that paper on fish farms and coral atolls that OCC commissioned a few years back?''

"But of course. I still use it as a model of the type of work we should be commissioning.''

"Mandy was a major contributor to that paper. Even if she never dives again, she's wasted in her present job. OCC needs someone who understands the ocean more than you need a girl Friday. I'd have given my eyeteeth to have Mandy along last year when I was trying to convince that little tin tyrant that his people needed an intact reef to attract edible fish more than he needed crushed coral to build roads for people who had no cars! I can think of a hundred times I could have used Mandy's advice in the last year. She's a hell of a lot more than a good-looking woman with a sassy mouth. She's intelligent and gutsy and—''

"Your lover," Anthea interrupted calmly.

"That, my dear aunt, is none of your business.''

She sighed. "Two more weeks?''

"Yes.''

"You'll have to fly straight to Darwin afterward. That man Peters doesn't get along with the aborigines as well as you did. Apparently he can't stomach the local delicacies. Without the support of the adults, we can do little for the children.''

Sutter grimaced at the thought of more baffling conversations, warm beer and charred lizard. On the other hand, there had been a few times in his life when he would have been glad to drink boiled beer and eat lizard, charcoal and all.

"We'll be into the monsoon season in a few weeks,'' Sutter pointed out. "It will be hell to get into the bush, much less to get out.''

"Then perhaps you could fly over for a few days now, patch things together and then have your two weeks' extra vacation.''

"Not a chance. There's no such thing as 'a few days' when you're dealing with a culture that has no concept of European time," Sutter retorted. He smothered a curse. "Two more weeks for both of us on the island. Then I'll eat goanna until I get things straightened out. Deal?"

"Deal."

"Good. You can use those two weeks to write out a job description for a resident OCC oceanographer."

"Damon..."

"Yes?"

"Have you changed your mind about marriage?"

Sutter held the receiver until his hand ached. When he spoke it was in a clipped voice that invited no confidences. "To quote my dear aunt, 'a discreet, mutually satisfying affair is far superior to the lackluster social convenience known as marriage.'"

When Anthea spoke, there was an indefinable sadness in her voice. "I meant that only for myself, not as blanket advice for my nephew."

"What's sauce for the goose, et cetera."

"Is that how Mandy feels?"

Sutter's temper slipped. "Do you think I'd be her lover otherwise?"

"That would depend on how badly you wanted her, wouldn't it? Or, perhaps, on how badly she wanted *you*."

"Thanks for the vote of confidence in my personal integrity," Sutter snarled.

"Damon, I didn't mean—"

"The hell you didn't."

Sutter broke the connection and spun toward the door in the same savage motion, startling the girl who was racking postcards. A few moments later the phone rang. Sutter was gone. The girl listened and then noted in the resort log that the couple in the unnumbered tent were extending their vacation for two more weeks.

The days became a sensual kaleidoscope for Mandy, a colorful wheel whirling faster and faster around her. Sutter made love to her with his smoky green glances and his long-fingered hands, with his powerful body and his hot, insatiable mouth; and she loved him in the same way, sweetly devouring him, taking and giving and sharing until the world splintered into colors and fell away, leaving only ecstasy behind.

One day Sutter came back from diving to find Mandy snorkeling within the lagoon's clear water. He watched for fifteen minutes, and then he had waded out and lifted Mandy into his arms, exulting in her success, giving her a deep kiss that had left both of them trembling with something more than triumph. On the first calm day after that, Sutter went with Mandy into the unbridled sea on the opposite side of the island, where waves swept in from a distant horizon. He led her to a place called the Garden, a favorite local snorkeling ground. There, beyond the creaming waves, she swam by his side, their bodies propelled by lazy movements of their flippers, their fingers interlaced, their masked faces turned down toward the extraordinary alien beauty of the coral growths.

For a week Sutter went scuba diving in the morning and snorkeling with Mandy in the afternoon. And then Mandy turned up at the dive boat in the morning with the other divers, her scuba gear in hand and her heart in her mouth. Sutter gave her a smile and a kiss that made her feel as though she could breathe underwater and to hell with air tanks and mouthpieces.

"Are you sure, love?" Sutter asked softly. "You don't have to."

"I want to. I'm scared, but I want to."

"What about being in the dive boat? It's hardly the *Queen Mary*."

Mandy hesitated, then smiled tremulously. "I won't know until I try."

Ray turned away from instructing a newcomer and saw Mandy standing next to Sutter, her tanks leaning against his. Sutter's fingers slid between Mandy's in a gesture of approval and sensual possession. He looked up from Mandy's red lips and saw Ray's smile.

"The boat will be a little crowded," Sutter said casually. "Mandy and I will wait until you drop off the first group."

"No worries, mate. Tommy is going to take this lot over to the Garden for a bit."

Tommy suppressed a look of surprise. One of the other divers started to say something, caught an elbow in the ribs and shut up instantly. Mandy's steady success in overcoming her terror of water was a source of very real pride to all of the divers. If Ray wanted to take Mandy and Sutter to the outer reef alone, then the rest of the divers could amuse themselves until the boat returned.

"Bloody good idea," one of the divers said. "I've been wanting a go at the Garden but the tide has never been right."

There was a ragged chorus of agreement as the men abandoned their scuba tanks and drifted down the beach to a point opposite the Garden.

"Right, here we go," Ray said to Mandy.

He took Mandy's tanks, waded out and hefted them into the dive boat, which was moored by a line leading from the bow to a sturdy little she-oak. Sutter scooped up Mandy, waded out and placed her carefully in the bobbing craft. He waited several moments.

"Okay?" he murmured.

Mandy let out a long breath. "Yes. It's…fine. Not like I thought it would be. Not nearly as bad as the plane was."

Sutter wondered which plane she meant, the one that had nearly killed her or the one that had flown her to Lady Elliot Island. He didn't ask because he didn't want anything to upset the balance of Mandy's control.

"If you change your mind," Sutter said, "don't fight it. Tell me right away. Promise?"

Mandy nodded.

Sutter signaled for Ray to bring in the bow line. After both men had hoisted themselves aboard with an easy strength Mandy envied, Ray set off for the diving grounds on the outer reef, which was on the opposite side of the island. Gradually Mandy relaxed. Before the accident she had spent many long, contented days in small boats, as opposed to only a few hellish hours after the crash. Most of her memories of small boats, unlike those associated with small planes, were good.

After a time Mandy let out a long breath and turned to Sutter with a smile, letting herself enjoy the gentle motion of the boat on the blue swells. Sutter smiled down at Mandy in return, watching her with affection and pride and the sensual hunger that was so much a part of him when he was close to her.

The boat turned, bringing the sun behind Sutter's profile. Mandy realized that sunlight and seawater had bleached his hair until it was incandescent shades of flax and gold, pale wheat and tropical sunshine. Dense, amber eyelashes shaded the green intensity of his eyes. The aggressive Scandinavian planes of his face showed cleanly beneath his taut, tanned skin. His male power and vitality were heightened by the black wet suit that was molded to his body. She watched him and wondered if she were pregnant, and which parent the baby would resemble.

Would our child be like you, beautiful enough to break my heart? Would our baby have your intense green eyes and burning gold hair, your incisive mind and your glorious passion for life? Am I carrying that child even now? God, I hope so! Believing that will give me the courage to let you go with a smile and a final, silent cry of love.

The boat came to a stop, shaking Mandy out of her private speculations. She realized she had been staring at Sutter for a long time. He wasn't disturbed by that, for he had been staring at her with equal absorption. She wondered what he had been thinking or if he had guessed her own thoughts.

"Over you go," Ray said to Sutter.

Sutter shrugged his tanks into place, checked the air feed and positioned his mask before he sat on the gunwale with his back to the water. If he had been diving with Americans he would have given the traditional thumbs-up before he went over backward into the sea. But he was diving in Australia, where that particular hand signal was an insult.

"Mandy? Want me to lift you over?" Ray asked.

She hesitated, then said, "Thanks. The first few times it would be easier if I didn't go in with a splash."

"No worries, luv. I never complain about the chance to get my hands on a good-looking Sheila. Put those long legs over the stern and your bum on the gunwale. I'll support you until you're ready to go in."

With Ray's help, Mandy maneuvered herself into position despite the cumbersome scuba gear strapped to her back. Ray braced her in place.

"Tell me when you're ready. No hurry, luv. I'm having a good time. You smell much better than the last diver I helped over the edge."

Mandy laughed. "Eau de wet suit, the new fashion sensation down under."

Despite her laughter, Mandy's hands grasping the gunwale showed white on the knuckles. There was a whole lot of ocean out there, blue on blue, fathom on fathom, swallowing the world.

Suddenly Sutter surfaced in the center of Mandy's vision. Even darkened by the sea, his hair still looked like a piece of the sun. He tongued out his mouthpiece, caught the stern with one hand and hung before her in the clear water, smiling up at her.

"The denizens of the Fish Pond must have passed the word about free lunches," Sutter said easily. "The finned hordes are waiting for their goddess to descend with manna."

"And me without a crust of bread to my name," Mandy said.

"They'll understand. That's the thing about friends, Mandy. They understand."

She looked into his green eyes, eyes so vivid that no mask could conceal them. Suddenly she understood what Sutter was saying: he wouldn't think less of her if she decided not to dive after all. Tears burned behind her eyelids. She took a deep breath, checked the airflow through the mouthpiece and nodded to Ray. He eased her over the stern and into the sea next to Sutter, not releasing her until she had a firm grasp on the boat's gunwale.

"Thanks, luv," Ray said when she was in the water.

Mandy looked up, startled.

"For trusting me not to pitch you in," he said simply.

Scuba gear prevented Mandy from speaking, so she squeezed Ray's hand, silently telling him that she had long since forgiven him for tossing her into the Fish Pond. Then she turned to Sutter and held out her hand. Strong, slick, wet fingers intertwined with hers. She released the stern and began sinking into the blue depths of the sea.

After the first burst of adrenaline passed, Mandy was able to regulate her breathing. It was still too fast, too shallow, but it no longer threatened to run through her supply of oxygen four times faster than normal. She looked at Sutter and gave him the thumbs-up signal, which he returned. Then he turned her around slowly until her back was to him.

One hundred feet away an immense, ragged wall rose from the sapphire depths to culminate just beneath the surface of the sea in a fantastic crown of multihued life. As enormous as the wall appeared, it was just one tiny fragment of a coral complex that went north for thousands upon thousands of square miles: the Great Barrier Reef.

Slowly Mandy swam toward the reef, drawn to its enormous, living presence as inevitably as a river is drawn by gravity to the sea. Sutter swam at Mandy's side, monitoring the bursts of bubbles she expelled, literally counting her breaths. With growing elation he realized that the longer she stayed in the water, the more her breathing slowed; her fear was diminishing, not increasing. Her breathing was still too fast, but no worse than his had been the first time he had found himself face-to-face with Lady Elliot Island's contribution to the immensity of the Great Barrier Reef.

Mandy didn't stop swimming until she was little more than an arm's length away from the reef. Six feet below the surface, bathed in warmth and light and nutrients, the section of reef that she could see was a fantastic garden of fixed animals and mobile plants, of individual lives so small she could barely make out their delicate shapes and of communal skeletons so overwhelming in numbers that man couldn't comprehend them. At each succeeding downward level of the reef there were more shapes and sizes and colors of coral, more varieties of life than seemed possible, a dazzling fecundity that shamed the land by comparison.

At the upper levels, staghorn coral grew in interlocking splendor, arms reaching into the warm sea to make a chaotic, living garden where tiny fish thrived, scattered among the prongs of coral like broken necklaces of citrine and emerald, amethyst and sapphire and gold. A soft coral grew in deeply sinuous array, its fleshy-appearing folds turned and refolded upon itself with muscular grace. Coral as intricate and as delicate as Irish lace shawls grew from a section of wall in stark contrast to the dense convolutions of maroon brain coral.

Starfish whose countless arms were as delicate as feathers and as flexible as whips clung to the living outer surface of the reef, adding bursts of magenta and white and red to the multihued coral display. Sponges whose shapes went from the ridiculous to the unbelievable grew from hollows and irregularities in the reef wall. An enormous shoal of tiny white fish wound across the face of the reef in a wild river. The fry of oceangoing fish hung against the reef like clouds against a rugged mountain.

Crevices and grottoes were everywhere, and each had its own inhabitants. At first they were only shapes hanging in the darkness. Then Sutter would flash a hand-held diving light, bringing the dark hollows and their dwellers into sharp focus. Sometimes the residents were vivid coral "trout" or muscular cod sporting freckles of electric blue, and sometimes there were banner fish whose long fins were breathtakingly graceful as they wove in fragile sine curves through the sea. Corals in the shape of enormous, deeply folded fans descended the face of the reef like gigantic footholds leading down and down and down to the levels where sunlight and warmth slowly were absorbed into the serene lapis depths of the Pacific Ocean.

Everywhere there was life. Mobile or motionless, camouflaged or shouting with colors, hunter or hunted, succulent or spined, wearing its skeleton on the outside or the inside or doing without altogether, graceful or grotesque, aggressive or shy, beautiful, ugly, haunting, overwhelming—Mandy barely had time to comprehend even the smallest fragment of the reef's stunning profusion of life before Sutter tapped her shoulder and pointed to his watch and then up to the surface. She was startled to find that nearly all of her dive time was gone. She was even more startled to discover just how far she had been drawn down the ragged face of the outer reef. The surface was far, far above, little more than a silver banner unfurled against the darkly luminous blue that surrounded her.

Slowly, reluctantly, Mandy followed Sutter back to the world of dry land and warmth, gravity and white sunlight.

In the days that followed, Mandy and Sutter spent every possible minute diving together, sharing the incredible beauty and infinite variety of the sea. After the first few dives fear stopped clutching at Mandy's heart and plucking unexpectedly at her nerves. Once more she was a part of the ocean, swimming easily in the clear water, cradled and at peace within the mother of all life. Mandy put away all thought of time, all fears, all knowledge of a life beyond the coral seclusion of Lady Elliot Island. It was the same for Sutter, no thoughts of what was to come, no bleak shadows of the past, nothing but the glorious reef by day...and by night a sensual beauty that grew until he could no longer measure it, he could only immerse himself in it as he did the sea, asking no questions, knowing no time, simply living within the endless, incandescent perfection of his lover.

The peace endured until the last day on Lady Elliot, then Mandy and Sutter emerged from the cradle of the sea and knew that their time together was almost gone. In silence they sat close while the dive boat was hurried back to shore by the wind, which was companion to the squall line that had pulled tangled skeins of cloud across the sky. At the dive shed, Sutter gently shooed Mandy off for a predinner shower while he supervised the packing of their equipment.

But later, when Sutter went to the tent, Mandy was nowhere around. Inside the tent there was only twilight dimness and the pearlescent, almost secret gleam of the white cowrie shell Mandy had placed at the head of their bed. Kneeling, feeling claws of sadness sinking and twisting through him, Sutter ran a fingertip over the shimmering beauty of the rare, flawless shell that would have to be left behind.

Sutter closed his eyes for a moment and his hand became a fist. Then he came to his feet in a rush and went in search of Mandy, needing her in a way he neither understood nor questioned. There was no one in the bathhouse. There was no one on the beach. The tide was higher than he had ever seen it, the wind was swirling over the crystal water, and tattered veils of warm rain were sweeping the surface of the lagoon.

Suddenly the breath rushed from Sutter's lungs as he saw a familiar, slender shape cruising facedown through the rain-washed, crystalline waters. He watched Mandy patrol the Fish Pond and then go out into the rest of the lagoon, propelling herself with very small, controlled flipper motions, her arms relaxed at her sides. When she headed back for the Fish Pond again, Sutter was chest-deep in the warm water, waiting for her. She swam up to him, reversed neatly and stood in water that came to her neck.

"It was too beautiful to give up just to eat dinner," Mandy said, sliding her mask onto her wrist, bobbing a bit in the chin-deep water, out of her depth but not frightened at all. "No weight, nothing dragging, just floating and the warm water everywhere, a whole world opening up around me."

Sutter smiled at Mandy, wanting her until he ached, wishing he had the words to tell her how much he enjoyed her renewed love of the sea. The setting sun sent a single, slanting shaft of light through the clouds, turning the beads of salt water on Mandy's mouth into pure gold. Sutter saw, and remembered a time when her lips had been silvered by rain and he had licked them until she moaned.

"I haven't thanked you," Mandy said, touching Sutter with sea-wet fingertips. "You've given me so much...."

"No," he said softly, kissing her fingertips. "It's you who have given so much to me. You're beautiful, Mandy. So elegant and determined." He smiled as his fingers gently caressed her cheek. "No matter what happens, no matter where I go or what I do, I'll never forget your courage." His big hands closed gently around her ribs, keeping her from drifting in the chin-deep water. "Give me a hug before you float away forever," he whispered.

Sutter's hands slid down Mandy's back to her thighs, lifting her slowly, anchoring her legs around his hips. The thin strip of cloth running between her legs didn't prevent her from feeling the hard, quintessentially masculine bulge pushing against Sutter's bathing suit. Her breath shortened as she realized that only two thin strips of cloth prevented her from taking Sutter into her body once more, here, now,

the heady warmth of the lagoon enfolding them, concealing their joined bodies beneath water turned incandescent
orange by the dying sun.

The erotic thought changed Mandy, sending softness
and heat flowing through her even as she dismissed the
idea as impossible. It was too light. Too public. Someone
might walk down the beach at any moment.

But that didn't mean that she couldn't enjoy a small
taste of the sensual pleasures Sutter brought to her. She
could rub her hands down his chest through the thick mat
of hair that concealed his nipples. She could kiss his neck
and taste the lagoon and wish that the salt had come from
elemental passion rather than the eternal sea.

As Mandy shifted slightly to reach the pulse beating in
Sutter's neck, the cloth between her legs rubbed over the
swollen ridge of male flesh. She made a ragged sound and
wished fiercely that it was dark and they were naked in
the sea and he was pushing into her with the hard, hot
flesh she loved to arouse and hold within her body.

"Sutter," she said raggedly, leaning back to look up
into his face, her body caressing him once more.

Blazing green eyes looked into her heavy-lidded ones.
"I know. Oh Lord, Mandy, I know what you're thinking
because that's what I'm thinking, too!"

She arched her back, rubbing lightly against him as she
brushed her lips over his mouth, whispering, "Tell me."

"You're thinking there's no one around, and even if
there was, the water is up to my collarbone and the surface
is scuffed by the wind and covered with burning colors,"
Sutter said in a low voice, shifting his grip until his left
forearm took the sweet weight of Mandy's hips and his
right hand was free. "Who would know if I untied just
one bow on your hip and you took me out of my suit and
guided me to that sweet, hot place between your thighs
and let me..." He groaned as his finger slipped beneath
the triangle of her bikini bottom. She was soft, hot, welcoming. "Let me," he said hoarsely, stroking her just

once. "Who would know, Mandy?" he asked, undoing one of the two ties that held the bikini bottom in place. "We'll be quiet and outwardly casual, just two people enjoying a sunset and talking and hugging up to their necks in water."

"Damon," Mandy whispered, feeling the warm lagoon caressing her most delicate flesh as he pulled the bikini bottom aside. *"Damon."*

"Take me, Mandy," he said in a low voice, running his fingertips over the softness he had uncovered, feeling her utterly open to his touch, wanting to join with her while the sky and sea turned to fire around them. "Take me," he whispered, "if you want me." His fingertips deciphered the message of her satin heat and shivering response as he probed her soft, feminine secrets. "Ah, you do want me," he murmured, caressing her with his hand and his voice. "Take me, love."

"Damon...we...can't."

"It will be our secret," Sutter whispered, watching Mandy through half-closed eyes, feeling her softness opening for him, yearning, wanting. "I'll be very slow, very quiet. Someone could walk by on the beach and be no wiser. I promise you, love."

The beach was deserted, the liquid warmth of the sea surrounded Mandy, and between her legs her lover's fingers slid and teased, parted and caressed her. She didn't know if she had enough self-control to act outwardly casual while Sutter was inside her, but when his hands moved to her hips, supporting her and at the same time leaving her bereft of all but the sea's lapping caress, she knew she was going to find out.

Mandy brought her hands down Sutter's muscular torso, all the way down, sliding her fingers inside the black strip of cloth that was all he wore. His breath hissed out as he felt her hands caressing him with small, secret motions. He tilted his head forward and brushed her lips with his own in a caress that would have looked quite casual from the beach.

"It's a good thing no one is within fifty yards of us," Sutter said in a low, raspy voice. "Your smile would give our game away for sure."

Mandy's only answer was a husky sound of pleasure and discovery as she stroked the potent male flesh she had uncovered. She looked up at Sutter, her eyes vivid with a combination of sensual mischief and frank passion. "You know," she murmured, her breath tight, rapid, "you bring a new meaning to some old phrases."

Sutter smiled despite the hunger racking him with each knowing, teasing movement of her fingers. "Like skin diver?" he suggested, flexing his fingers into her naked hips.

"That's one of them," she agreed, squeezing him with loving deliberation. "Then there's 'stand up and be counted.' Or take 'standing ovation,' that's another one. Or take 'a stand-up guy.' Or take—"

"Me, love," he interrupted, groaning. *"All of me."*

The husky command sent desire glittering through Mandy, scattering her thoughts, focusing her on the naked thrust of Sutter's arousal and the moist heat of her own response. Watching his face, wanting him wildly, she tugged his suit down just enough to give her the freedom of his body. His hands shifted as he moved her slightly, holding her just in front of the blunt, hungry flesh she had freed. Smiling, he watched her eyes as he felt himself brought closer and closer to her satin sheath, touching, teasing, nuzzling for heart-stopping seconds until he penetrated her with a slow, smooth pressure, watching her eyes take on a haze of pure sensuality as he filled her.

Mandy's breath unraveled in a soft, exciting thread of sound that went no farther than Sutter. She discovered that she could control her outward movements but not the secret, rhythmic shivering deep inside her. Her slick, intimate stroking pulled a throttled groan from Sutter. He smiled rather ferally at her and bit her lips in a wild caress that made them as red as the sun sliding deeply into the sea.

"Much as I'd love to do the same to your breasts," he said in a low voice, "it would be..."

"Indiscreet?" she offered.

"Very. It would be even worse if I...moved."

With heavy-lidded eyes, Mandy watched Sutter's taut expression. "What if I move instead?" she murmured.

"Same problem. Why don't we just count backward from one thousand in Sanskrit and look at the sunset until it's so dark that..." Sutter's breath was sucked in suddenly as he felt Mandy's torso tighten and then relax, stroking him as surely as if she had visibly moved. "Love," he said through clenched teeth, sucking in another whistling breath as she stroked him secretly once more, "this isn't fair to you. Taking you...like this...is too...hot. No more movements...like that...or I'll lose control."

Sutter barely restrained a wild shudder as he felt Mandy's body tugging invisibly at his. She saw his response, felt it in the steel of the muscles bunched beneath her hands, tasted it in the suddenly salty moisture above his upper lip. She flexed her legs, pressing herself over him, pushing him even more deeply into her body. Then she clenched the muscles of her torso once more, stroking him, loving him in secret.

"Like this?" she murmured.

Sutter's nearly closed eyelids quivered as he focused on the incredibly erotic feel of his lover's satin depths caressing him, and at the same time he fought not to lose his control. "Yes, love...like that...like...that...." He groaned very softly and clenched his teeth. "Mandy," he whispered, opening his eyes, looking into hers, "love..." wanting to watch her, "yes..." wanting her to watch him while he gave himself to her, *"yes..."* with countless deep, ecstatic pulses, *"just...like...this."*

Mandy whispered Sutter's name as she watched his face and loved him with hidden movements of her body. Without warning, waves of pleasure shimmered wildly up from her core, stealing her breath, her body, her soul, giving them to the man who was secretly joined with her, pouring all of himself into her caressing, welcoming heat. For a time neither he nor she could move, or even breathe, for they were too deeply embedded in each other and in the rapture weaving them together with hot, invisible lightning.

Finally Sutter reclaimed himself by tiny increments, a breath, two breaths, the ability to think, to hear, to speak.

"Mandy," he murmured, brushing his lips across her forehead, her eyelids, her lips. "I've never known anything…like this…like you."

She smiled up at Sutter, the last of the glorious sunset reflected in her eyes, wanting to tell him of her love and knowing that she must not. He hadn't come to her for that. Just a vacation affair between consenting adults. She had promised him that because it was all he wanted, all he would accept. So she kissed him softly and substituted a lover's words for the vastly greater truth that was consuming her.

"I love…being…with you," Mandy whispered, kissing the line of Sutter's jaw and the corners of his smile, holding him within her. "I love having you in my body, in my arms, in my mind. I love…"

The last words were breathed into Sutter's mouth as Mandy kissed him. Then they held each other in silence until the sunset was little more than a thin carmine flush across the horizon. Finally they separated slowly, reluctantly, rearranged their bathing suits and walked hand in hand back to the tent, where Sutter once more licked the sea from Mandy's body, loving her, dying within her and being reborn again when she lay between his thighs, tasting herself and the sea on him, loving him.

Those were the memories Mandy held tightly in her mind when the little white plane taxied up to the dive shed the following morning. She scrambled in without help and strapped herself into her seat in the same way, knowing that Sutter would break every bone in his hands rather than confine her again in a place she feared. When he sat next to her she took his big hand and held it between both of hers. This time she forced herself to look out over the island and the maze of interlocking coral structures that surrounded it and carpeted the floor of the azure sea.

Memories of Sutter's voice husky with passion and warm with praise helped Mandy when the plane began its steep descent to Bundaberg's small airport. Memories of being cherished, desired, consumed; memories of laughter and triumph, passion and release, sleeping and waking and diving through beauty that knew no end; those memories gave Mandy strength when Sutter helped her to the apron, touched her temple, her cheek, her lips...and then turned away without a word.

Mandy stood motionless, watching Sutter, desperately hoping for a word, a wave, a look, anything to tell her that he cared just a little for her beyond the self-imposed boundary of their passionate affair.

There was neither a word, nor a wave, nor a look; simply another small plane waiting, two men rushing forward to shake Sutter's hand and pull him aboard, and the rising whine of engines revving as the plane started to turn toward the runway.

Don't look back. Don't look. Don't.

But in the end Sutter could not prevent himself. When the plane paused at the end of the runway he turned back, looked...and saw only empty tarmac and lightning dancing against towering, slate-bottomed clouds.

Chapter 14

The couple in the picture were tanned and healthy. Salt water beaded like diamonds on their skin, their fingers were interlaced, their mouths smiling, and all around them was a blinding-white coral beach, turquoise water and scuba gear glistening from recent immersion in the sea. The big photograph was an unexpected gift from Ray, who had wanted to commemorate Mandy's victory over her fears.

And now she couldn't look at the photograph without wanting to laugh and to cry with bittersweet pleasure. It was the same for the lab report telling her that another life was growing in her body...sweet triumph and only a few salty tears. What the sea had once taken from her, Sutter had returned. She had what she wanted. She could dive, she was using her scientific knowledge toward making a better world for the next generation, and she was carrying a piece of that future within her own womb. All she lacked was the man who haunted her every dream, her every silence, even the breaths she took.

"Mandy, did Jessi give you that study on coral reefs and petroleum seeps?" Steve asked. "Yo, Mandy. Anybody home?"

With an effort Mandy focused on Steve rather than on the lost past or the unreachable future.

"Er, coral reefs, seeps, study…let's see." Trying to keep her mind on the task and off a man with blazing green eyes and hair the color of the sun, Mandy sorted through the mounds of scientific papers that Anthea had heaped on the desk. "Reefs from old cars…oil pollution…natural tar on beaches…edible reef fish of the…ah, here it is."

Steve took the bound sheets, read the concise summary Mandy had attached and smiled. "Don't know why you spent the past year hiding your light under a cabbage leaf, kid."

"I think you mean under a basket. Kids are what you find under cabbage leaves."

"Knew there was a reason I hated gardening. Thanks," he said, waving the study as he walked away.

With ambivalent feelings, Mandy turned back to the remaining papers. She knew busywork when it was piled under her nose. OCC might need a marine expert from time to time, but at the moment there was no special niche waiting to be filled. It was catch as catch can—a summary of a scientific study here, a word of advice there, a flat thumbs-down on a shortsighted scheme to turn inedible reef life into fertilizer for the export market.

Yes, there was work of a sort at OCC for Mandy, but her future lay elsewhere. No one knew that fact better than she did. She had to be gone before her pregnancy showed. Anthea would know instantly that Sutter was the father. What Anthea knew, Sutter would learn just as soon as he emerged from the Stone Age amenities of the Australian bush in monsoon season. With the first phone call Sutter made, he would know that his neat vacation affair had suddenly leaped the agreed-upon boundaries.

He would be furious, and justifiably so.

Mandy refused to let that happen. Sutter had given her too much. She wouldn't go back on her promise and hold him responsible for a child he had never wanted. He had told her he couldn't protect her and she had told him that was all right. She had meant it. The pregnancy was her choice, her responsibility, her joy. She didn't want Sutter to feel guilt or anger, treachery or betrayal. Each of them had achieved his separate desire. *Just a vacation affair between consenting adults.*

And now the vacation was over.

Even if Mandy weren't pregnant, she wouldn't have hung around OCC like the Ghost of Vacation Past. She had heard enough gossip during her time at OCC to know that when Sutter was finished with a woman, he was finished. Mandy had promised him there would be no fuss, no muss, no tears, no loose ends. The only way she could keep that promise was to be gone when he returned. She simply couldn't face having him walk into the office and nod civilly to her as he would to any OCC employee, nor could she stand seeing him and not touching him.

Mandy could endure a great many things, but not that. Not that.

The only thing holding her at OCC right now was the hope that Sutter had missed her as much as she missed him, that he would call from Australia and tell her that he couldn't sleep for wanting her, couldn't watch a sunset without remembering her, couldn't taste the sea without tasting her, couldn't breathe without remembering how it had felt to be completely joined to her....

He haunted her.

With fingers that trembled very slightly, Mandy reached for another report. She read quickly, making notes, trying not to think about anything beyond the words printed on the page in front of her. She was successful to the point that the phone had to ring four times before it got her attention. As she picked up the receiver she automatically glanced at the clock. After six. Vaguely she remembered saying goodbye to Steve and the others as they left for the day.

"Our Children's Children," Mandy said into the phone,

the words automatic, her voice sounding odd from lack of use in the past few hours.

There was a background of static and voices and a loudspeaker saying something Mandy couldn't understand. The caller cursed and spoke loudly.

"Sutter here. Give me Anthea."

For a moment Mandy thought she was drowning. She was dizzy, couldn't breathe; her whole body felt weak. Without a word she punched in the hold button and rang Anthea's office.

"Yes?"

"Sutter. Line one," Mandy said, fighting to control her voice.

"Wonderful! How is he? Is he coming home? Did he get the job done?"

"He didn't say."

There was a pause while Anthea absorbed Mandy's colorless voice. "Thank you, dear. Don't leave yet, if you don't mind. He might…"

But Mandy had already hung up. She stared at her desk without seeing it. There were two possible explanations. One was that Sutter hadn't recognized her voice. The other was that he had but hadn't wanted to talk with her. Neither explanation was comforting.

There was a lot of noise on his end. Maybe that's why he didn't recognize my voice. He must have been exhausted and hungry and harried and it was noisy and there's no reason he should have recognized my voice, he's never said more than twenty words to me on the phone. But Anthea will tell him I'm here and then he'll…

Mandy didn't realize what she was doing until she had the knob of Anthea's office door in her hand. She opened the door soundlessly but made no move to go farther into the room. Anthea's back was to her.

"Dear boy, my heart goes out to you. I can't imagine eating lizard once, much less for three weeks. And leeches…!" Pause. "Well, of course, I understand that the

leeches were eating you rather than vice versa." Pause.
"Two days? Wonderful. I'll have Man—er, someone—
pick you up." Pause. "Don't be foolish. You sound terrible. It only makes sense for someone to pick you up at
the airport. When will your plane land?" Pause. "You are
in an exceptionally vile mood, Sutter. Perhaps it's just as
well that no one meet you." Pause. "Is there anything you
need taken care of on this end? Any messages for me to
pass on?" Pause. "I see. Well, then, I'll talk to you in two
days. Try to spend the whole time sleeping."

Mandy's mind was too numb to get her body moving
in time to evade discovery. She was still standing in the
doorway when Anthea turned around to hang up the phone.
The older woman gave Mandy a compassionate glance.

"I'm sorry, dear. I've never known Sutter to be like that
except for the time after we got him out of jail in that
wretched country. He wouldn't let anyone near him. He
hated being helpless."

"Yes. He told me."

Anthea's eyebrows climbed. "Did he? How odd. He's
never spoken to anyone about that."

"He was trying to make me feel less a coward for being
afraid of the water, that's all," Mandy said, turning away.

"Mandy? Are you all right, dear?"

She stopped and faced Anthea once more. "Don't worry
about me," Mandy said in a strained voice. "I'm a sur-
vivor."

"Mandy," Anthea said hesitantly, "do you understand
that Sutter doesn't mean to be cruel? He just…doesn't trust
women. Give him time. He'll learn that you're different,
that he can trust you."

Unconsciously Mandy's hands moved to cover her
womb, where life grew, a secret that couldn't be kept.
"No," she said, her voice low. "He'll think that I'm no
different." She saw the distress in Anthea's face and added
softly, "Don't be unhappy for me. Sutter gave me far more
than he took. I have no regrets. Not one." She turned away

again. "Better hurry. You're scheduled for cocktails in half an hour. With downtown traffic the way it is, you haven't a moment to spare. I'll lock up behind you."

Long, long after Anthea left, Mandy sat and worked, skimming and summarizing scientific papers until nothing of importance remained on her desk. Finally she pulled out a clean sheet of office letterhead and picked up a pen, only to discover that there was too little to say. Or too much. Finally she wrote two words, clipped the sheet to the photo and left them on Anthea's desk.

After that, there was nothing for Mandy to do but go to the apartment and pack. With luck she would be far away before Sutter's plane even landed.

Sutter leaned over the sink at the airline terminal and splashed cold water on his face. The water was refreshing, but it wasn't eight hours of sleep. It was all he had, however, so he splashed more water over his hair and skin, trying to chase away the fatigue of the past few weeks. He hadn't slept but a few hours a night; and when he had slept, he had dreamed of holding a graceful, golden-eyed mermaid in his hands, bathing himself in her beauty, and then she was receding from him, swimming faster and faster until she vanished and he was left exhausted and alone in a cold midnight sea.

He looked in the mirror and grimaced. Bronze stubble and black circles, his hair wet and roughly finger combed, his mouth set in a flat, angry line. He had spent a lot of time like that in the past few weeks. Angry. He wasn't sure why, but he suspected that he had committed some irretrievably stupid act. His problem was that he couldn't decide whether the stupidity resided in ending his affair with Mandy or in not wanting it to end.

With an impatient curse Sutter picked up his baggage and hunted down a cab. He knew he should go home, sleep for a day, shower, eat, sleep; and then maybe, just maybe, he might feel whole again instead of only half-aware, half-awake, half-alive, the other half missing, lost and alone in a midnight sea.

The cab dropped Sutter off in front of OCC's offices. He took the elevator up, pushed open the office door impatiently and strode into the lobby. A new girl was at the receptionist's desk. She started to ask Sutter if she could help him but he brushed by before she could say two words. There was another strange woman sitting at Mandy's desk. Sutter didn't even hesitate. He went to Anthea's office, opened the door and slammed it shut behind him.

"Where is she," he said flatly, a demand rather than a question.

"Welcome home, Sutter," Anthea said, eyeing him rather warily. "You look like death warmed over."

"Where is she."

"Who?"

"You know damn good and well who I mean," Sutter snarled. "Where is Mandy!"

"I don't know."

"Is she sick?"

"I don't know."

"Why isn't she at work?"

"I—"

"Don't know," he interrupted savagely, finishing Anthea's sentence for her. "What *do* you know, dearest aunt?"

"Many things, dearest boy," Anthea purred. "Is there any particular area of inquiry you wished to pursue?"

"Don't push me, Anthea. I'm not in the mood for it."

Anthea's eyebrows climbed, but she said only, "When I arrived at work yesterday morning, there was a note on my desk and this." She handed over the note and the photo.

The note said, simply, *Thank you.* The photo made Sutter's breath hiss out as though at a blow. He had never seen a woman so incandescent…or a man so damned pleased with life.

"Go on," Sutter said tightly, struggling to contain his anger at himself and life and the woman who had promised a neat, no-strings affair.

But she had lied. She haunted him.

"That was all," Anthea said. "It covered the ground adequately, don't you think? As they say, a picture is worth a thousand words."

Sutter knew his aunt was baiting him again, but it no longer mattered. Nothing mattered but getting his hands on Mandy and teaching her…

What? What did he want her to know? How could he teach her what he didn't know himself?

"There wasn't anything else, no message for me?" Sutter asked.

"Were you expecting one?"

"She didn't even give notice? She just left? Of all the ungrateful—"

"Yes," Anthea agreed, cutting across Sutter's anger. "It certainly was ungrateful of the wretch to leave before you were through with her. What is this younger generation coming to when a girl doesn't wait around for her lover to break off the affair? So impatient to get on with life. No time for all the amenities. No sense of proportion at all. And after all you promised her, too."

"I didn't promise Mandy a damned thing," Sutter retorted.

"When a man declares his love to a woman, there is an implicit—"

"I didn't say a damn thing about love to her, either!" he interrupted curtly.

"In that case, dear boy, what on earth are you complaining about? You enjoyed her, you walked away from her, and now she's gone."

Sutter closed his eyes on a wave of fury so great that it

could barely be contained. He swore in an icy monotone until there were no words left, only ice.

"Where did she go?"

Anthea flinched at the clipped words and savage green eyes of her nephew. "There's no point in being angry with her," Anthea pointed out. "She was only doing what any—"

"Where did she go?"

Anthea gauged the sound of her nephew's voice accurately and gave up all attempts to bait or reason with him. "I don't know where Mandy is."

"Where are you sending her paycheck?"

"I'm not. Damon, believe me, I don't know where she is!"

"Call her apartment."

"I did. The phone has been disconnected. The apartment is empty."

Sutter shook his head in denial even as he felt the chill of truth condensing around him. "The post office."

"She left no forwarding address." Anthea hesitated, then said softly, "She made a very clean break, Damon. She even pulled her job application from the file. We have no previous addresses for her, no names of family members, nothing. It's as though she never walked through the door of Our Children's Children."

"My God. How she must have hated me."

"She loved you," Anthea said in a flat voice. "She loved you, and you didn't even speak to her when you called from Australia. Why?"

"I could barely hear myself think. I didn't know it was Mandy until it was too late. And what should I have said?" Sutter asked harshly. "That I can't sleep for wanting her? That I can't smell the sea without remembering what it was like to fall asleep with her in my arms? That I can't look at a woman without seeing Mandy, tasting Mandy, needing her until I think dying would be easier than living without her? What could I have said to her, Anthea? There are no words to describe the hell I've been going through!''

"Try 'I love you.'''

The words were like a knife gliding between Sutter's ribs into his heart, twisting. He turned away, saying nothing, for the only words that mattered had already been spoken.

Mandy was gone.

November rainstorms swept down over Northern California, carrying the chill of the distant Aleutians in each slashing gray drop. The tidal flats around Monterey Bay were deserted except for disgruntled sea gulls and a lone figure walking along the rocky shore, pausing from time to time to pick up a bit of sea life stranded by the falling water. The wind gusted suddenly, roughing up the sea and rushing over the land in a long, sighing moan.

Mandy shivered and turned up the collar of the red-and-black-checked lumberjacket she had bought at a garage sale. The coat was too large, but its thick wool defeated the wind and the big scarlet checks always looked cheerful against the winter land. When worn with a sweater, scarf and waterproof fisherman's boots, the coat kept her warm on her long daily walks around the bay.

But it was time to get back to the little beach cottage she was caretaking in lieu of paying rent. Soon it would be dark. She didn't want to take a chance of stumbling or falling on hidden rocks. She wanted nothing to happen that might jeopardize the baby growing within her. Not that she had any reason to worry—her doctor had assured her that everything about the pregnancy was normal.

Groping in her pocket for her key, head bent against the wind, Mandy had no warning that someone was on her front step until she ran right into a solid wall of flesh.

"What—?" she gasped, looking up. "*Sutter!* What are you doing here?"

"Freezing my butt off waiting for you."

"How did you find me?"

"In the telephone book, under Dr. S. Blythe-Cameron, the same name on the OCC paper you wrote."

He took the key from Mandy's fingers, opened the door and pushed her in ahead of him. The door thumped shut with the help of his solid heel. After the chill outside, the room felt almost tropical. A single glance took in the huge, colorful throw pillows scattered about, the lush plants and the open futon that was doing double duty as Mandy's bed.

"Sutter, what—"

"Later," he interrupted, catching Mandy's face between his cool hands. "First I want some answers of my own."

Mandy felt the heat of Sutter's breath, the sudden thrust of his tongue between her lips, tasted him, and the world came apart around her. Her breath jerked out in a shattered moan as her arms circled his neck. She didn't know if he was real or a waking dream; she only knew that she had to taste him, had to feel his power and warmth, had to feel fully alive with him once more.

Sutter had been expecting Mandy to fight or flee or freeze, anything but the wild answering hunger of her mouth mating with his. He lifted her off her feet, wanting to know all of her sweet weight pressed against his body. But even that wasn't enough. He had to feel her hair, her skin, taste her warmth, her passion; yet everywhere his hands moved they found only cloth and more cloth.

"My God, you're wrapped up with more layers than a Chinese puzzle box," he muttered.

Impatiently he unwound the wool scarf from Mandy's head, kissing and biting her lips lightly every few seconds, finally spearing his fingers into the warm, silky mass of her hair, groaning with pleasure at the remembered silk and scent of her. He caught her lips once more, rubbed his fingers against her scalp and slid his tongue into her mouth, tasting her with a slow, rhythmic intimacy that unraveled her.

Mandy's hands stroked continuously over Sutter's chest,

probing through his heavy jacket for the heat and feel of his body. More by accident than intent her fingers found the cold metal tongue of the jacket zipper. She pulled it down and thrust her hands inside, feeling his vital heat and the power of his flexed muscles. Her nails raked down his spine to his hips, making him shudder heavily. Without lifting his mouth from hers, he undid the buttons of her heavy jacket, only to be confronted by the much smaller buttons of her cardigan. He pulled it free of her waistband and eased his big hands beneath her sweater.

The feel of Sutter's cool fingers caressing her skin made Mandy gasp with pleasure. When his thumbs skimmed repeatedly over the tips of her breasts, her gasp became a moan and liquid heat spread through her body. Her hands slid up his back from his hips, rubbed down his chest to his waist and then lower, seeking and finding the ridge of hard flesh that burgeoned beneath his jeans. Suddenly the world spun and Mandy found herself flat on her back on the futon with Sutter's big body moving against her in an agony of need. With a thick, broken sound, he rolled aside and fought for self-control.

"I'm sorry," Sutter said hoarsely. "I was just going to kiss you, to see if it was half as good as I remembered." He put his forearm over his eyes and shuddered. "It was twice as good. Three times. Four." Suddenly he rolled over onto his side and said angrily to her, "There aren't enough numbers, enough words. You're a fire in my body, in my mind, in my soul. *And you left me.*"

Mandy touched Sutter's beloved face with fingertips that shook. "That was what you wanted," she whispered. "You wouldn't touch me after that first time until I promised no strings, no tears, just a vacation affair. The only way I could keep my promise was not to see you again. So I…left."

"I've changed my mind. I want you, Mandy."

Her beautiful, sad smile sliced through Sutter's passion and anger to the fear that lay beneath. He knew before she could speak the words forming on her lips that she was slipping away from him, receding like the golden mermaid of his anguished dreams.

"No," he snarled. His hand went between Mandy's legs, anchoring her in place. "Damn it, you want me as much as I want you. Don't try to deny it, Mandy. I can feel the heat of you!"

She closed her eyes for a moment, unable to face the fear that had haunted her since she had discovered she was pregnant. She wanted to remember Sutter with desire in his eyes, not disgust for the woman who hadn't kept her promise. But she had learned that running from fear simply wouldn't work. She had tried to run from this moment, but it had come to her just the same. Slowly she opened her eyes and looked at the man she loved.

"Yes," Mandy said tightly, "I want you. If it matters, I'll want you until the day I die."

"If it matters?" Sutter said. "Of course it matters! What the hell are you talking about?"

"I'm pregnant."

Sutter went completely still. "What?"

"*Enceinte,*" Mandy hissed, angry at having to explain the obvious, "as in 'expecting a blessed event,' 'with child,' 'eating for two.' Ah, the light dawns."

Even the narrowing of Sutter's eyes couldn't wholly conceal the savage blaze of his emotions. "You told me—"

"I told you there could be no such thing as an *unwanted* pregnancy for me," Mandy said, cutting across Sutter's words, wanting to get it over with so she could crawl away and lick her wounds in peace. "That was the exact truth. I want this child!"

"You're carrying my child," he said in an odd voice.

Mandy started to demand that Sutter tell her whether he had any doubts about the paternity when she felt the warmth of his big hand sliding caressingly over her womb, and the ability to speak deserted her.

"My child," he breathed.

Biting her lip, unable to hold back the tears spilling down her cheeks, Mandy watched as reverence replaced anger in Sutter's face.

"Is everything...normal?" he asked hesitantly. "Are you all right? Is the baby?"

"Everything is fine," Mandy said. "The doctor told me I couldn't be healthier."

Without a word Sutter turned and began pulling off and discarding Mandy's boots and socks. Then his hands went to the waistband of her jeans and stopped suddenly, as though he had just realized what he was doing.

"May I?" he asked huskily. "I want to see...."

She nodded.

Very gently Sutter slid Mandy's jeans and underwear from her legs. The skin of her abdomen was warm, still tanned from her island days, and taut with the first swelling of her pregnancy. She trembled and bit back a cry at the sweet touch of his hand over her womb.

"I'm sorry," Sutter said instantly, retreating. "I didn't mean to hurt you."

"You didn't," Mandy said, taking his hand and pulling it back to her body. "It's just that I've...I've dreamed of you touching me like that...wanting the baby as much as I do."

Sutter closed his eyes and fought for self-control. It was impossible. Her words had moved him beyond bearing.

"Mandy," he whispered, bending down and kissing the warm skin he had uncovered.

Sutter tried to say more but his throat had closed, leaving him no voice, nothing but the tears that brushed over Mandy's skin as he turned his head from side to side, bathing his senses in her, cherishing her, absorbing her presence, feeling her hands softly stroking his hair even as his face caressed her. For a long time there was only silence and the sound of their ragged breathing.

Suddenly Mandy twisted beneath Sutter. His arms tightened around her waist, not wanting to end the healing embrace.

"Mandy?"

"There have been other changes, too," she murmured, twisting again, throwing aside the last of her clothes. "Don't you want to see them, too?"

Sutter's breath wedged in his throat when he looked up and saw that Mandy was nude, a smile trembling on her lips, her golden eyes radiant with tears and happiness. Without looking away from her, he began stripping off his own clothes, not stopping until there was nothing between their bodies. Only then did he bend down to her, giving in to the wild, oddly tender hunger that was ravishing him.

Mandy's breasts were taut and golden, their centers darker than Sutter remembered, fuller, and they tightened into velvet crowns at the first brush of his tongue. He barely restrained a thick sound of need, but his caresses were as gentle and reverent as his hand over her womb. Very slowly he sat up and looked at her, missing nothing of her beauty.

"I understand now why some cultures worshiped the female figure," Sutter said huskily, stroking Mandy lightly from her temples to the soles of her feet, lingering over each subtle sign of her pregnancy, cherishing her very femininity. "They were really worshiping life." His hand spread over Mandy's womb as he bent to kiss the same breasts that would someday nourish his child.

"Half of that life is your gift, not mine," Mandy said, biting back a low moan of pleasure as Sutter's tongue moved over her.

"My mind knows that," Sutter murmured, kissing her breasts, tasting them, making her shiver, "but my emotions are a hell of a lot more primitive. I see life welling up in you, Mandy. I've always seen it in you, life that's hot and sweet and wild and clean, and I want to bathe in that sacred upwelling, taking some of your life into me even as I give myself to it."

Mandy whispered Sutter's name against his lips as her hands found and cradled his hungry masculine flesh. His shuddering reaction made her feel as though she were holding lightning pooled within her cupped hands. Answering fire streaked through her when Sutter's large hand moved down between her legs to caress her. His husky sound of pleasure as he cherished her was echoed by her unraveling words.

"Is there anything else I should know before we're married?" Sutter asked, smiling down at Mandy as he smoothed his palm over her, caressing her with her own sultry heat.

"The baby is growing so fast..."

Pleasure radiated hotly through Mandy, taking away her words. Sutter watched, smiling, caressing her, calling more torrid rain from her gathering storm.

"Yes?" he murmured encouragingly.

"The doctor is...talking about...twins," she said, moving against Sutter's hand, seeking a deeper joining.

"Twins," Sutter said, sucking in his breath, then laughing with delight. "Twins. My God." Still smiling, he knelt between Mandy's legs to kiss the swelling mound that might contain not one of his babies but two. "Any other miracles that you've been saving for a rainy day?" he murmured.

"Just that I love you."

Sutter's whole body froze in the instant before his breath came out with a husky, ragged sound.

"I love you, Mandy. I must have loved you since I carried you off that damned plane. That's why I couldn't get enough of you no matter how many times we made love." As he spoke he kissed her womb, her breasts, the pulse beating beneath her throat, her trembling lips, smoothing his words into her skin as he slowly joined his body to hers. "You're my life and I didn't know it until you walked away. But I know now. I'm going to spend my life loving you."

Mandy tried to tell him that she loved him in the same way, but he was moving within her, stealing her thoughts, her breath, her words. With a cry she gave herself to him and took him in the same instant, moving with him, chain lightning weaving between their bodies, ecstasy calling a passionate rain from the depths of their love until they could bear no more and slept deeply in each other's arms.

Within six months a son and then a daughter were born from Mandy's body into Sutter's gentle hands. Later, as he put each babe to suckle against her breast, she smiled and wept and whispered her love to the man who had returned to her twice what the sea had once taken.

When the babies were full of milk and love and sleep, Sutter put them in their bedside cribs before sliding into bed with the woman he loved. Even as he gathered her into his arms, she came to him, holding him. They slept as they would always live, body to body, breath to breath, love to love…complete.

* * * * *

A VEILED JOURNEY

NELL BRIEN

Learning that her birth mother was a
Saudi Arabian concubine who gave up
her infant daughter to save the child's life,
Liz Ryan takes a journey that will change
her life. Accepting a job in Jeddah, she is soon
transported into the heart of a land as beautiful
as it is ruthlessly savage. And into the intimate
and hostile world of the women behind the veils.
It is a journey that will threaten all she believes...
and ultimately her life.

On sale mid-September 1999 wherever paperbacks are sold!

MIRA

Look us up on-line at: http://www.mirabooks.com   MNB528